Gorgeous Gruesome Faces

Gorgeous Gruesome Faces

LINDA CHENG

ROARING BROOK PRESS

NEW YORK

Published by Roaring Brook Press
Roaring Brook Press is a division of
Holtzbrinck Publishing Holdings Limited Partnership
120 Broadway, New York, NY 10271 • fiercereads.com

Our books may be purchased in bulk for promotional, educational, or
business use. Please contact your local bookseller or the Macmillan Corporate
and Premium Sales Department at (800) 221-7945 ext. 5442 or by email at
MacmillanSpecialMarkets@macmillan.com.

Library of Congress Cataloging-in-Publication Data

Names: Cheng, Linda, author.
Title: Gorgeous gruesome faces / Linda Cheng.
Description: First edition. | New York : Roaring Brook Press, 2023. |
Audience: Ages 14-18. | Audience: Grades 10-12. | Summary: Disgraced
teen idol Sunny comes face to face with Candie, her former bandmate,
and the demons of their shared past when the two enter a K-pop
competition that devolves into a deadly nightmare.
Identifiers: LCCN 2022057230 | ISBN 9781250864994 (hardcover) |
ISBN 9781250865007 (ebook)
Subjects: CYAC: Contests—Fiction. | K-pop (Subculture)—Fiction. |
Lesbians—Fiction. | Chinese Americans—Fiction. | Korean Americans—
Fiction. | Horror stories. | LCGFT: Horror fiction. | Novels.
Classification: LCC PZ7.1.C497524 Go 2023 | DDC [Fic]—dc23
LC record available at https://lccn.loc.gov/2022057230

First edition, 2023
Book design by Samira Iravani
Printed in the United States of America

ISBN 978-1-250-86499-4 (hardcover)
1   3   5   7   9   10   8   6   4   2

ISBN 978-1-250-32519-8 (international edition)
1   3   5   7   9   10   8   6   4   2

To JM,
For every adventure we've gone on,
and every storm we've weathered

Prologue

THEN

Two years ago

Candie predicted I was going to ruin everything months before it all happened. When we were told that our sophomore album was put on hold and our show wouldn't be renewed, I knew she was right. Our careers were officially over.

She said I was selfish and stupid, that I was throwing away everything we've worked for, that my bad decisions were going to cost us our futures. I called her an egotistical glory hound who doesn't give a shit about anyone's feelings or anything other than fame. And Mina, always the peaceful mediator, was caught in the middle of the storm yet again, doing her best to hold her umbrella of nonpartisan support over both our heads as Candie and I lashed out at each other.

The truth is, I think that fight was what broke us for good, not what came after.

I said a lot of terrible things I shouldn't have. But isn't that what "best friends" are for? They alone can reach into your core, scoop out the ugliest bits, and hold them up to your face so you can see exactly what kind of damage you're carrying around.

No. That's an excuse. I said those things to hurt her.

The three of us have spent the past several years conquering stage and screen together, hand in hand, in matching costumes. Our bond was forged under the burn of spotlights and the intrusion of cameras, stewed in the sweat we poured out in practice rooms, sworn in with the blood that dripped from the blisters between our toes. I thought what we had would last forever. Now all we have is a scandal-tainted legacy and a surplus of unsellable merch.

The only reason Candie's meeting up with me today is because we agreed that, for Mina's sake, we need to set aside the crimes we've committed against each other and go check on her as a united front.

Mina hasn't been herself since we attempted the ritual.

The last time we saw her, bubbly, happy Mina, who reliably banishes dark moods and has an inspirational glass-is-half-full speech for every occasion, she didn't smile or say a word, even as our manager unloaded a metric ton of bad news on us. No anecdotes of encouragement, no soothing hugs. Afterward, she left without a goodbye. Then she stopped answering her phone.

Mina moved out on her own a few months ago. At first, I thought there was literally nothing cooler than living in a fancy downtown apartment with barely any adult oversight. But with her family on the other side of the country, there's no one there to look after her.

Candie's BMW is already in the visitor's spot when I pull into Mina's building. At the same time, we step out of our cars into the dim fluorescent lights of the parking garage. I struggle to meet her eyes.

"Has Mina responded to you?" Candie's voice echoes against the concrete.

I force myself to look up. "No. She text you back?"

Candie shakes her head, bone-straight hair bending gently against her clavicle. Our world is imploding around us and she still looks radiant and assured, her outfit precisely put together, while I barely managed to put on a bra and wrangle my hair into a messy bun. She's in a blazer, a skirt, and her favorite oversize sunglasses, the ones that make her look like a total movie star. Like she was born to be pop royalty.

Standing beside her has always made me acutely aware of the differences between us—the way my eyes don't shimmer with alluring depth, how my cheeks are chipmunk round instead of high and defined, the coarse texture of my wavy hair compared to her shampoo-commercial-grade locks. The glow she exudes is mesmerizing, like a light shining down from an otherworldly place. When she performs, it's impossible to look away from her.

But if you cross her . . . that's when the idol vanishes, and a whole other persona surfaces.

I want to ask Candie if she's still angry with me. Her shoulders are rigid, her expression closed off. The emotional distance between us spans a few more feet, and for one frantic second, I consider reaching out to catch her wrist and pull her back before she can float further away. But then Candie turns and walks into the building. My hands stay where they are.

The elevator ride up to Mina's floor is pin-drop quiet, Candie and I occupying opposite corners of the silent gray box. The doors slide open before I can work up the nerve to ask how Candie's feeling. I shouldn't even be thinking about us right now, I remind myself. We're here for Mina.

Candie uses the spare key to let us into Mina's apartment. The interior is pitch-black.

"Mina? It's us," Candie calls out into the darkness.

I feel for the light switches. "Are you home, Minnie?"

The overheads come on with a click, illuminating the front hallway. A sample of Mina's colorful heel collection forms orderly lines on the rack, undisturbed. We remove our own shoes and leave them beside hers. In the living room, the walnut coffee table is free of clutter, the plush pillows on the sectional couch neatly propped. Nothing appears out of place.

The walls of Mina's apartment are a curated collage of her life. *Sweet Cadence* promo posters and magazine covers hang in frames among candid pictures of family and friends. My favorite of her displays is a photo strip from our early era, before anyone knew our names. I remember that day so clearly, the three of us squeezed into that smelly mall photo booth, our faces pressed together, arms looped over necks and shoulders. Our show had just premiered, and between us there was only trust and cama-raderie. No cruel words said out of spite, no awful secrets that pushed us apart.

I'm pulled from the whirlpool of nostalgia when I notice something strange about that photo strip. I lean in and squint.

There's a brownish-red smudge smeared across Mina's face in each square.

And it isn't just that photo strip. Mina's face is vandalized in *every* photo and poster on the wall. The glass over each shot of her face is caked over in the same brown muck, leaving dark blots between Candie's and my shining photo-shoot smiles.

"Candie, look . . ." My voice trembles. "Is that . . . what I think it is?"

Beside me, Candie's eyes are already wide with alarm. It jolts me every time I see cracks in Candie's composure. Like standing on an empty beach as the ocean suddenly recedes. A warning that something terrible is coming.

We call out for Mina again and again.

The kitchen and the rest of the living area are empty. We turn down the hall toward her bedroom. At the end of the corridor, the door to Mina's room is cracked. There's someone muttering inside. For the second time, I fight the urge to reach out and grab on to Candie. Our feet pound in unison as we hurry down the hallway. When we reach the door, Candie doesn't hesitate, pushing it wide open.

There's a shadow of a person sitting on the edge of the bed, back facing us.

"It's not right. It isn't mine," the shadow whispers.

Candie reaches for the light. I gasp in relief to see that it's Mina, that she's here, she's home, she's safe.

"Minnie, didn't you hear us calling for you?" I rush forward.

Candie's left arm shoots out, a sudden barrier across my midsection. I freeze at the abrupt impact.

"Careful." Candie points to the floor. There's broken glass all over the carpet.

Before I can fully register the warmth of her touch, it's already gone. Candie steps past me into the room, carefully dodging the shards as she makes her way to Mina.

I follow her and find the source of the mess. The full-length mirror on the wall has been completely shattered. So has the mirror on her vanity table. My stomach clenches into a solid knot. I hurry to Mina's bedside to join Candie, who's already kneeling down, her brows pinched in concern.

Mina's head is hung low, the ends of her short bob trailing forward, obscuring her face. There's a handheld mirror in her lap. The glass is broken as well, scattered in a jagged halo at her feet. Her hands and nails are filthy. Like she's been digging in dirt.

"It's not right," Mina mumbles.

"What's not right? Are you feeling sick?" I brush my hand across Mina's forehead, and then I flinch. "Oh my god, Minnie, you're burning up! Here, lie down, I'll get you some ice—"

"Ice won't help," Candie says. "She needs to come with me."

"To *where*?" I snap. "And you better say the hospital!"

Mina looks up, finally, and I suck in a breath. Her face looks . . . different.

At first, I think she's wearing makeup. It's as if a beauty filter has been applied to her features, shifting and heightening them to uncanny proportions. Enormous eyes turn up to me, alien wide. Her pupils are massive. Is she wearing circle contact lenses? Her nose is thinner, pixielike, her mouth miniature. Her jaw seems daintier, curving down to a tiny, pointed chin. Did she contour to change the shape of her face? Mina has always preferred natural looks, secure and comfortable with herself in ways I can only dream of being. The girl sitting in front of me looks almost like a complete stranger.

"Minnie?" I ask in a faint whisper.

"It isn't right." Mina looks down at the broken mirror in her lap again. "It's not my face . . ."

"I'm going to call her parents." I reach for my phone with shaky hands.

"No!" Candie shouts. "I can help her; I just need her to come with me."

Mina starts scratching at her cheeks with her dirty hands. "This isn't my face!" she cries, clawing at her neck, her jaw, brown nails sinking in, dragging out red marks down her paper-white skin. *"This isn't my face!"*

I jump to my feet. A sliver of glass presses into my heel as I step back, but I hardly feel it. All I can feel is my thundering heart about to burst.

Candie grabs at Mina and wrestles her hands away from herself. "Mina, calm down! Everything is going to be okay; we're here to help you!"

"I want to go! I have to go! Let me go!" Mina screams.

I stumble back a few steps as Mina starts to sob, long animal howls of anguish. I've never heard her make sounds like that. I've never heard anyone sound like that.

"This is happening because of me, isn't it?" I turn to Candie, like I always do, for her guidance, for her care, things I have no right to ask for anymore. But I'm spiraling, panic choking me, my breaths raging faster and heavier. "It's because I stopped the ritual . . . Because I couldn't go through with it . . ."

Candie looks up, and the second her attention is split, Mina breaks free from her hold. Mina bolts out of the bedroom, her bare feet slapping across the glass shards littering the floor.

"Mina!"

We race after her out into the living room to see Mina throwing open the balcony door. The night breeze lifts the sheer curtains, enveloping her in a white shroud.

Time congeals. Everything churns in slow motion. We run toward her, arms stretching, fingers reaching. Candie pulls ahead of me, and the grip of terror eases because I know she will fix this.

Candie will make Mina come back inside.

Candie will save her.

But Mina doesn't stop. She starts to climb, pushing herself up to stand on the balcony railing. Behind the billowing curtains, she spreads her arms out wide as she turns to face us, and we hear her say:

"I want to go home."

Then Mina's body tips, and she drops backward into the night.

Chapter 1

NOW

I'm never wearing anything cute or doing something glamorous when I get recognized these days. Either some TMZ photographer's trying to get pictures of me eating a burrito from a deeply unflattering angle or I'm in a sweatpants–flip-flops combo on day three of not washing my hair, standing in the frozen aisle of Kroger.

The lady hovering next to me pretending to look at Eggos while not so covertly examining my profile waits for me to drop the sixth frozen meal into my shopping cart before she shuffles forward.

"Excuse me, dear, I don't mean to bother you, but I just wanted to ask, were you on that TV show? The one about the Asian pop group?"

The fact that she didn't use my name or the title of the show is enough to tell me that the best course of action here is to show myself out of this potential social disaster by offering her a polite "Sorry, you've got the wrong person."

But the corners of my mouth lift and the words are spilling out before I can stop them.

"Yes, I was!" My voice automatically pitches into a higher register, the one that makes me sound younger, friendlier. "That's me."

The lady lets out an excited whoop. "Oh my gosh, would you mind taking a quick picture with my daughters? Just one? They absolutely adore you!"

"Of course."

The rational, self-respecting part of me floats away, untethered, glancing down in disappointment at the lesser me left behind—the one who still craves the validation of strangers.

"Aubrey! Anya! Come here, quick!" the lady hollers. "You're not going to believe who I just met!"

Two tween girls come bounding around the other end of the aisle. One has locks of purple twisted into her curls, and the other's got streaks of blue weaving through her high ponytail. They look twelve, thirteen at most, but their style is impeccable, their makeup stunning enough to be on a Sephora ad. They probably have a dance video out there that's got eight hundred thousand views. The next generation of trendsetters, here to step all over the corpse of my career with their rhinestone sneakers.

"It's Candie—from that show you love!"

The name lands like a gut punch, and I bite the inside of my cheek as the pang hits.

Even during the height of our popularity, Candie and I still got mistaken for each other all the time. I used to get happy butterflies when it would happen, thinking that it meant people thought we looked alike. It took me a while to realize they merely thought of us as interchangeable.

The mother presents me like she's unveiling a prize, and the girls' faces progress through a slow-motion car crash of emotions, shifting from surprise to recognition to alarm to disappointment to unbearable secondhand embarrassment. And finally, to pity.

"Um, no, Mom, that's—" Purple Curls attempts to correct.

"*And* she was nice enough to agree to a picture!" The woman's already got her phone out and she's shoving her daughters forward, arranging them next to me, one on each side, like we're estranged relatives being forced into a family photo.

I flash Purple Curls and Blue Pony a tight smile, hoping to assure them with my eyes that I won't make this any more uncomfortable than it already is and that the sooner we get this over with, the sooner we can all be released from this awkward circle of hell. The girls cooperatively stay silent and lean into me as their mother snaps a picture of us against a backdrop of frozen peas.

"Thank you so much!" the woman gushes.

"Yeah, thank you," Blue Pony mumbles.

"Uh, good luck with everything," Purple Curls adds.

"It was nice meeting you both," I tell them, forcing myself to maintain the smile until the girls rush their mother away into the next aisle. The lady's voice comes sailing over the top of the shelves.

"What's the matter with you two? What are you upset about? I thought she was the one you liked."

"Mom, you are *so* embarrassing; that wasn't Candie—that was Sunny!"

"We have literally never liked Sunny; she was such an annoying character, and then it turned out she was trying to steal Jinhwan from Brailey—"

I flee out of the aisle before I can hear the rest of the indictment. Even with two whole years' worth of new celebrity scandals, the internet is forever—and no matter how far from the limelight I retreat, the long, ugly shadow of my mistakes always finds a way of reaching me.

On my way to the front of the store, I pass by a long shelf of fashion and tabloid magazines. Instead of the current models and actresses on the covers, all I can see is the past. *My* past. I see our debut, the three of us posing in our trademark formation.

The headline says: **Meet the stars of *Sweet Cadence*: the K-pop inspired musical hit!**

Candie stands in the middle, the centerpiece of the show. I'm on her right, my elbow propped on her shoulder, in a cheerleader outfit. And to the left, Mina. The heart and soul of our group, with her bob cut and freckled nose, nothing but the purest joy reflected in her smiling eyes.

When my eyes move across the rack, the headlines and covers change.

K-pop star Jin-hwan Woo phone-hacking scandal! Leaked nudes!

Teen pop triangle feud ends in heartbreak.

Splashed across the front of *People* magazine are photos of Jin-hwan and me. Stills from his cameo on our show. Pics taken backstage at an award show, his hand on my waist, me leaning in with a smitten smile. Pap shots of me getting into his car.

I push my shopping cart down the aisle, and the headlines change again.

Tragic accident halts production on teen music show.

Sweet Cadence star Mina Park dead at age 18.

Mina's face stares back at me from another glossy magazine cover; it's the black-and-white memorial photo they used at her funeral.

I tear my gaze away from the magazine rack. Suddenly, it seems like everyone in the aisle is turned toward me, staring, their faces look strange, eyes too large, chins too small—

My fingers release the cart's handle and I run, abandoning my groceries in the aisle. I run away, like I always do, as if I can somehow outpace the oncoming panic attack, narrowly avoiding colliding with the other shoppers as I race out the doors.

Out in the parking lot, I keep glancing over my shoulder, terrified I'll see that face right behind me. Once I'm safely in my car, I try to do the breathing exercises my therapist taught me but give up when I can't remember if I was supposed to hold my breath for four counts or six before exhaling. I throw the car into reverse and peel out like I'm fleeing a crime scene, cursing the loss of this convenient location because I can never set foot in this Kroger again.

After we lost Mina and *Sweet Cadence* was canceled, my mother moved us from LA to Atlanta.

"It'll be a fresh start," she explained as I watched the movers load the furniture onto trucks. "For both of us."

But mostly for her. With all the film and show productions shooting in Georgia, the move felt like a decision made to benefit her career as a producer more than anything else. She sold the relocation to me as a perfect chance to get away from the toxic LA scene so I could focus on "recovery" and "re-centering myself." Now that I've graduated high school with tentative plans to take a gap year, Mama's been bringing up work again.

"Maybe we can get you a small role on a superhero movie," she'd try to pitch while driving me to therapy. "Or a CW show?"

But no matter how many opportunities my mother concocts for me, I haven't gone to a single audition. When everything ended, the limitless future that once spread out before me like a glittering carpet turned into an endless black tunnel, the walls steadily crushing in against my body as I descended from "before" to "after," from celebrity to obscurity.

We had a tutor on set, so when the show ended and I transitioned back to regular school, it was already senior year. I could barely force myself out of bed every day; there was nothing left

in me to rebuild a social life with, especially this close to grad-
uation. And after I found out the girls in my grade had a group
chat dedicated to my scandal, I stopped trying to make friends.

As expected, the house is empty when I get home from the
store. When my mother left this morning, she said she'd try her
best to make it home to have dinner with me, but her "best"
is an arbitrary sliding scale of effort that's entirely dependent
on her work schedule. I don't know why I still get my hopes
up. It's pilot season; she doesn't have time to nurture our fading
mother-daughter bond when she's trying to launch a new network drama.

I take out the last frozen entrée from the freezer and pop it
into the microwave, then carry the flimsy plastic dish up to my
bedroom to eat in front of my computer. I fully intended to pull
up the trashy reality show I've been bingeing, but instead I navi-
gate to Candie's vlog.

It's been a long time since I've looked at any of her accounts,
but that Kroger encounter has thrown me right off the wagon.
She's posted several new videos since the last time I checked. I
click on the most recent one, with the word *announcement* hand-
lettered across the thumbnail.

"Hi, sweeties, welcome back. Thanks for joining me today."

Candie waves at me from the other side of the screen. She
has bangs now.

There's always a moment when I'm watching her vlogs where
it feels like she's actually here, sitting across from me, and we're
talking just like we used to, late into the night even with a 6:00 A.M.
call time. Like we're squeezed in front of a bathroom mirror

trying to lance the zit on my chin. Like we still mean the world to each other.

When I first moved away, I tried to reach out to her a few times. She rarely responded. She's busy, I told myself. She's trying to start over. Trying to heal. We both were.

Through her posts, I received curated updates of her post-*Sweet Cadence* life. There was Candie's new bedroom. Here were Candie's new clothes. These were Candie's new friends. My texts to her would sit for days without an answer. It was almost a year before I realized she'd stopped replying at all.

The sound of shuffling steps drifts into my room from the other side of my door. Someone is coming up the stairs. I look away from the computer screen.

"Mama?"

The light thuds travel up to the second-floor landing, the floorboards in the hallway creaking. I didn't even hear the garage open, or her coming into the house. The slow footsteps grow closer, stopping just outside my door.

"Mama, is that you?" I call out. Nobody answers.

I push up from my chair and open my bedroom door.

"Mama? Are you home?"

The hallway outside is empty. I step out farther, wandering over to the top of the stairs to glance down. The living room below is dark and silent. There's no sign of my mother.

Suddenly, from back inside my room, a bout of familiar laughter floods out of the speakers. Laughter that doesn't belong to Candie. My entire body tenses.

It's Mina's laugh.

I hear my own chattering voice, too, along with Candie's

gentle chastising. It sounds like footage from the dailies, or something we filmed ourselves backstage.

Candie never talks about me or Mina in any of her videos. She avoids all questions about *Sweet Cadence* in her Q and As. Why would Candie put something like this in her vlog?

I dash back into my room, nearly crashing into my computer desk. On-screen, Candie is talking about the benefits of exfoliating facial scrubs to the same sleepy ambient music. I scrub back through the footage. There's no clip of the three of us. Only Candie speaking. I click to the beginning of the video and watch it over again. Same thing. I click around frantically and find no other tabs or windows open on my desktop. Candie stares back at me from the screen, her deep brown eyes blinking slowly.

A familiar chill crawls up my spine, notch by notch, before clasping around my ribs. My breath catches.

Is Candie doing this? Is she making me hear things that aren't there? Screwing with my head from several states away?

The Candie in these videos, the charming starlet who smiles all the time while openly inviting strangers to peer into the private corners of her life . . . is a complete act.

I know who Candice Tsai really is. What she's really like. The things she can do.

"*I have some pretty exciting news I wanted to share with everyone,*" Candie says. "*I'll be taking a brief hiatus because I've been selected to participate in the SKN workshop in Atlanta next month. The chosen finalists will get to travel to Korea to become trainees under top producers who are putting together a new girl group. Thank you to everyone who has supported me all these years; I hope you'll continue to cheer me on.*"

My mouth falls open. I'm stunned by the way she's glossing over such a momentous part of her life—*our* lives—and all those horrific things that happened. Not only that, she's planning to mount a comeback in Atlanta, where I *live*?

Her gentle smile carves open every half-healed scab, and the hurt feels fresh all over again.

This is it. This is her leaving me behind for good, fully cutting ties with *Sweet Cadence*. She's going to win this contest, move to Korea, and debut as part of the hottest new girl group next year. She's going straight to the top, the place she once promised we'd someday stand together. Why does she get to have all that when I'm still cowering in shame, haunted by memories and terrorized by her fans in grocery stores?

When her video ends, I immediately google the words *SKN workshop Atlanta*. The splash page is sleek with a deep plum velvet texture, the header image featuring girls in various popstar dance poses, the photo cropped to only show the bottom halves of their faces.

They're still accepting applications.

The program is being run by an entertainment company I've never heard of. The K-pop world is notoriously hard for non-Koreans to break into, and the only Korean I know are the five phrases I've learned from watching K-dramas. The last time I auditioned was for my role on *Sweet Cadence* when I was barely fifteen years old. And the last time I performed in front of an audience was at our final concert two years ago.

But my brain leaps over all those logistical obstacles and latches on to the fact that this workshop is my way back to Candie. Back to all the things that I've lost. I have so many questions about what happened to Mina, and Candie is the only one who has answers. If she wants to pretend the past no longer exists, then I'll just have to show her how wrong she is.

I won't let her forget about Mina. About me.

I drag the cursor down the page and click on the big button that says APPLY NOW.

Chapter 2

NOW

The audition for this supposedly prestigious workshop is at some nondescript brick building tucked inside a back alley in Midtown.

As I walk up to the door, all I can think about are the horror stories of idol hopefuls who signed their souls away to the K-pop industrial machine only to get scammed, exploited, or trapped into yearslong "slave contracts" with unethical companies, leaving them with nothing but shattered aspirations and mountains of debt.

After my online application was accepted, I got an email with instructions for the in-person audition. It included a link to a dance routine I was expected to learn and perform for the judges.

The video submission I sent in with my application was focused almost entirely on my vocals—my best asset. Back then, even after putting in tons of extra rehearsal time, I was still the weakest dancer in the group. I don't have Candie's natural talent or Mina's ballet training, and for the past two weeks, I've done nothing but practice the routine until the choreography was burned into my muscles and the backs of my eyelids. The second I stopped practicing and turned off the music, a highlight reel of all the nastiest comments I've ever read about myself would start playing in my head instead.

Can they just recast her pls? tired of looking at her face.

She's a total nepo baby, her mom's like some famous producer.

Home-wrecker! You're nothing compared to Brailey!

I've never seen anyone so incredibly FAKE and UNTALENTED!!!

I didn't tell my mother I was trying out; she would have gone full momager and hired a team of instructors and consultants to whip me back into shape, or worse, contact the workshop herself to demand that they give me a spot. My mother wasn't a producer on *Sweet Cadence*, but she was incredibly invested in me landing the part and repeatedly assured me of all her close studio contacts. I never asked my mother outright if she influenced the casting process of *Sweet Cadence*. But I've never stopped wondering.

This time, I want proof that I can do it on my own.

But my resolve crumbles when I step up to the door and catch an eyeful of my reflection in the glass. Long, loose T-shirt and tights chosen to maximize range of motion and conceal my weight gain, frizzy flyaways already escaping the bun at the back of my head, my features nowhere near the unrealistic photoshopped perfection expected of Asian pop idols, just another desperate face in an ocean saturated with beauty and talent.

I don't smile a lot these days. I'm not the same starry-eyed preteen drawn to the glamour of show business and addicted to the attention fame brought me. But I can't deny that I miss it.

I miss the stage. The lights. The fans. The ritualistic chants backstage. I miss late nights practicing in the studio and early mornings getting ready on set. I miss being part of something meaningful, something much larger than myself.

I miss Mina. And I miss Candie.

I step up and press the number on the intercom. The door buzzes open.

Inside, I take the elevator up to the fourth floor, where the directions told me to go. When the elevator doors ding open, I fully expect to be greeted by a line of fifty stunning girls waiting to audition.

But there's no one. Just one long, empty hallway with no windows or doors on either side. The whorled gray carpet is dizzying. Faint nausea crawls up into my throat. What did I have for breakfast? Eggs? Toast? Oatmeal? Anything?

I remember this feeling. The cold spike of dread. The pinch of my lungs constricting. The fear of failure, of being mocked, of being a disappointment. Suddenly, I hear Candie's voice, clear as if she's right beside me, murmuring in my ear.

You really think you can face me again? she says. *You can't even make it down the hallway.*

I take in a long breath. Candie isn't here. That voice I hear is my own self-doubt.

My feet lift, and I walk forward. The hallway seems to get narrower as I make my way down, and my steps speed up until I'm practically sprinting to push through the double doors at the other end.

Light floods my vision. The room is massive. Floor-to-ceiling windows on one wall, full-length mirrors and a ballet barre along the other. In the center of the studio, four women sit side by side at a folding table. I close the doors behind me, and when I turn, all four of them are looking up at me in unison.

Go on, then, Candie's voice says. *Show me you still have what it takes to stand shoulder to shoulder with me.*

The stage smile blooms wide across my face. I approach the table.

"Hi, I'm Sunday Lee, here for my audition for the SKN workshop."

I can't help it, the second I open my mouth, my voice instinctively hitches higher. Just like it always does.

The judges are all dressed in similarly plain outfits. White blouses, black bottoms. The only hints of color on them are the varying shades of red lipstick. All four women are East Asian, with long black hair and smooth, poreless skin. They look like those ageless actresses who can pull off playing a teenager on one show and a married mother of three on another. A camera is set up on a tripod next to the table.

"Sunday." One of the women stands, pushing her chair back. "It's great to see you."

She comes around the table and wraps her arms around me

in a light embrace. It takes me another second to finally recognize her.

"Oh, Ms. Tao!" I gasp. "It's so good to see you!"

Vivian Tao was Candie's talent manager who Mina and I both eventually signed with. She took us under her wing, didn't coddle us when the execs talked down to us, and encouraged us to speak our minds when producers told us how we should behave. After everything fell apart, Mama fired my entire "team," including Ms. Tao, and I haven't seen or heard from her since we moved away from LA. I always assumed it would be difficult to encounter people from that time of my life again, but it's actually a relief to see a familiar face. Well, somewhat familiar. She looks younger than she did two years ago. I should ask for her plastic surgeon's number; Mama's in the market for a new doctor.

"Let me take a look at you," Ms. Tao says, hands resting on my shoulders. "You're eighteen now, right?"

"I'll be nineteen next month."

She takes a step back and gives me an appraising once-over, cocking her head to the left. "You look good. A little fuller around the hips, but nothing we can't fix."

Her smile is so loving it almost softens the blow. Almost. Ms. Tao turns to sit back down at the table, and the row of eyes lands on me once more.

"Whenever you're ready," Ms. Tao says, folding her hands neatly in front of her.

I drop my bag down against the wall and settle into position in the center of the room. A few deep breaths, a few tosses of my head to relax my neck, then I nod.

The music starts. Five, six, seven, eight.

Turn and step, reach and pose.

Five, six, seven, eight.

Turn and pose and step in, step out.

Five, six, seven, eight.

My body is fluid; my energy is high. I'm feeling confident and landing all my steps. I turn into a spin. Behind me, one of the doors leading to the hallway is open. I could swear that I pulled them shut?

One, two and three and—*shit*, did I miss a beat? Five and six and seven, eight—

The tempo picks up and my turns grow faster, legs pumping, hips swaying. My arms shoot up, then out, bending and flexing. I try to block out the blaring music and focus on counting the beats.

One, two and three and turn—

Something snags at the edge of my vision. I glimpse a flash of pink and white, a pinwheel of skirts. There's someone standing in the doorway, watching me.

I spin forward again to face the panel. There's no emotion on their faces, no telling what they're thinking, which mistakes they're marking down; I can't mess this up, don't mess this up—

When I spin back toward the door again, I see her.

It's Mina. Standing in the doorway. Her face is exaggerated, her eyes are large and vacant, her mouth small and puckered. Dirt-covered hands reach up to her face.

I let out a silent scream as I fall out of the turn at a bad angle, crashing to the ground onto my side. A soft gasp comes from the judges' table. I push my head up and look again.

The doorway is empty.

Every last breath of air rushes out of me. The room tilts sharply even though I'm not moving. My cheekbone throbs.

"I'm sorry," I gasp, scrambling to my feet. "I—I can't do this—"

"Sunday, wait!" Ms. Tao calls out, but I don't stay to hear what she says.

I grab my bag and flee from the audition room. When I burst through the doors and rush into the hallway, there's nobody standing on the other side.

Chapter 3

THEN

Four years ago

It's a few months before my fifteenth birthday, and I'm sitting with my mother and about a hundred other girls who've made it through to the semifinal round of open casting.

Mama's been drilling it into me for weeks now how the show I'm auditioning for is A Big Deal. All it said on the casting call is that it's a "K-pop-inspired musical series," but according to my mother's inside sources, the studio plans to use the show as a launching pad to debut a new pop group.

"It's a tried-and-true formula, and they're jumping on that Asian pop train before it leaves the station," she reminded me for the third time when we showed up to the auditions. "Plus, a network show with multiple Asian American leads? Opportunities like this were nonexistent when I was going out for roles."

After she graduated high school, Mama defied her Taiwanese

immigrant parents and moved to LA to be an actress. Her dream didn't last very long and she ran out of money in a year, but she was way too stubborn to go crawling back to my grandparents. She met my father, a Hong Kong film producer, when she was cast as a minor character in one of his movies (Female Victim 4 on IMDb). They didn't last very long, either.

He went back to Hong Kong after the movie wrapped, and she walked away from that relationship with two things: a three-month-old me and the epiphany that rather than fighting every actress in LA for scraps, she could move behind the scenes and be the one to call the shots like my father did.

We have no contact with my father, and my grandparents never forgave Mama for rejecting the path they had paved. I know she's under a lot of pressure. She worked incredibly hard to build a life for us, and she wants me to be successful where she failed.

Going to auditions is a treasured ritual of ours. I love to sing and perform, but what I love the most is the shining pride in her eyes, the way she gives me pep talks while she straightens my hair and paints the lids of my eyes with a soft brush.

We've been in a holding pattern for hours, and for the last ten minutes, Mama's been on the phone arguing loudly with my grandmother, not giving a single damn about the bothered glances other parents are shooting her way. Every few years there's an attempt to begin peace talks between my mother and my grandparents. So far, none have resulted in a happy reunion, and this one doesn't sound like it's going to go very well, either.

Mama's speaking in Mandarin, and I can only understand bits and pieces of the conversation until she suddenly switches to English.

"—I have given you *plenty* of opportunities to see her. If you wanted to, you would have made it happen. No. *No.* Don't turn this around!"

I shrivel into my seat when I realize they're talking about me. More people are staring now.

"I'm going to the bathroom," I toss out, springing to my feet and fleeing before Mama drags me into this fight and I end up on the phone trying to fumble through a conversation with my embarrassing broken Mandarin.

The convention-room floor is packed with every flavor of dazzling star: child actors who have probably been in block-buster franchises, doe-eyed undiscovered hopefuls, pageant princesses texting on their phones, aspiring singers showing off elaborate vocal exercises, dancers posing like they're in a music video. There's probably some prodigy here who's been winning music competitions since kindergarten.

I'm not a complete amateur, but my demo reel isn't all that impressive, either. I've done a few commercials and lots of back-ground work. I got pretty far in a major televised singing com-petition before getting the ax. Being surrounded by incredibly beautiful girls who already look like full-fledged K-pop idols, however, batters my already shaky confidence and I feel a sud-den urge to run out of the building.

But I know I can't. Mama's waiting for me.

She believes in me, has supported me the way her mother never did for her. My mother and grandmother seem incapable of having a single pleasant conversation. I don't want my relation-ship with Mama to ever become that.

I can't let her down.

Around another corner, down a different hallway, I finally find the restroom. Right as I'm about to step into a stall, I hear muffled sniffling coming from the end of the row.

Someone is having a quiet meltdown.

I stand there for a few uncomfortable seconds, wondering if a stranger is any of my business. Eventually, sympathy overrides awkwardness, and I make my way over. Before I can raise my hand to knock, there's a flush, and the door swings open.

The girl who emerges startles, not expecting someone to be standing right outside. I'm shocked, too, because I recognize her instantly.

A quick glance down at her name tag confirms it.

She's Candice Tsai.

I was just watching one of her videos last night.

Candice isn't a hugely popular influencer, but I've been an avid follower of hers for almost a year now. Alone in my room, I'd listen to Candice sing cover songs, try out her makeup tutorials, and when Mama worked late, I'd eat dinners in the company of her mukbangs. In most of her videos she's just in her bedroom talking, about what she did that day, new music she's listening to, which couples she's rooting for in the latest drama she's watching. And while I'm fully aware that Candice Tsai has no idea who I am, it feels like I'm meeting a dear friend for the first time.

Candice blinks her dark eyes at me, and I seem to shrink on the spot, becoming more insignificant, just another amateur wannabe standing in the presence of a genuine star. Everything from her tailored outfit to her flawless makeup to the Swarovski crystals on the tips of her nails looks like it was designed by professional stylists. Her sleek waist-length black hair shines even under the poor bathroom lighting. If not for the hint of pink at the corners of her eyes and the fact that I had just heard her, there would be no evidence that she had been crying.

"Are you . . . all right?" I venture.

She doesn't answer the question, just motions for me to step aside. "Excuse me."

"Right. Sorry." I step back, and she sweeps past me toward the sink.

I watch her check her makeup in the mirror, then open up her clutch to pull out a mascara wand. She applies mascara to her thick lashes carefully and dabs another coat of gloss over her lips, cleaning the excess from the corners of her mouth with her pinkie.

I'm nowhere in her field of vision. I might as well be a hand dryer on the wall at this point. Even though she's here to audition, just like me, it's as if I'm having a chance encounter with an actual celebrity, and I can't let a golden opportunity like this slip by.

"Not to sound like a total stalker," I say, stepping toward her and raising my hands up in an *I'm harmless, I swear* gesture, "but I really love your videos."

Candice pauses in the middle of spritzing herself with puffs of citrus-scented mist. She turns to glance at me over her shoulder.

"Your skin-care routines literally saved my life last year when my forehead was seventy-five percent acne," I say.

When she doesn't respond immediately, I laugh a little and try to power through the silence. "I was about to start putting toothpaste and Windex on my face; thank god your suggestions worked."

Finally, she gives a small smile. "You're welcome. I'm glad it helped."

She's clearly not in the best headspace right now, so I don't blame her for being less friendly than she appears online, but her smile is, in fact, *more* stunning in person.

"Whatever it is you're upset about, don't let it get to you, okay? You're an amazing singer and dancer; I bet they're writing up your contract right now." Her smile makes me feel warm all over, and I ramble on, emboldened. "If some asshole made you cry, I wish them failure in all their future endeavors. May they step on dog turds every day for the rest of their life."

Her smile fades. Her shoulders tense, and her eyes shift down. I immediately realize my mistake. She was trying to have a private vulnerable moment, and here I come with my big mouth loudly exposing her. I panic and start to stutter out a retraction, but Candice snaps her clutch shut and turns away from me. "Good luck with the auditions."

She brushes a strand of stray hair over her shoulder and exits the bathroom, leaving me standing stiffly in her wake, this dazzling girl who seems leagues ahead of me. A cold understanding washes over me. I may think I know Candice Tsai, but I don't. She isn't my friend at all. She is untouchable. Unreachable.

When I make it back to the waiting area, Mama is waving her arms madly at me like her jacket sleeves are on fire.

"Where did you run off to?" she shouts. "You missed the whole announcement! You made it to the final rounds!"

I can tell Mama is annoyed that I'm not displaying the proper amount of excitement. But I can't shake the mortification of how poorly that bathroom interaction went. Candice's videos have gotten me through some really tough and lonely days, and I wanted so badly to return the favor. Instead, I probably made her feel worse. I should have left her alone.

That night, I spend an unreasonably long time writing and rewriting a three-sentence DM. I contemplate tacking on a heart emoji at the end but decide against it.

> Hi Candice, this is Sunny, the girl you met in the bathroom today at the auditions. I just wanted to apologize for getting in your face like that. I hope you're feeling better!

For an entire week, I leap out of my skin every time my phone goes off. Afterward, staring at an empty inbox, I'm forced to admit how silly it is of me to expect a reply.

Candice Tsai is obviously not going to message me back.

Chapter 4

NOW

"This is it," **Mama** says, cutting the car engine. "We're here."

We're thirty minutes out from the city, in the heart of Y'allywood—the collection of sprawling movie lots and studio complexes that sprung up when film productions moved south.

The building before us looks like it belongs on the cover of an avant-garde architecture magazine. The facade is built out of geometric shapes slotted together at bewildering angles, with long windowpanes sliced into the walls, surrounded by wide lawns of unnaturally green grass.

This is where the SKN workshop is being held. Where I'll be spending the next several weeks.

A personalized acceptance letter from Ms. Tao showed up in my inbox a day after my disastrous audition. Turns out, she isn't just a judge—she's the director of the whole workshop.

Dear Sunday,

Your submission package to the SKN workshop has been reviewed by the panel, and I'm delighted to inform you that you have been selected to join our summer workshop. While I know the audition was not your best performance, this program is about unearthing and nurturing true potential. Taking into consideration your industry experience, I believe that you deserve a second chance. Please find the full details and forms for the program attached, and don't hesitate to reach out to me if you have any questions. I'm looking forward to working with you again.

Sincerely,

Vivian Tao

SKN WORKSHOP PROGRAM DIRECTOR

Even if this is just a handout because Ms. Tao feels sorry for me, and even though my subconscious keeps conjuring up phantoms that aren't really there . . . I can't look back now. There were so many days when all I could do was curl into myself and hide in my room where nothing and no one could ever hurt me again. Somehow, I've climbed out from the wreckage of myself. The answers I want from my past and the hopes I have for the future are just beyond those doors. I only need to take this one last step and unbuckle my seatbelt.

I stare out the car window at the building. My hands stay motionless in my lap.

"Go on, then," Mama urges. "You wanted to do this on your own, right? Or do you need me to go in with you?"

I shift my gaze toward her. "Are you still mad at me for not telling you about the workshop?"

"Of course not."

"Because you sound mad."

"I'm glad you took the initiative." With her sunglasses blocking the top half of her face and the bottom half frozen by a vigorous Botox regimen, it's impossible to tell how she actually feels.

". . . What if I mess it all up again?"

The question that's been endlessly plaguing me forces itself out, looming like a foreboding omen.

"Don't think like that," Mama instructs. "For the next few weeks, don't think about the past and just focus on moving forward, okay?"

"Okay." I nod.

"Remember to drink tons of water."

"I will."

"And make sure to properly stretch; the last thing you want is an injury."

"Uh-huh."

"And don't forget to use under-eye cream; your eyes always get swollen when you're stressed."

"All right, *I got it*," I huff. "I'll try my best."

Mama adjusts her sunglasses. "I know you will."

I consider reaching out for a hug but decide that it's best

not to ruin a good moment by testing the boundaries of my mother's low tolerance for physical affection. But then Mama leans over and wraps her arms around me. I shut my eyes against her shoulder, and we stay like that for a few brief moments. The embrace feels surprisingly natural but also weighted with every unsaid word stored up between us over the years.

"Thanks, Mama."

I step out of the car, pulling my little suitcase behind me, and watch as my mother drives out of the lot.

Past the set of towering glass doors, the lobby has an aggressively modern art-gallery vibe. A soaring ceiling and blinding white walls and floors so polished I can see my own nervous reflection. The reception desk looks like it was carved out of one massive piece of wood. A large painting hangs on the wall behind it—a colorful row of dancing women, their faces blurry, mid-spin. There's nobody at the desk.

"Hello?" I call out.

My voice echoes in the cavernous space. A long hallway stretches back, leading into the building. I venture a few steps past the reception area, craning my neck, and spy someone at the end of the hallway. A girl, facing away, with her back turned to me.

Her dress is dramatic and hard to miss even from a distance. Sparkly bodice, tiers of pink-and-white skirting. It looks like a stage costume. Short black hair curves against her nape.

"Hello? Excuse me?"

The girl doesn't turn.

That's when I notice. Her outfit. It looks familiar. Like I've seen it somewhere before. The girl slips around the corner just then, the ruffled edges of her dress disappearing behind the white wall.

The urge to chase after her grips me, but I stop myself. I'm probably not allowed to go inside without checking in, and I don't want to start my first day by setting off security alarms. I turn back toward the lobby and nearly jump out of my skin. A smiling receptionist is standing behind me.

"Welcome to the SKN workshop, Sunday."

The receptionist has the same silky hair and airbrush-smooth features as the judges who were at the dance audition. There's probably a certain look required to be hired here. Young, slim, pale—the devil's triangle of Asian beauty standards.

"Please follow me," she requests. "Ms. Tao is expecting you."

She leads me down the hallway where I saw the girl in the pink dress. But when we turn the corner, there's no girl on the other side, only a vast open atrium with a wide spiraling staircase at the center. I glance up at the hallways of the second and third floors, squinting against the bright rays pouring down from the skylight. White pillars blend into the white walls that extend to the white ceiling, and I quickly look down before vertigo sets in.

The receptionist heads up the stairs and I rush to catch up, listening for the other participants—any girlish laughter or excited chatter—but there's only the tap-tapping echo of our footsteps. The atrium is silent, and so is the second-floor land- ing. Either I've arrived too early or the soundproofing in this place is amazing.

We make our way down another identical hall and through the open doors of an elegant office—sleek ivory shelves and spotless floors like the rest of the building. The rapid clacking of keyboard keys pauses as Ms. Tao looks up from her computer.

"Sunday, please, come on in." She gestures to the cream chair in front of her desk. "We're absolutely thrilled to have you."

The door shuts behind me, the receptionist already gone.

"Thank you again for this opportunity," I emphasize as I take a seat. I doubt every workshop attendee is getting a personal meet and greet with the program director. "I can't tell you how happy I am to be here."

Ms. Tao's fashion choices have gotten a lot bolder. Sitting there with blowout waves, a bloodred blazer, a tight pencil skirt, and a plunging-neckline blouse, she looks like a cutthroat producer who power lunches with music execs then goes club-hopping with her much younger boyfriend.

"It's been too long." Ms. Tao sighs. "How's your mother?"

Since Ms. Tao last saw her, Mama has had a slew of new relationships, including two broken engagements, and has issued one restraining order.

"She's great. Ratings for her new show are through the roof."

"She must be so happy that you've refocused on your career."

My smile tightens. "Definitely. She's been very supportive."

"Know that I'm absolutely here to support your growth and healing, as well. Please don't hesitate to let me know if there's anything you need. Do you have any questions about the information I sent you, or the consent forms?"

"Oh, um—" I pull my phone out from my jacket pocket. "I'm supposed to give you this?"

"Ah, yes, the device policy." She nods sympathetically. "I

know that taking away a teenager's phone is like asking them for a limb, but one of my main goals for this program is to create a space devoid of outside distractions, so that our attendees can focus all their attention on reaching their goals."

I look down at my phone for a few more seconds before handing it over. She's right—I don't need the temptation to google myself or read hate comments at two in the morning.

"Don't worry, you won't be completely cut off, there's a computer lab that you're free to use during your downtime." Ms. Tao takes my phone and sets it next to her keyboard, out of my reach. Then the cordial smile fades from her face, her eyes grow somber, and I know what's coming.

"Sunday, I'm so incredibly sorry I wasn't able to be by your side during that difficult time. I'll forever carry the pain with me, as well. My door is always open if you want to talk."

By the end of *Sweet Cadence*, everything had devolved into a mess of compounding disasters. Mama moved us out of LA immediately following Mina's funeral, and she fired Ms. Tao over the phone. I never even got the chance to say goodbye to her.

"I meant what I said in the acceptance letter," she tells me. "I know that audition wasn't representative of your capabilities. Your personality shines when you step onstage. You have great screen presence, a unique voice, and most importantly, a strong work ethic. I saw the way you pushed harder than anyone else to improve yourself. And that is why you have been selected for the workshop. Not because of our personal history. But because of your talent and potential. Because you deserve to be here."

The relief I feel when she tells me this is tremendous. "Thank you. That . . . that really means a lot."

Her smile blooms again as she clasps her hands together. There's not a single crease in the skin around her eyes and mouth. "Let's get you settled in before orientation starts, shall we?"

We leave Ms. Tao's office and head down what I thought was a different hallway, but we end up at the same central staircase.

"The facility's very nice," I comment as we ascend the grand stairs.

"My investors and I are hoping to turn this complex into a performing-arts academy soon. The workshop is a bit of a trial run," Ms. Tao explains.

The third floor has dormitory-style doors lining both sides of the hallway. So far, I've only seen one piece of wall art and it was the blurry image of those dancing women down in the lobby. Without a single drop of color elsewhere, the whole building feels like a sterile, disorienting maze. We stop in front of the room numbered 309.

"This is your room. The communal bathroom is just down that way." Ms. Tao knocks on the door before pushing it open.

The room is larger than I expected. There's a window on the far wall, and the space is split precisely down the middle, with an identical dresser, desk, chair, and bed on either side. White interior, just like the hallways outside. And it looks like someone has already claimed the left side of the room.

There's a water bottle on the nightstand, a handbag on the desk, and a suitcase open on the floor. On the bed, there's a turquoise throw pillow with an illustration of a French bulldog eating a donut on it. I know that pillow. I've seen that pillow before.

"I thought it would be nice for the two of you to be roommates," Ms. Tao says, gesturing to the other occupant.

My heart hammers, rapid-fire. I turn to the left.

Candie looks up from where she's depositing her clothes into a dresser drawer.

For a few horrible seconds, I'm convinced that I've been tricked. That I've misread some crucial fine print in the contract and this is actually a classic reality-show setup where two people with a complicated past are forced to live and compete together—and for all I know there are hidden cameras everywhere recording my dumbstruck face.

Candie's lips bend up slightly into a soft smile.

"Candice tells me you two haven't spoken in a while." Ms. Tao looks exceedingly pleased that the three of us have reunited. "I'm sure you have a lot of catching up to do."

Chapter 5

NOW

"**Orientation will begin in** about fifteen minutes in the atrium," Ms. Tao tells us. "I'll see you girls downstairs."

Neither of us moves as Ms. Tao turns to leave. As soon as the door closes, Candie's demeanor changes.

The flawless stage smile vanishes first. Her body language shifts into an unwelcoming stance. She's not the charismatic YouTuber giving skin-care tips or the sparkling pop idol who can command the attention of a stadium full of screaming fans. The real Candice Tsai lying beneath that cloyingly sweet princess facade is an uncompromising, jawbreaker-hard tyrant who is capable of anything.

She was the person I once held closest to my heart. She promised me she would always be there for me and then promptly walked away when everything fell apart. I've spent whole days imagining various reunion scenarios and crafting the witty and exacting statements I might deliver when I saw her again.

". . . I like your bangs" is what comes out.

Candie lifts a hand to her face and brushes her fingertips against her hair before dropping them back to her side.

"What are you doing here?" Her tone is accusatory, like my presence is a personal affront to her.

"Same thing you are." I cross my arms. "What? You can try to be relevant again, but I can't?"

The defensiveness is instinctive. Toward the end of our relationship we were always at odds with each other, and Mina was stuck playing peacemaker.

But Mina is not here anymore.

"I'm not trying to pick a fight, Sunny. I'm just surprised."

The patronizing use of my nickname like we haven't been estranged for two years cuts deep enough to sting.

"If this is too awkward for you, I can ask Ms. Tao for a room change," I offer flippantly.

She glances at me steadily, without blinking. "Why would this be awkward for me?"

Two seconds, three seconds go by, and I crumble under her challenging gaze, thoroughly losing the staring contest. "Well. Because. We . . ."

Several knocks land on the door just then, and Candie turns from me to answer it. Suddenly, the doorway of our room is bursting with enthusiastic chatter. A few other workshop participants have evidently gathered for the express purpose of meeting the famed Candice Tsai.

"We just wanted to come by and say hi! I'm Jessica!"

"Oh my god, I watch your channel religiously."

"We're so excited you're here!"

The girls don't address me at all, rendering me an irrelevant shadow lingering in the corner of the room. Candie interacts with them easily, her expression open and gracious, the mask firmly back in place.

The gulf between us has never felt vaster.

The atrium is packed with girls.

Rows of them, an army of lean bodies and glossy hair and spark-fueled eyes focused straight ahead, all locked on the same goal. Ms. Tao addresses us from atop the first step of the staircase, haloed in light shining down from the circular skylight.

"It's my pleasure to welcome you all to the SKN workshop. The team and I are so excited to spend the next five weeks helping you reach your dreams."

I once orbited the very epicenter of this universe. Stuck my flag into the holy grounds all these girls are marching toward. But now, standing at the back of the crowd, I feel like an interloper sneaking into a land I was exiled from. My eyes unintentionally seek out Candie. She's in athletic wear, her hair loosely pinned up with barely any makeup on, surrounded by her new admirers. Even in a room teeming with lovely, attractive faces, hers is still the one that stands out.

She's always the one who stands out.

"—I'm sure you've all read the details already, but I just wanted to remind everyone that we will be scoring each of you during your sessions on your skills, presentation, and potential,"

Ms. Tao says. "Scores will be tallied at the end of each day and will determine which girls will advance to the finals and be chosen to join the trainee program abroad. Those with unsatisfactory scores will, unfortunately, be cut from the program. If anyone has any questions, feel free to ask them now."

The crowd is silent.

"Wonderful. I'll give everyone a quick tour of the facilities, and we'll head straight into our first session."

Ms. Tao walks us through the lounge area decorated with beige sofas, past the fitness center, and around the corner to the cafeteria full of white dining tables and chairs.

"Breakfast is served at seven, and the first practice session begins at eight thirty. After lunch will be the afternoon sessions that focus on vocals, acting, and stage presentation. We want everyone to be as healthy as possible, physically and mentally. There won't be any weigh-ins or diet restrictions," Ms. Tao informs us. "Our catered meals are nutrition—not calorie—based."

As she's giving us the "healthy bodies, healthy minds" spiel, I remember the way Ms. Tao's eyes had lingered on my waist at the audition like she was taking measurements, calculating exactly how far off I was from the ideal weight.

I remember the way Mama used to keep sugar away from me like contraband, reminding me that she had a round face at my age, too, and this was how she lost the baby fat. The way every move I made was scrutinized and used to critique my character, every part of myself dissected and packaged for the public's enjoyment. I remember all the vicious online comments about the size of my thighs and shoulders compared to the slim, lithe limbs of Candie and Mina, the criticisms of how I'm too short, too dark, too western-looking, that I would never be popular in Asia where I'd have to compete against *real* idols.

It makes Ms. Tao's words sound a little canned, a little disingenuous, like an obligatory disclaimer given to gloss over the poison of weight and body obsession the industry makes us drink at the door: *Side effects of being an idol may include headaches, nausea, loss of appetite, dehydration, malnutrition, depression, anxiety, body dysmorphia, poor self-esteem, eating disorders, suicidal thoughts, and in some severe cases, death. Always consult your doctor to see if being an idol is right for you.*

Even if Ms. Tao doesn't expect us to look a certain way, I have the screencaps to prove that the rest of the world does. Dread and doubt fill my stomach along with a familiar pressure. The pressure of performing, touring, endless press, and living life on display.

What have I gotten myself into? Am I really doing this again?

I grapple for that initial reason, that burst of conviction I felt when I first applied.

"The fitness center and private practice rooms are open until ten. Curfew is at eleven—everyone must be back in their rooms."

As we make our way through the first floor of the building, whispers and murmurs bubble up all around me. When I turn to look, heads whip away quickly, and I only catch fleeting glimpses of the judgment and speculation in the other girls' eyes.

Ms. Tao concludes the tour by leading us into the main dance hall, a huge studio with light hardwood floors and mirrors spanning the whole length of the room. "Please allow me to introduce Yuna, our wonderful dance coach."

I recognize Yuna as one of the judges from my audition. Or is she? She definitely looks familiar. She must be a new protégé of Ms. Tao's, with that straight-backed ballerina posture and the same ageless beauty.

"Let's get started, everyone," Yuna tells the crowd.

I steal another glance at Candie, who's focused straight ahead, and suddenly the doubt gives way to razor-sharp clarity.

I used to make all my choices based on what other people wanted.

This time, I'm choosing what *I* want.

I want to show Candie that I'm still here. I want to prove to her, to Mama, to all the fans I've let down that I'm not an embarrassing disappointment. That I can be worthy of their love and respect again.

But more than anything, I want to learn the truth about what happened to Mina.

And I can't leave until I get it.

Chapter 6

THEN

Four years ago

I can't believe it. It doesn't feel real.

A dream this incredible can't possibly come true so easily.

I've been cast as one of the three leads in the new teen musi-cal dramedy *Sweet Cadence*.

What's better, my costar is none other than Candice Tsai herself. We're going to be costars. Groupmates, even, if they decide to debut us as a pop group.

Best of all, we might actually become real friends.

And I'll be a real actress, just like Mama wanted. I'll be fol-lowing in her footsteps, across the same stages. Mama is over the moon when we get the call from the casting director. For the first time in a long time, my mother seems truly happy.

Mama is in such a state of bliss that she finally does the thing she's been putting off for years. She drives us down to San Diego to see my grandparents.

Two hours down the I-5, and we pull to a stop in front of a little blue bungalow. As we walk up to the door, I picture a plump, five-year-old version of my mother playing in the front yard, drawing chalk artwork on the sidewalk, Rollerblading down the driveway. I imagine a sixteen-year-old version of her, fresh out of braces, kissing boys in their cars in the spot we just parked in. I think about her flicking her parents off the day after she turned eighteen and driving away to LA in her old green station wagon that she still speaks of fondly. I wish I could tell that girl that she made it, she succeeded despite the odds, that we are now are fulfilling her dreams, together.

Both my grandparents are shorter and frailer than I remembered.

"Agong. Amah." I greet them as Grandpa and Grandma politely.

Amah immediately starts speaking to me in Taiwanese, the words too fast for me to follow, and I start to panic about having to puzzle together an entire discussion centered around me. I barely understand enough Mandarin to keep up with casual conversation; throw in Taiwanese, too, and we might as well start playing charades.

Amah ushers our feet into plastic house slippers, and Agong guides us into the living room. I sit quietly on the couch next to Mama and stare at the plate of cut fruit on the coffee table that nobody is eating. Amah and Agong speak in a combination of Taiwanese and Mandarin with the occasional English words

tossed in, and I try my best to keep up with this trilingual conference. Then Mama delivers the big news.

I know this because my grandparents fall completely silent.
The looks on their faces need no translation.

"You are going to be an *actress*?" Amah asks me in English,
pointing to the TV set behind her.

I want to answer yes in Taiwanese, but I'm so nervous I'm
blanking on even the most basic of vocabulary. I nod stiffly.

"What about school?" Amah demands.

"We'll figure it out," Mama answers.

"She has to go to school! Children go to school!"

"She doesn't have to be in school to receive an education!"

"She is a little young, don't you think, Shu Jing?" Agong
chimes in finally, and it's not to voice his support.

"You have not learned your lesson!" Amah berates. "You're
going to let your daughter make your same mistakes!"

"She's going to be on a big show, bigger than anything I've
ever done!" Mama retorts.

"She's going to end up pregnant, like you! Or do drugs!" Amah's
yelling now.

"Why are you so obsessed with failure? You wanted me to
fail, and now you want Sunday to fail, too!"

They switch to Mandarin again, and I retreat into silence. I
don't know why I thought this would go smoothly. A few heated
exchanges later, Mama stands from the couch.

"We're leaving," she announces.

"What?" I blurt. "We just got here!"

"Get your bag." She leans down to grab the handle of her

suitcase, yanking it behind her as she turns toward the door. "We're going home."

"But—!"

"*Now*, Sunday. I'm not asking."

I look between Mama's retreating back and my grandparents' scowls. They make no move to stop her. I bow my head apologetically to them before rushing after Mama. The front door has been left open. Mama's already halfway to the car.

As I shove my heels into my sneakers, a dry, wrinkled hand grasps my wrist. I turn. Agong stands behind me in the front hall with a remorseful smile. He slides a white envelope into my hand.

"Take care," he says, fingers slipping away from my arm.

When I get into the passenger seat, Mama says only one thing to me.

"Forget everything you heard in there. You're going to prove them wrong."

I feel the full weight of her expectations as she rests them soundly on my shoulders.

It makes me feel important. It gives me purpose.

"I'll try my best, Mama," I promise her.

When we're stopped at a gas station, I take a peek inside the envelope Agong gave me while Mama's picking up cigarettes and coffee. It's full of fifty-dollar bills.

I see where Mama learned it from now. The way she uses material goods as expressions of love and care. How she buys me Chanel handbags instead of telling me she's proud of me.

According to Mama, no matter how far up the social ladder she climbs, it still won't amount to anything in her parents' eyes. Working in the entertainment industry is not reputable, and having a child without a husband is shameful. I didn't quite believe her when she told me this before, but now I've experienced that harsh rejection firsthand. Mama wasn't exaggerating.

I comfort myself by watching fancams of my latest obsession, Jin-hwan Woo, on my phone. He only debuted a month ago, but in the time it took me to finish watching the music video of his first single, I had broken up with all my other idol loves and pledged my devotion to this beautiful boy.

Jin-hwan's voice croons at me through my headphones, and I daydream about him sitting next to me instead of Mama, winking from behind the steering wheel, his smile capturing that elusive angle between charm and arrogance, a single lock of his bangs falling over his left eye as he drives us up the PCH and into the pinkish-orange sunset.

I meet my other costar, Mina Park, on the first day of rehearsals.

The experience is the polar opposite of my encounter with Candice.

Mina rushes straight at me, a blooming sunflower of a girl with an adorable bob cut and a freckled nose, overflowing with enthusiasm and positivity.

"I'm *so* excited to work with you, Sunday!" she gushes, and hugs me like we've been costars for ages.

She reminds me of the intrepid heroines of my favorite

K-dramas. Like she could befriend anyone and tackle any challenge with her effortless girl-next-door charm and dimpled smile. Mina is sixteen, and when she finds out I'm nearly two years younger than her, she immediately assumes the eonni role and promises to look out for me on set, assuring me that I can seek her advice for anything I need, anything at all.

"Is this your first major TV role?" she asks.

I nod sheepishly. "I don't think being a background patient on *Boston Medical* counts."

"Mine too!" she says without a hint of embarrassment. "I heard that Candice was someone the producers discovered online?"

"Is Candice here?" I immediately turn my head to glance around.

Mina nods. "She was the first one to arrive!"

My palms start to itch, and I rub them against the side of my shorts. I must look really anxious, because Mina wraps an arm around my shoulder and gives me a tight squeeze. "Don't be nervous, Candice is super nice, come on!"

I don't correct her that Candice and I have, in fact, already met.

When we walk together into the room where the table reads are being held, Candice is seated at the table, talking to the production crew.

She's wearing glasses today and a white eyelet sundress, her hair twisted in a loose braid over the ivory curve of one shoulder. I'm pretty sure she's only a year or so older than me, but there's a sophistication to her look that makes my floral-print shirt and jean shorts feel like something off the spring catalogue of OshKosh B'gosh. Surrounded by the production crew,

Candice is chatting and laughing with ease, the Candice I know from her videos.

Mina drags me over and plants me squarely down in the chair beside Candice. "Candice, this is Sunday, our third musketeer!" Mina introduces me, blissfully unaware.

When Candice turns to us, I give her a tentative wave. She smiles at me, and once again I'm hit by the same heated pangs of admiration that struck me in that bathroom.

"It's nice to meet you," Candice says pleasantly. "I'm so glad we get to work together."

Of course. Of course she doesn't remember me. I force my smile to stay intact.

"I can't believe this is happening!" Mina chimes in.

"Hello, syndication and world tour!" I declare loudly, trying to hide my small heartbreak by being obnoxious.

We have our first table read, and it goes perfectly. The showrunner is clapping, the producers are praising us, and my mother looks exceedingly pleased when she picks me up afterward. It was incredibly easy to get into character; Mina and Candice already felt like the big sisters I'd never had. It was a real inspirational moment—our newly formed trio set to embark on a life-changing journey together.

Except, the movielike training montage culminating in a total pop-star transformation I envisioned for myself doesn't happen.

When rehearsals begin, I'm overwhelmed by all the lines I need to memorize, the marks I have to hit, the choreography I have to learn, the lifetime of hopes and dreams my mother is expecting me to fulfill for her.

I got all the information about this show from my mother, and it turns out, there's way more dancing involved than she let on. My character is a cheerleader, and I'm expected to learn actual cheer moves. I'm confident in my singing and comfortable in front of the camera, but the only dance experience I have is a year and a half of jazz and tap when I was five.

The physicality is grueling and the learning curve feels impossibly steep. Candice and Mina dance effortlessly, gracefully, but I struggle every session to make my feet coordinate with my arms.

"You're putting too much pressure on yourself, Sunny. Remember, deep breaths, and relax your limbs," our dance instructor reminds me. "Watch how Candice does it."

Naturally, everyone is enamored with Candice, showering her with praise and glowing feedback, such as: "This is what a future superstar looks like."

Mina provides a constant stream of moral support, but Candice smiles at me less and less, and there's an edge of irritation in her eyes as she watches me stumble. When Mama comes to rehearsals, she wears a similar expression, her mouth pulled in a taut line, and I'm terrified that she's disappointed by what she sees.

It's two days before filming begins, and I'm still messing up the same sequences.

"Damn it!" The curse slips out of me when I turn in the wrong direction and nearly collide with Mina. "I'm so sorry; can we try again . . ."

Candice walks over to the stereo and stops the music. The

studio sinks into sudden silence save for our harsh panting breaths and Candice's marching steps. She comes up to me, sweat slicking down her face, her eyes scalpel sharp.

"We start shooting on Monday. Why are you still messing up? Unless you can nail your parts within the next forty-eight hours, I don't know how this is supposed to work."

She doesn't pull me aside to tell me this. She declares it loudly in front of our choreographer, the musical director, and all the production assistants. Her voice is stinging, lacking any of its usual warmth. My face burns. My hands go numb. I've never seen Candice look so fed up, and I can't think of a single response that doesn't involve a dumb joke, or groveling.

Mina steps between Candice and me, her easygoing smile a disarming buffer. "Come on, Candie, it's not that serious! We're all really tired; I think we just need a break!"

Candie shoots her eyes at me again. She opens her mouth, and I turn immediately, not wanting to hear another harsh word, and rush out of the dance studio. I run straight down the hall and out the back door of the building, into the darkened parking lot. The moon hangs high in a cloudless night sky. We've been at it since 9:00 A.M. I collapse onto my butt on the sidewalk.

I'm shaking. From humiliation or exhaustion, I don't know.

Or maybe from fear.

There was something so unpleasantly cold about the way Candice looked at me. Like I was an obstacle that needed to be cleared from her path.

I fold my arms over the tops of my knees and drop my head.

I wanted Candice's approval and friendship almost as badly as I wanted to do well on the show. And I might have just blown my shot at everything.

The building doors open behind me with a loud crack, followed by the sound of padding footsteps. Someone's walking toward me. It's probably Mina, or our dance instructor. But when I raise my head to look, Candice is bending to sit down beside me.

She doesn't say anything for a while, so neither do I. We sit quietly under the fluorescent hum of the parking-lot lights, watching streams of traffic rush by.

"I didn't mean to blow up at you," Candice says finally. "I'm sorry."

She does look apologetic, but I still feel like trampled garbage. "If you wanted me off the show, you could've just told the director."

Her head whips around at me. "That's not what I want."

"You're the *superstar*. If you say things like *I don't know how this is supposed to work*, they'll replace me."

"Nobody is getting replaced."

"Maybe you're right, though." I drop my head back down against my knees. "Maybe I'm just not good enough."

"That's not true," she states firmly. "Out of all the people who auditioned, they picked you. I want to help you get over this hurdle. Tell me how I can help you."

"I don't know." I shake my head in despair. "I don't know why I keep screwing up."

"Do you want to talk about it?"

I don't.

But I end up telling her everything.

About the crushing pressure from my mother, how she holds an unshakable belief that I'm about to become a breakout star, while my grandparents are actively hoping that I crash and burn. I tell her about my secret hope that my father will somehow see me on this wildly successful television show and regret that he's not in my life, that he's never tried to reach out to me, not even once.

"I think I'm just really scared that I'm going to let my mom down," I admit.

"I understand," Candice says. "My family expects a lot of me, too. And all I want is for them to be proud of me."

There's a quiet sorrow in her eyes, and my chest tightens. This is the first time she's ever mentioned anything about herself.

And I realize that when Mina and I would gleefully chatter about our favorite K-pop idols and dramas and shoujo mangas, Candice always orbited our periphery, rarely breaking into the conversation. I feel terrible now for not making more of an effort to include her. I was so intimidated by her that I'd fallen into the trap of assuming her rosy online persona was an accurate reflection of who she actually is.

"How do you deal with the pressure?" I ask.

"By crying in public bathrooms," she answers with a straight face.

An eruption of surprised laughter bursts out of me. "So you *do* remember; you were just too embarrassed to admit it! You're sneaky, Candice Tsai; I'm onto you."

She shrugs as though dismissing my accusation, but the corners of her lips curl around a held-back smile.

I poke a finger against her shoulder. "You know, I messaged you afterward, but you never replied."

"I don't really check my messages," she explains. "What did it say?"

I open my mouth, then close it. "... Nothing important." Another car zooms past us, and I look down, away from the glare of the headlights. "I really hope the pilot gets picked up."

"It will," Candice says with the kind of effortless confidence I hope to have one day. "Come on." She stands. "I'll practice with you all weekend if we have to. We're going to nail the shoot on Monday." She holds out her palm to me. "Together."

I grasp her hand, and Candice pulls me up from the pavement, breaking me free from the dark spiral of anxiety and self-doubt.

"Together." I smile.

Chapter 7

NOW

I can barely move by the end of the first morning dance session.

There's a stabbing ache in my side and tight knots in my calves. Even my kneecaps hurt from all the drops to the floor, and I'm one muscle cramp away from collapsing at Ms. Tao's feet and admitting I've made a terrible mistake signing up for this when the most cardio I've done in the past two years was the time I took up jogging for a month.

I nearly cry tears of relief when Yuna dismisses us for lunch.

In the cafeteria line, I introduce myself to a few girls. They politely entertain my small talk, sharing their backgrounds. Most of the attendees are Korean American, but there are also several, like me, who aren't. There's Wei Yen, a Chinese teen model who just returned from walking in a Shanghai fashion show. Julianna, a Filipino American who's been crowned Miss Teen Asia USA two years in a row. Anisa, who apparently made swear her gaze lands right on me—"I hope to see improvement in tomorrow's sessions."

Prove to me that I was right to grant you another chance, Ms. Tao's eyes say.

My resolve reignites. Candie's at the top of the mountain and I'm languishing at the bottom, whining and crying after just one dance session.

I can't get eliminated before I've had a chance to confront her about everything.

I need to get my ass up and start climbing. *Fast.*

At dinner, I'm sitting alone again in the cafeteria, sipping vegetable soup that's really just broth, when someone sets their plate down at my table and drops into the seat across from me.

"I couldn't double-check on my phone, but you *are* Sunday Lee from *Sweet Cadence*, right?"

I look up, the spoon hanging from my half-open mouth.

The girl sitting in front of me is beaming, her starry eyes stretched wider than my soup bowl. She looks really young, but I'm not sure if it's because of her birthday-kid-standing-under-an-exploding-piñata energy or the fact that she's drenched head to toe in pastel colors. From her bubblegum pink curls to her soft-hued makeup down to her outfit and sneakers. It's been a long time since anyone's looked at me with those eyes—the eyes of a fan.

I smile a little and nod.

She lets out a high-pitched squeak, like a mouse being stepped on.

"Oh my god! I can't believe it! I can't believe I'm here with *both* of you! This is the first time I've made it through the auditions; it's just, such a dream come true! *Sweet Cadence was* middle school for me; every day after school I'd go over to my best friend's house and we'd watch the show together—"

Through her blinding joy and bright cheer I see shadows of my old self. The me that was easily starstruck and rambled when nervous and still had a rosy view of the industry and the world.

The me who doesn't exist anymore.

"When I saw Candie at orientation I nearly peed myself! I haven't tried talking to her yet; she's so intimidating—" The girl stops herself abruptly, the shells of her ears turning red. "I'm talking too much. I'm so sorry. I'm just . . . really excited."

I shake my head. "Don't be sorry. You're the first girl to say more than three sentences to me today. What's your name?"

She laughs nervously, like she just realized she hasn't introduced herself. "I'm Faye. Like the singer, Faye Wong. My mom's a huge fan. And, yeah, nobody's really talked to me, either." She picks up her fork and stabs half-heartedly at the broccoli florets in her salad.

Faye. She's the other low scorer.

I lift my glass of water to her. "Cheers to not getting eliminated on our first night here."

"You absolutely shouldn't have been on the bottom; I mean, you're an actual celebrity!" She looks intensely offended on my behalf.

"Not anymore." I glance quickly over Faye's shoulder at

the dinner crowd. Still no Candie. I stir my spoon, chasing the tiniest piece of carrot around the bowl, trying to quell the disappointment.

Faye leans forward, looks me in the eyes, and tells me in the most unabashedly heartfelt voice, "You are one of my biggest inspirations. And you always will be."

The affirmation that I'm important to someone, that I'm special, hits my brain like a dopamine bomb and I cradle that sliver of approval greedily in my palms.

"Thank you." I smile the first genuine, unstrained smile I've managed to muster all day. "That means so much to me."

Her expression of joy shines straight through all the shuttered windows boarded up around my heart.

"I'm thinking about hitting the practice rooms after dinner," Faye continues. "If there's any hope of me moving up from the bottom, I need to be using every second of my free time to practice." She sucks on her bottom lip, worrying it with her teeth, before venturing on. "Would you, maybe, want to join me? You could give me some pointers?" Her eyes brim with hope.

Past experiences have brewed in me a heavy suspicion toward anyone trying to get close to me. But in this moment, I think I would have said yes to anything Faye asked.

"Sure," I agree. "Good idea."

Faye squeals again and practically lunges across the table to hug me.

All the practice rooms are full except for one. I peer into the rooms that have windows, the girls inside whirling like windup dolls in glass displays.

"Everyone is so talented," Faye says as we flip on the lights in the empty room. The space is large enough for a small group to comfortably practice a routine together, with a full stereo system and a flat-screen TV mounted on the wall. "The choreo is so hard, I don't know how they all learned it so instantly. It really makes me want to push myself, you know?"

Just as Faye gets the music set up, the door to the room swings open. A group of girls stroll in, laughing together like they're already lifelong best friends sharing a priceless inside joke. When they see us, the expressions on their pretty faces shift sharply from humor to annoyance. I recognize a few of them from the table openly discussing me during lunch.

One girl steps forward—tall, stunning, an armor of bold assurance draped across proud shoulders. The leader. The other girls promptly fall in line, troops rallying behind their commander. She looks at Faye and me like we're pieces of gum caught beneath her red-soled designer shoes.

"Hi, Eugenia!" Faye greets her hurriedly with an uneasy, forced cheer.

Eugenia Xin, I remember. One of the top three.

"You have to sign up for these practice rooms to use them," Eugenia says.

Faye's already petite, but standing in the attack path of a domineering queen bee, she looks like a tiny critter cowering at the feet of a predator. "You're right, I'm sorry. I—I forgot."

"It's my fault," I say, stepping up to Eugenia. "I thought the rooms were first come, first served."

Eugenia is nearly a head taller than me, and she uses every extra bit of height to her advantage, staring down her chiseled nose at me.

"Were you not listening during orientation? Or do you think the rules don't apply to you just because you know Ms. Tao?"

She's practically taking a Sharpie and writing *nepotism* across my forehead.

I used to be obsessed with converting every hater to a fan, convinced that I needed everyone to like me, and felt absolutely crushed when they didn't.

After the scandal, I've learned that no matter how many backflips I do to please the critics, there will always be people who loathe me like it's their full-time job, and I will never win the hearts of people who enjoy being cruel.

"You're right." I shrug. "I'm very close to Ms. Tao. She's practically my godmother." I say the lie as confidently as I can.

"She must be disappointed, then." Eugenia's lips pull into a mock pout. "That was really rough this morning. Honestly, I was embarrassed for you. But let's face it, everyone knows you can't dance. You're always going to be remembered for the way you threw yourself at someone else's boyfriend."

On cue, the assembly behind her snickers.

Word must have spread that drama is going down; there's now twice the amount of people crowded around the doorway, waiting to watch the show unfold.

"You do realize it takes two people to cheat, right?" I'm ashamed of what I did, but there's no need to deny what happened. "I've suffered the wrath of both Jin-hwan *and* Brailey's fans for two years now. At one point they had three different 'cancel Sunday Lee' hashtags trending. I've had my life threatened by stalkers. So if you're trying to intimidate me, you need to step up your game, Eugenia. You can't scare me just by acting like a huge bitch."

Eugenia's eyebrows shoot up into her angular bangs. "What did you call me—?!"

"—I'm done with my practice room, if one of you wants to use it."

Heads turn toward the new voice, and bodies part to reveal Candie standing in the hall. She glances at me for the first time all day, and suddenly I'm angrier at Candie than I am at Eugenia.

It's so like her to give me the cold shoulder just to swoop in for a rescue when I'm at the end of my rope like she's doing me a huge fucking favor.

Eugenia opens her mouth to speak, but I've exhausted my fight reflex.

"Come on, Faye."

I brush past Eugenia, past Candie, muscling my way through the crowd into the hallway.

Chatter immediately breaks out over my shoulder, but I don't look back. The only things I focus on are the sound of my furious footsteps and Faye's voice bouncing off the walls behind me.

"Oh my god, I can't believe you *said that*!"

Chapter 8

NOW

This isn't how I wanted my reunion with Candie to go.

I wasn't expecting an emotional reconciliation where we admit to all our mistakes, make up in a tearful embrace, exchange "I'm sorry" and "No, *I'm* sorry" for a few rounds, and bury the horrors of the past into the ground where a pristine, unsullied relationship will spring anew. Too much has happened. Too many things we can't erase, can't take back.

I don't know *what* I was expecting. But it hurts that Candie is treating me with so much indifference, like I'm just another person in the crowd, like we don't have all this grisly, convoluted history between us.

"You always seemed so nice and cheerful; I had no idea you were this much of a badass!" Faye exclaims as she follows me up the staircase to the third floor, away from all the practice rooms.

"That's . . ."

Not who I am anymore. I'm not a nice, cheerful person. Most of the time I feel numb. The rest of the time I'm angry.

". . . I'm used to dealing with bullies by now," I explain.

"Her face, though! God, I wish I had my phone to take a picture!" Faye cackles at the memory. "I'd make extra-large prints and send them out as Christmas cards."

"You don't have to let people like Eugenia push you around," I tell her. "They're just cowards looking to prop themselves up by making everyone else feel small."

"Maybe, but . . . I'd never have the guts to say something like that to her." Faye looks like she's ready to snip off a piece of my hair to make a talisman, or pledge her firstborn to me in exchange for protection.

"Don't worry. I got your back," I promise. "We'll stick together, all right?"

Faye's ecstatic smile lights up her entire face.

"Sorry we didn't get to practice. Let's try again tomorrow." I roll my achy shoulders. "I think I'm going to turn in. See you in the morning?"

Faye looks a little down when I tell her I'm cutting the night short, but she perks up again quickly, nodding. "See you at breakfast! Good night!"

She bounds down the hall, and I turn and make my way back to my room—*our* room—kicking off my shoes before collapsing onto the bed. From the other side of the room comes a faint whiff of citrus body mist. I turn my head, my gaze landing on the empty desk, the neatly made bed.

And I wait.

I'm halfway done wrapping my ankle with athletic tape when Candie finally comes through the door.

She slides off her shoes wordlessly and drops her bag next to her bed. Walking over to her desk, she sets her water bottle down and pulls the elastics out of her messy bun, letting her waist-length hair tumble free past her shoulders and down her back.

We've spent countless hours in close quarters like this, sharing our meals, schedules, hotel rooms, tampons. We've seen each other at our most disheveled and unpolished—without a stitch of makeup on, retainer pressed into gums, massive eye bags, extensions falling out, every pockmark, blemish, and ingrown hair that otherwise gets covered up or airbrushed away. Grief flares unexpectedly when I'm reminded of how close we once were.

Candie spins her chair toward me and sits down. We stare at each other steadily from across the room. Candie speaks first.

"If Eugenia bothers you again, I can—"

"I'm a big girl now." I cut her off before she finishes the offer. "I don't need you to fight my battles anymore."

"I can see that."

There's a note of incredulity in her voice, and I relish the fact that she's realizing she doesn't know me as well as she used to. That the Sunny who trailed after her all day long like a dumb puppy, who she spoiled then abandoned, has come back to her with longer claws and sharper teeth.

"People change, Candie. I'm sure you've changed more than just your hairstyle."

I'm mocking her a little, and she picks up on it immediately.

"I'm trying to be nice." She frowns.

Like how you ignored all my calls and texts? That was real nice. The heated words fill my mouth, but I swallow them back down.

"Why are you here?" she asks me again.

"I told you. Same reason you are."

Candie shakes her head. "You and I both know you're not cut out for this business."

I try not to let the hurt show on my face at her easy dismissal. She always knew exactly what to say to build me up, and with a single sentence level me to the ground again.

"I'm happy to see you again. I am." Her tone softens for a brief moment. "But after everything that happened, I think it's best that you drop out."

"After 'everything'?" I let out an unkind laugh. Even she can't bear to put it into words. "You mean after what we *did*? What *you*'ve done?"

I had wanted to find the most opportune time to talk openly about our past. But instead, the accusation comes rushing out. The shutters slam down hard over Candie's expression. Her jaw tightens.

"I'm telling you this for your own good," she says.

"I think my days of letting you dictate what's good for me are over."

"I'm not kidding, Sunny. You should leave."

"Or what?" I know I'm getting close to crossing the line, but I push toward it defiantly. "You're going to make me?"

Candie's eyes harden into flints.

It's the same admonishing look she used to give me, and it elicits the same response—I recoil a little, fighting the instinctive urge to give in to her.

She still thinks I'm weak. That I'm a pathetic people pleaser. That I'll do as I'm told, satisfy her every whim, that I'll let others use me for their own amusement, then get on my knees and thank them when they toss me aside.

That's not who I am anymore.

"You said I was your family, once. But in the end your promises meant nothing. I'm not giving up what I want again just because it doesn't align with what *you* want," I tell her. "I want to win this thing. I'm not going *anywhere.*"

"If that's how you feel, then there's nothing left to say." The pitiless chill of Candie's words scratches down my spine. "You're right. Things are different now. You might not be scared of Eugenia, but you know better than anyone what happens to people who get in my way."

I'm shocked into silence.

No matter how tense things got between us, she never directly threatened me. I realize that I've successfully struck a nerve. I've upset her.

Candie pushes up from the chair, turning away sharply as she retreats to the other side of the room to ready herself for bed.

I do know better than anyone. I saw it. The brutal horrors

Candie inflicted upon another person. The ease with which she did it. The satisfied gleam in her eyes when they screamed.

The thought of Candie being my enemy, of standing toe to toe against her on the same stage, fills me with deep dread. And at the same time, a secret, feverish thrill.

Chapter 9

THEN

Sweet Cadence **is a** massive hit.

Our characters are strategically named using our real-life nicknames so it'd be a seamless transition when we debuted as a pop group—

Candie: the perfect immigrant daughter, excels at academics, training to be a classical musician but secretly desires to be a pop idol.

Minnie: the undiscovered talent, an introverted outcast who's hiding her ambitious dreams and a powerhouse voice.

Sunny: the bubbly cheerleader, torn between wanting to fit in with the school's popular crowd and embracing her love of Asian pop music.

The plot follows our journey from regular teens to idol stardom while balancing friendship woes, family expectations, and romances in what critics call a "positive and nuanced" portrayal of Asian American girlhood.

After only a few episodes, several of our featured songs are topping the streaming charts, and by the time season one is wrapping up, fans are recognizing me on the street, at the mall, in movie theaters, restaurants. Once someone shouted at me from their car while I was stopped next to them at a red light.

The sponsorship and merchandise deals come pouring in, and suddenly I'm being shown prototype lunch boxes and pajamas with my face on them. Candie's manager, Ms. Tao, took over as *Sweet Cadence*'s music manager, and she keeps our itinerary packed with filming, rehearsals, appearances, interviews, and photo shoots.

As a fan, I've always wondered what it was like for idols to live such an elevated existence, where you're no longer a person but a symbol, a living embodiment of obsession. And now that I'm on the other side of the television screen, I finally have the answer.

It's *a lot*. Like fireworks and parades going off on an hourly basis, like waking up and going skydiving every single day. It's tens of thousands of strangers embracing you at once, telling you that you're beautiful and talented and special, that you are so, so loved.

It's the best feeling in the world.

But with the incredible highs come sharp falls. Large swaths of people are suddenly convinced our show is either too pandering or too whitewashed. Multiple opinion pieces are published about how the writing tries to paint a pretty face on the ugly realities of the pop-idol industry, and how our characters actually enforce harmful Asian stereotypes. And then come the calls to boycott, people bombarding us with messages ranging from *Go back to your country* to *You should be ashamed to participate in the commodification of our culture.*

And then there are the creeps. The gross DMs. The uncomfortable comments about our bodies. The middle-aged men counting down the days till we're legal. Mina's strategy is to block and ignore, and I know that Candie doesn't read her messages, but I can't stop myself. I read every comment, try to respond to every concern; I want so badly to please everyone, but I only end up digging each hole deeper, and everything I post spurs another round of fiery debate until Mina has to threaten to put me in phone jail.

Candie and Mina both have huge fan bases, and I try to remind myself that's how it was designed to be. Candie is the beautiful idol princess, Mina the down-to-earth sweetheart, while my persona is the "baby" of the group, and I'm starting to worry that I come across as the inferior little sister trying to crash my much cooler older sisters' party. The envy has me constantly scrolling through my mentions and browsing the hashtags to see what's being said about me.

Every once in a while, though, I get a really nice message from a fan that makes my entire week.

Hi Sunny, I really liked this week's episode, you were so funny. I don't have a lot of friends at school, but when I watch Sweet Cadence it's like the three of you are my best friends and I feel less alone.

I smile to myself as I type out a reply.

That is the SWEETEST, thank you so much! I feel lonely sometimes, too, even when I'm surrounded by people, but knowing that I'm able to make someone else's day brighter makes me so happy <3 <3 <3

"—I was thinking that when we're back in the studio next week, we could try . . . Sunny. Are you listening? Can you get off your phone for a second?"

"Uh? What?" I look up from typing and am greeted by Candie's aggravated face.

"I was talking to you," she says.

"I've been listening to people talk at me all day; my brain is a pile of mush right now," I groan, sliding my phone away.

The clean edges of her brows knit together, and I brace myself for the incoming lecture, but it's my lucky day and Candie simply turns away to continue packing up her things. I breathe a covert sigh of relief.

We'll get there together.

Candie has kept her word. She's always ready to do that extra round of practice and runs lines with me anytime I want. She doesn't seem to share any of the insecurities I have about whether people like me, whether I'm good enough. Candie doesn't compare herself to anyone.

Working alongside Candie has been a dream come true, but it has also meant getting to know the real Candice Tsai: the critical, temperamental, obsessive perfectionist.

I watch Candie collect the last of her belongings, her expression faraway and stormy—the face she wears when the cameras are off and she doesn't think anyone is looking. The slope of her shoulders spells loneliness, a withdrawn solitude shadowing her frame. She's the beloved star of a hit show with legions of fans who hyperventilate at the mere sight of her, but Candie rarely seems . . . happy.

I think about the first time we met, about Candie's pink eyes, her quiet sobs.

I wish there was something I could do to make her happy.

"Minnie's coming over to my house tomorrow night to watch a movie," I tell her. "Want to join us?"

She turns to face me, the solemn look already wiped clean, replaced by what I now know is her practiced false smile. "Maybe next time."

I frown. "You're busy?"

"Yes."

"Doing what?"

She doesn't answer, and I lean forward conspiratorially. "Seriously, why do you always turn us down? Are you double-booked because you're living some kind of real-life Hannah Montana situation?"

She huffs out a dry, placating laugh.

"Or maaaybe you're in a forbidden relationship with a K-pop star, forced to only meet up in secrecy because of the dating ban?" I gasp, putting on a scandalized expression.

"Yep. That's it. You caught me," she says, deadpan.

"I'm *totally* onto you." I point my finger at her, swirling it around in the air like I can bait her into giving me her secrets. Candie rolls her eyes and bats my finger out of her face.

I heave an overwrought sigh. "I know our relationship has progressed beyond the cringey parasocial era, but I still feel like I know nothing about you."

Candie stares at me like she doesn't understand what the issue is. "What do you want to know?"

"Um, *anything*? What do you do when you're not working? What about your family?"

She shrugs. "I read. Play music. Make videos. I live with my aunt and little cousins, but I've been in boarding school the last few years."

"Oh . . ." It doesn't escape me how she very pointedly says nothing about her parents.

Just then, Mina pokes her head into the studio through the doorway. "You guys ready to go? My dad's here."

Mina's parents didn't hesitate to embrace Candie and me as additional daughters. Mrs. Park fawns over us and brings us Tupperwares full of japchae whenever she visits the set, and Mr. Park makes sure we never work a minute over the allotted hours dictated by child-labor laws and always offers to drive Candie and me home at night. Mina was raised with such an abundance of unconditional love that she can't help but radiate with it.

I point an accusatory finger at Candie, not wanting to let her wiggle off the hook. "She said no to movie night. Again."

Mina turns to Candie and puts her hands on her hips in the eonni power stance. "That's, like, the fifth time you've blown us off. Come on, Candie. We're about to be stuck in this building all summer working on our album; you can't take *one* night off to hang out with us?"

Candie's eyes shift with guilt at getting called out on the spot. I love it when Mina pulls seniority. Finally, Candie sighs and concedes. "Okay, okay, I'll come."

"At last, we're granted an audience with her excellency!" Mina pronounces dramatically.

"Oh, what a glorious day!" I throw a hand over my eyes like I'm about to faint. "Behold, her highness hath smiled upon us!"

Candie shakes her head. "Never mind, I don't want to go anymore."

Mina laughs and links an arm around Candie's left elbow while I slide my arm through Candie's right elbow on the other side, ignoring her fake protest. We parade her like a captive out of the studio and up to the front of the building, where Mr. Park is waiting to pick us up.

"Candie?"

An unfamiliar voice calls out, and I glance up. A young man I don't recognize is loitering at the other end of the corridor. I rack my brain, trying to recall if he was one of the sound engineers we met today.

Candie's arm goes stiff against mine. I turn to her, and the look on her face sends an uneasy anxiety curling down my spine.

The man is approaching us slowly, almost cautiously, but the closer he gets, the more tense I feel. There's a hostility in his gait, an unnerving intensity in his stare. "You wouldn't talk to me, so I had to come to you."

"Who are you?" Mina demands from the other side.

"You did a shout-out to me in your last video; we had a connection!" The man is only a few feet away from us now.

Candie hasn't updated her channel in a while due to our schedule, but I do remember the last one she did. The shout-out was to her "followers who have been with her from the beginning."

"I'm sorry, but y-you can't be in here." I try to keep my voice steady, forceful, but the demand comes out trembling. "If you don't leave, we're going to call security."

The man pulls a black object out from his jacket.

My eyes register the shape of the object he's holding—barrel, handle, trigger, gun, it's a *gun*—but my brain stutters, lags, can't process what's happening. My mind is stuck on how unreal this is, that we're being held at gunpoint inside the halls of a recording studio, and how strangely normal this man looks. Like a college student who works the cash register at Target. Clean-shaven face, sandy hair beneath a baseball cap, gray hoodie jacket and jeans. He doesn't look like a maniac.

Mama went to work before I woke up this morning. I didn't say goodbye to her before she left the house . . .

"Please, don't hurt us," Mina begs him. She sounds like she's crying.

"*She's* the one who hurt *me!*" He raises the gun and points it at Candie's face.

One thought rises above the suffocating fear: *He's going to shoot her.*

My body moves on instinct. I turn and throw my arms over Candie's shoulders, tackling her to the ground, shielding her body with my own. Mina screams. The gun goes off, and it's so shockingly loud that in the aftermath of the bang I can't hear anything at all, just a muffled ringing and my own wild breaths.

Candie and I are sprawled on the ground. I don't feel any pain, don't see any blood. Candie pushes up onto her elbows and wraps an arm around my shoulders, holding me tight against her.

"Put the gun down," Candie's voice says next to my ear, clear as a bell, unyielding as steel. I blink up in confusion at her, but she's not looking at me, she's staring straight ahead at the man, her eyes hard and unflinching. Beside us, Mina's whole body is trembling, her face soaked with tears.

I want to scream at Candie—*What are you doing, why are you trying to talk this psycho down, we need to get up, we need to RUN*—but my lips are quivering too much to form words.

Suddenly, like a flipped power switch, the man lowers his arm, fingers uncurling one by one. The gun clatters onto the ground.

"Get down on the floor, on your face," Candie says. "And don't move."

The man drops down onto his knees, then lays his body forward until he's facedown on the floor, fully prone. He goes as still as a slab of wood, completely silent, and he stays like that until the security guards come racing around the corner.

Everything after that is a blur.

The guards surround us, talking at us, some of them kneeling down to detain the unmoving man on the floor. Someone drapes their jacket over my shoulders. Police sirens blare outside, red and blue lights flashing through the windows. Mr. Park is there, holding Mina as she sobs into his shoulder. Officers are in my face asking questions: *What happened? Are you hurt? Did you know this man? We've contacted your mother; she'll be here soon.*

I stand there mutely, dazed through it all. I don't answer any of the questions I'm asked. I can't explain what I saw. Candie told the man to drop the gun, and he did. She told him to get on the floor, and he did. I don't know *how*, but she stopped that man.

She saved us.

Candie is sitting next to me in the conference room, giving a statement to the police. Her breathing is shallow, and her face is stark. As composed and brave as she had been earlier, she looks like she's in shock now, too.

Her gaze shifts to me when she notices me staring at her. Under the table, her fingers brush against mine, and she takes my hand in hers.

She doesn't let go for the rest of the night.

Chapter 10

NOW

I'm pushing through layers of velvet.

Inky drapery falls on me from all sides, collapsing onto my head, shoulders, arms, swallowing me into its black folds.

My body feels weightless. I don't know where I am.

Am I dreaming?

There's somewhere I need to be. I think.

Off in the distance, there's rhythmic clapping and faint cheering.

"Sunny! Sunny!"

The crowd is calling for me.

Hands out, fingers spread, I force a path forward through the heavy fabric. Finally, I break free. I'm backstage, standing beneath massive rigs, surrounded by stacks of equipment boxes and instrument cases. Disorienting stage lights strobe overhead.

"Sunny! Sunny! *Sunny!*"

The chanting is feverish. The front of the house sounds

packed. For a venue this size the backstage should be bustling. But there's no one. Where's the crew? Where are the stage-hands and techs? I step over the webs of thick electrical cables spread across the floor, wandering through a towering forest of amps and speakers.

Finally, I see people.

It's our crew of backup dancers. They're holding hands, heads bowed low in the middle of the preshow ritual.

"Where the hell were you?"

Candie's voice booms in my ears, and I turn. She's right behind me, arms crossed, her costume glimmering like she just emerged from a bath of jewels. Her expression is shrouded by the darkness, but I know she's angry with me.

Please don't be angry with me.

I'm in costume, too, the layered skirt-petals blooming out from the stem of my waist.

"Let's go," Candie says. "It's time."

"But—" I look up, lost. "What's the set list? And where's Mina? We can't go on without her."

"She's up there already." Candie turns and struts, her sleek ponytail swinging behind her, stiletto heels sharper than knives.

The backup dancers break open from their huddle and flat-ten into a line, a troop of dutiful soldiers ready to be deployed, a procession of shadowed faces watching me as I chase after Candie.

The black drapery behind them billows. I squint. Something is moving behind the curtains. Something large, bulging. The shape of it pushes up against the fabric, like a sea creature lurk-ing just beneath the surface of still water.

"Candie—" I don't know why, but my voice comes out as a whisper. "Candie, do you see that?"

A horrible, pungent stench wafts toward me, like burning plastic and charred hair. Rotting meat and open wounds. Sulfurous. My eyes water and my stomach curdles. Candie doesn't seem to notice at all, not the smell, not the thing under the curtains crawling closer and closer. She just keeps walking forward until we reach the base of the staircase leading up to the stage. The crowd on the other side is ceaseless in their shouting.

"You ready?" Candie turns to me.

I have no idea where we are or what I'm doing, but I nod. Unpreparedness is anathema in Candie's world. She reaches out and takes my hand. We ascend the stairs, one at a time, up up up.

I follow.

I always—

follow.

The spotlights flash like flares and we're there, onstage, encased within the velvety innards of a gilded theater, the focal point at the center of an enormous opera house. Private viewing boxes line the chamber walls like rows of glittering teeth. Cherubs with rosy faces peer down at us from the clouds painted across the trompe l'oeil ceiling. The crowd below is ecstatic, alive, a writhing mass of raised arms and red, open mouths, hungry and pleading. For a second, the rush of pleasure from receiving all this unfiltered attention overwhelms me—*Yes, that's it, that's the feeling, more, more—*

"Look." Candie points. "She's about to perform."

A spotlight drifts over the crowd, the beam climbing until it lands on—Mina. Up on the mezzanine.

The audience turns away from the stage to look back at her. Her costume matches ours, sparkling pink and creamy white, skirt puffed up with layers of tulle. She blows a kiss below, and it elicits more whistles and cheers and pledges of eternal devotion. She places a shushing finger to her lips, and the crowd instantly quiets like she pressed a mute button.

Mina bends at the waist into a deep bow. Then she starts climbing up onto the railing.

"Wait, Mina..." I take a few steps forward as icy dread begins to drip steadily down my neck.

When I reach the edge of the stage I stumble back in shock. Where the orchestra pit should be is a deep, gaping trench, separating the stage from the crowd. I peer down into the gorge and see no bottom. The stairs on either side of the stage leading down have vanished. There's no way across.

On the other side, the masses are mesmerized, all eyes fixed on Mina. That awful smell is starting to permeate the stage. I don't dare turn to look; I know the thing lurking behind the curtains is right there. In front of me, the yawning black canyon stretches on.

Up on the second floor, Mina balances delicately on the railing, wobbling slightly before righting herself. She raises her arms out to the sides, elegant as a swan spreading its wings in preparation for flight. She tips forward—and for a brief moment looks gently suspended in midair—before she dives off the balcony headfirst.

"*Mina!*"

Inside the silent theater, the loud *crack* of a body breaking open against a hard surface echoes endlessly. The audience rises to its feet as one, the applause drowning out my cries.

I jolt upward, gasping and choking like I've been held underwater.

I'm—in a dark room. In bed. For a few confused seconds, I wonder where all the posters on my bedroom wall went, until I remember where I am.

The workshop.

My hair lays in a tangled mess across my face, and I reach to push it out of my eyes. My palm comes away sticky with sweat. My whole forehead is wet, and so is the pillow. My nostrils sting from the memory of that awful stench and I gag again, doubling over as I cough.

On the other side of the room, Candie exhales softly and shifts onto her back. The silhouette of her hands resting on her chest looks like some fairy-tale princess waiting to be roused by a lover's kiss.

A bitter impulse strikes me and I want to go over there and shove her awake, turn on all the lights and shine them directly onto all the unsightly things wiggling and festering in our past. How can she sleep so soundly when I'm forced to endure these vivid night terrors, constantly torturing myself with what-ifs about things I can't change?

I stopped taking meds a while ago when it seemed like I wasn't having panic attacks as often, but I'm pretty sure I stuffed some emergency sleep aids in my bag.

The dim digital haze of the workshop-issued alarm clock on the nightstand is the only light source in the dark room. As I shift to get off the bed, I see something in the corner of the room.

A hunched shadow. There's a person there. Standing a few feet away from my bed, looking at me.

All at once I'm hyperaware of my T-shirt collar against my neck, the quick hiss of my breath as it leaves my nostrils. I want to pinch myself, slap myself, to make sure I'm fully awake, but I can't move a single muscle.

The person is shrouded in darkness, but I can see the outline of a puffy skirt, the edges of a short bob haircut. The shadow reaches its hands up to its face and starts clawing.

The sound is awful, nails scraping, like frenzied rats trying to tear out of a trap. That horrible scratching reverberates inside the room, inside my skull.

A scream rises and lodges in my throat, forming a painful bubble, cutting off all airflow. I can't tell anymore, can't tell if I'm imagining things or if I'm still dreaming.

Finally, my body throws itself into motion. Like a terrified child, I yank the blankets over my head and tuck myself into a fetal ball, squeezing my eyes shut, my hands fisted tightly into the blanket, wrapping it around myself like it can somehow protect me against the horrors outside.

The fabric shifts, despite my hold. The mattress dips. The person is crawling inside my blankets. Ice-cold fingers curl around my ankle and start to pull.

I scream and thrash, yell and kick, my body spasming as I try to throw off the hand that's gotten ahold of me. Suddenly, there's a heavy pressure against my arms. Someone is trying to hold me still. It makes me panic more, my whole body twisting wildly.

"Sunny, Sunny! Wake up."

My eyes open. Candie is sitting on the edge of my bed, gripping my shoulders. Her expression is solemn under the dim glow of the clock, her brow furrowed. I blink again and again. There are no ghostly shadows in the corners. Nothing under my sheets.

"It's just a nightmare," Candie repeats. "Just a dream."

Tears flood my eyes.

I *am* in a nightmare, one I haven't been able to escape for two years. I'm still dreaming of Mina, still seeing her staring at me from darkened corners with a face that's not quite hers. I throw my arms around Candie's neck and cling on to her as hard as I can, gasping into her hair over and over, "I'm sorry, I'm sorry, I'm so sorry, I'm sorry . . ."

Chapter 11

NOW

The sound of rapid knocking jolts me awake.

"—Sunday?"

I blink against the morning light. More urgent knocking. It feels like bony knuckles rapping directly on my cranium. When I finally force my eyes open, I find myself in bed, the blanket pulled up to my chin. Images from last night filter through in hazy fragments, then wash over me in one sweeping wave.

The stage. Mina falling. The shadowy figure crawling into my bed. Candie's calm voice in my ear. Me clinging on to her for dear life.

I glance over to the other side of the room. Candie's empty bed is made up, the sheets folded and pillows arranged like a furniture-store display.

Did she help calm me down last night? Or was *all* of it a dream?

"Sunday, are you in there?" Faye's voice calls from outside.

"Come in; I'm just getting up," I call out, swinging my legs over the side of the bed and fighting a swoon of vertigo.

The door slides open, and the top of Faye's pink head pokes inside. "You didn't come to breakfast, so I thought I'd come check on you . . ."

She ventures in with polite cautiousness, like she isn't entirely sure she's allowed inside my private space even though I've already granted her permission. Her outfit today is just as dreamy as yesterday's, eyes and lips dusted with glitter. Plenty of idol girls try to go for the eternal baby-doll persona; the producers encourage it, and the male fans eat it up. But Faye's kind personality feels real, nothing forced or artificial, and I recognize it as the same affable charm that made Mina so popular.

There's a hint of concern and an undercurrent of disappointment in her voice, and I remember then that I promised to meet her for breakfast. I rub the heels of my palms into my eye sockets.

"Sorry, I had a rough night. Didn't sleep very well. My head is killing me."

"Oh no." She reaches out a hand and brushes her fingers gently against my forehead like she's checking for a fever. "I think I have some Tylenol back in my room; I can run and get it for you?"

Before I have a chance to respond, she's already distracted, spinning on her heels to survey the room. "Wow, you only have one roommate? You're so lucky! I'm sharing my room with three other girls . . . not that I'm complaining or anything. It's just that I'm an only child so I've never had to share a room like that before. You're an only child, too, right, so you know what that's like?"

Faye's such a sweet girl, but her flittering thoughts and off-the-charts enthusiasm for life are hard to handle first thing in the morning.

"What time is it?" I mutter groggily.

"Um." Her eyes shift uneasily. "We have maybe ten minutes until our first session?"

"What?!" I throw the sheets back. The clock on the nightstand reads 8:17. "Shit!"

I haven't even unpacked yet. I dive toward my bag and start tearing through the contents. There goes my plan of coordinating my makeup and outfit today so that my look is immaculate and screams "Come at me" to all my rivals. Instead, I toss on the first pieces of clothing I grab—a tank top and a pair of loose dance pants—and slap on some concealer and eyeliner. Which I apply crooked. *"Shit!"*

I used to have a lot of trouble waking up on tour. Maybe it was the stress, but I would always oversleep unless I set several alarms. There were a few close calls and nearly missed flights, but Candie was always there to make sure I got up.

She has no reason to look out for me anymore.

Faye and I make it into the dance hall with exactly two minutes to spare. The room is already full, every workshop attendee present, looking refreshed and ready to go, some chitchatting away, some doing warm-up stretches, none of them looking like they just rolled out of bed ten minutes ago. I barely have time to drop off my bag at the lockers before Yuna starts the session.

"Good morning, everyone."

From the back of the hall, I see Candie standing tall at the front of the group, surrounded by her new loyal followers. It shouldn't hurt as much as it does. But the reminder hits me like a hot poker jabbing into the space between my ribs. The spot next to her used to belong to *me*.

"Now that we've gone over the choreography, you'll be splitting up to begin the group performance training," Yuna announces. "When I call out your name, please join your group members for rehearsals. Group one members are Grace Zhang, Mali Saelim, Victoria Oh, and Faye Kwok."

"Wish me luck!" Faye says with rushed excitement, and I give her a quick wave before she bounces up to join the other girls.

Eyes shift from side to side as names are listed, everyone sizing up their neighbor, quietly assessing which of their competitors would be most valuable or detrimental to have as a teammate.

"The next group," Yuna calls out. "Alexis Tran, Hannah Park, Sunday Lee, and—"

My head jerks up when I hear my name.

"—Eugenia Xin," Yuna concludes.

A vein in my forehead twitches. Same group. Eugenia and me.

"You have two hours for the initial practice. Group leaders should be selected among yourselves," Yuna instructs after the teams are assigned. "At the end of the session, we'll be doing an evaluation of all groups. Please make your way to the practice rooms."

The dance hall erupts in a flurry of motion as the countdown begins.

If anything, this will be a good opportunity to retrain my cheek muscles to hold a cheery smile while I'm seething on the inside.

I spy Alexis first, her dyed blond hair a brilliant contrast against tanned shoulders. She radiates athletic SoCal vibes, like she spends a lot of time at the beach playing volleyball in a bikini. Hannah joins us next—a tiny bird of a girl, even smaller than Faye, with a conventional idol face and a timid smile. I can easily see her on the roster for one of those mega groups that boasts fifty members.

And finally, Eugenia Xin graces us with her presence. She's dressed for battle: a cropped shirt that shows off her entire toned midriff, and leggings so formfitting they might as well be body paint on her thighs. Alexis and Hannah exchange uncomfortable glances. I'm sure everyone has heard by now that Eugenia and I went for each other's throats yesterday. They're probably simultaneously cursing their bad luck for getting stuck with the both of us.

"Great. Just great," Eugenia scoffs at me.

"What's wrong?" I chime in. "I thought we really bonded last night."

"You better not drag our score down." She jabs a threatening finger at me. "I'm not wasting my practice time propping up someone who's basically already eliminated."

"Remind me again which one of us has a platinum single?" I shoot back.

"All right, put your claws away," Alexis cuts in, stepping between us. "Can we go practice already? We've only got two hours."

Eugenia snaps her mouth shut, but not before sending her eyeballs into a dramatic spin.

That's right, I think spitefully. *You can't sabotage me without crippling yourself.*

I'm not sure this is what they mean by *keep your enemies close*, but so far, it's working in my favor.

After we file into one of the smaller practice studios, Eugenia immediately appoints herself the group leader.

"I was in the top three, so I should take the lead," she declares, proud of her own airtight logic.

For the sake of the greater good, I decide to hold my tongue and be cordial. I'm not sure if Eugenia plans to do the same.

Somehow, the rehearsal goes well.

Shockingly well.

I'll give it to her: Eugenia knows her stuff. She divides up the vocals and choreography, assigning them among the four of us, arranging and transforming what was once a solo act into a group performance.

"Got it? Okay, let's do a run-through."

Eugenia hits the PLAY button, and music pours through the speakers. Bass and drums only at first, a deep, thrumming heartbeat. Then a cascade of otherworldly electronic notes layered over sighing strings, a synthesis of modern and classical sounds. I didn't think much of this track during practice yesterday, but hearing it again right now, it seizes me and reels me in against the vibrations. It's soothing. It's hypnotic. It's making my blood rush. It's cyclical and looping, flowing outward then folding back in on itself, a melodic ouroboros. It's beautiful.

Together, we lift our arms and voices.

I move effortlessly, muscles no longer burning. I feel cloud light when I leap and immensely powerful when I stomp down. I only learned these steps and lyrics yesterday, but my body recalls the words and dance moves like I've delivered them for years.

In the mirror, Eugenia and I reflect and complement each other's angles and rhythm, our voices melding, and I recognize all the things flaring in her sharp cat eyes—the fire, the drive, the intense, desperate, relentless pursuit of this shared dream. The unforgiving words we spat at each other are momentarily forgotten, and we move as one. Language isn't necessary anymore. Thoughts dissolve into physical instinct. The four of us unite into a single force, expanding and contracting with the beat, arching back then rushing forward.

Again and again.

I don't know how many times we run through the routine—it feels like twenty—and then we're back in the main dance hall, in front of everyone, performing under Yuna's scrutinizing gaze.

The song crescendos and ends.

We're suspended in the silence, like hung marionettes, our breaths huffing loudly in the empty space where the music once cradled us.

When I look up, there's no cheering, no applause. Just a room full of calculating, judging eyes. Yuna doesn't smile or frown, offering no indication of whether she was pleased or disappointed by what she saw. She simply waits for us to shake out of the final pose and line up to receive her assessment.

"First of all, Eugenia," Yuna begins without preamble.

Eugenia snaps to attention, stepping forward out of the lineup.

"You're stiff."

Yuna's review drops like an ax.

"Your movements are still too measured. You're so focused on technique that you're losing fluidity in your lines. It's not about getting all the steps right, it's about creating a dialogue, a connection with your audience. You need to make them feel something, and I couldn't feel any emotions watching your performance. I've already given you these notes yesterday, but you haven't addressed any of them. Just because you were top ranking yesterday doesn't mean you'll stay there. You need to do better."

Eugenia nods, her eyes cast down. ". . . Thank you. I will."

"Next. Sunday." Yuna looks to me.

I step on the chopping block and prepare to be eviscerated.

"Your form still needs work, but that was a great improvement from what I saw yesterday. Your voice is really strong; I'm impressed by the way you sustained those crisp high notes during the movement-heavy segments. I can feel your energy and personality, and I want to see more of that. You captured my attention and held it. Well done."

A flash of pink bobs at the corner of my eye, and I turn slightly to see Faye's elated face in the crowd, clapping her hands together lightly in muted applause, and I smile, relief buoying me up.

Yuna finishes the rest of her critique and sends us off. "Next group."

We exit center stage, and Hannah leans in toward me, whispering, "Good job; you were really great!"

"Yeah, that was awesome," Alexis adds from the left.

"Thanks, guys, it was a group effort," I tell them, buzzing from the praise and the thrilling possibility of new friendships. "We were really cohesive."

Speaking of "we," I cast a sideways glance at my right toward Eugenia. She stares resolutely forward.

As I sit down with my group, Candice leads her team up. I watch her, my nerves jittery with anticipation. Even though she seems to have drawn a line in the sand, I still find myself awaiting her performance with the eagerness of a die-hard fan, the threats she threw yesterday as good as forgotten.

Candice stands front and center in the principal position, the other girls flanking her. She raises her hand, a lithe conductor's baton, and the pulsating beat begins. The music is the same, but their group's interpretation of the choreography is wholly unique, and I can see Candie's stylistic guidance throughout.

Watching her perform again, in person, not on a screen . . . is pure joy.

Footwork so delicate it's like she's skimming over water, and the next second her moves burst with explosive power. Her voice glides effortlessly from the lowest purring range up to the most soaring, angelic register. The other girls in her group may as well be her backup dancers. They don't compare, can't match her, not even close.

Now and always, Candice Tsai is in her own league.

The rest of us can only hope for the privilege of standing in her dust as she storms past us.

Just as the song reaches its climax, the girl to Candie's left suddenly falls out of step. The choreography comes apart like knocked dominoes. Candie stays focused on the dance sequence, seemingly confident that they can recover, until the girl starts to scream.

She falls to her knees onstage, crying like she's scared, like she's in pain. Her hands come up, and she scratches wildly at her face and neck, her fingernails digging in deep.

Pandemonium sweeps through the room. Shocked gasps. Panicked shouts. Yuna stops the music and rushes up. The girl is starting to draw blood.

"Oh my god, Blake!"

"Blake, are you okay?"

"What's happening, is she hurt?!"

I freeze. All I can do is stand there and stare as this awful, familiar scene plays out before me.

Everyone is gaping in horror at the injured girl—Blake, the other top scorer from yesterday's ranking. Through the commotion, I see Candie reach toward Blake and take hold of her shoulders, anchoring her and speaking in a low voice. I can't hear what she's saying, but it looks like she's attempting to calm Blake down. Then Yuna is there, the two of them forming a blockade around Blake as they rush her to the door.

"Please practice among yourselves" is all Yuna says before she and Candice escort the howling girl out into the hall, deserting us in the disordered aftermath.

The rest of the group evaluations are canceled, but the afternoon sessions continue as if nothing has happened.

We try our best to carry on with the training, but the haunted look in everyone's eyes is the same. Before I realize it, I've bitten the nail of my thumb so low it bleeds.

At the end of the day, we gather back in the main hall to hear Ms. Tao's announcements.

"I know everyone is worried, but we are taking care of Blake, and she has received prompt medical attention. We'll update you on her status as soon as we can," Ms. Tao assures us. "I'm glad to see that everyone still remained calm and focused. Today's top scorers are Rebecca Hwang and Sunday Lee."

I blink as the clapping starts, completely stunned at her calling my name. A whole room of eyes land on me. I can practically hear the thinly veiled thoughts in the false smiles and lukewarm applause.

Why her?

Wasn't she almost eliminated?

She doesn't deserve this.

Even more unexpected is the elimination that comes right after.

"The lowest scorers are Eugenia Xin, Tessa Meng, and Carly Yun. I'm sorry, Tessa and Carly, but tonight will be your last night with us," Ms. Tao announces.

I should be basking in sweet victory. This is what I wanted. My first win in a long, long time, while one of my enemies has been cast down.

But all I can think about is Blake. About how she was hurting herself the same way Mina did. The same way that nightmare phantom I saw in my room did.

How Candie was standing right next to her when it happened.

This can't be a coincidence.

"Congratulations!" Faye pops out of the crowd and hooks her arm around mine. "I knew you'd get a top score today. Your group was amazing!" Then she leans in and winks. "Except Eugenia. Serves her right."

We *were* amazing. But after what happened to Blake, I can't bring myself to celebrate.

At dinnertime, the cafeteria is emptier than it was yesterday. The few stragglers keep to themselves at separate tables. After the initial burst of excitement, Faye's been quiet. I briefly wonder if she's feeling down on herself, especially after we had bonded over the shared shame of being on the bottom that first night.

Before I can offer her encouragement, Alexis and Hannah drop down at our table with their trays. The first thing Alexis says is "Holy shit, that thing with Blake was nuts!"

"Do we even know *what* actually happened?" Hannah poses the question of the day to the table. "It looks like she just got a second-degree burn out of nowhere. Nothing even touched her!"

"Have you heard anything from Yuna or Candice yet?" Faye asks me.

"No. I haven't seen Candice since this morning," I tell her.

"Blake will probably need to drop out after this," Hannah says gravely. "I mean, it looked bad. Like, really bad."

"Everyone is saying she probably had a severe allergic reaction to something," Faye supplies.

"That didn't look like any allergic reaction I've ever seen," I mumble.

"Hope she's okay. But at the same time"—Alexis twirls a forkful of spaghetti and lifts it to her mouth—"that's one less person to compete with for a spot at the finals."

"Oh my god, Lexi, how can you say that?!" Hannah protests, her brow furrowing with distaste. "Blake could literally be in the hospital right now!"

"Don't act like you're not thinking it, too. The competition is stiff enough as it is, no offense." She glances at me. "And what's up with this arbitrary scoring system? What are they even grading us on? It seems like anyone could be eliminated at any time."

I stare down into the ground meat of my red Bolognese sauce as Hannah and Alexis argue.

Blake's wounded face overlaps with Mina's in my mind, and I lose my entire appetite.

Chapter 12

THEN

Three years ago

Work on our album is paused while the record label secures a new studio.

The PR department is quick to release statements. The official story reported by the press is the truth—the gunman broke into the studio, fired a shot at us, then was detained by security.

Except the story is missing one crucial detail—it wasn't the security guards who saved us.

After comparing and contrasting both of our versions of events, Mina and I arrive at the same conclusion: Candie was the one who stopped the stalker.

"We *have* to ask her about it. It's the only way we're going to know," Mina says to me on the video call.

"I mean, we can try. She's got *Matrix* reflexes when it comes to dodging personal questions," I point out. "My theory is hypnosis. Like that magician who goes around Venice Beach making people act like they're zoo animals?"

"You can only hypnotize someone if they let you do it," Mina points out. "What Candie did was . . ."

"*Whatever* she did saved our lives," I interject, feeling suddenly defensive, as though we were accusing Candie of something terrible behind her back.

Mina pulls the camera in close to her face like she's the protagonist in a found-footage horror movie about to reveal the plot twist. ". . . I think, maybe, she might have some kind of power."

I can't help the incredulous laughter that escapes me.

"I'm being serious," Mina huffs at me.

"I'm sorry, I know, this is all extremely serious, but . . . *powers*? Aren't you a good churchgoing Christian? Don't they frown on that kind of stuff?"

"I go to church because it's important to my parents." There's a rare hint of defiance in her voice. "But I've always believed in, well . . ."

"In what? Mind control?"

"We both saw it! He did exactly what she told him to," Mina argues. "We shouldn't rule anything out until we speak to her."

"So. The plan is we invite Candie over and ask her about it directly?" I confirm.

"Exactly."

"Cool. Just be ready to back me up and grab her legs if she tries to run."

When I get off the call with Mina, there's an unread text from Candie waiting.

> Are you sure you're ready to go back to work tomorrow? If you need more time I can talk to the producers for you.

It's almost eleven o'clock at night, and Candie is thinking about me. Being considerate of me. A pleasant warmth blooms in my chest as I type back:

> I'm totally fine! My mom is driving me nuts, I NEED to get out of here. What about u?

Mama's been in a paranoia-and-guilt-fueled frenzy since the incident. Her phone is glued to her hand all day feeding her live updates from her real-estate agent, because she's convinced stalkers are going to break into our house and we need to move ASAP. I don't even remember the last time Mama cooked me breakfast, but suddenly it's like I'm waking up in an IHOP every morning, and at night, I fall asleep to the sound of Mama canvassing the house checking and rechecking all the locks.

> Don't worry about me. It's late, you should get some rest.

> Ok ok tucking myself in rn. See u
> tomorrow, C!

I add on an entire row of kissy face emoji for good measure. After a few seconds, I get a text back that reads simply:

> Good night, S

Candie, who never used to text me, just sent me a good-night message.

I throw myself back on my bed, smiling at the ceiling. A swift and awful realization strikes me like lightning on a clear day.

I'm enjoying this.

I know it's wrong. I know I shouldn't feel this way. But here I am basking in Candie's attention, swimming in it, doing the backstroke through the tidal waves of affection and worry, and a sick, horrible voice in my head whispers: *Maybe it was worth it.*

The next day, Ms. Tao drives the three of us to our new work location—a private studio hidden deep in the hillsides of Laurel Canyon instead of the flashy building in downtown LA. I crank my smile to its brightest setting as I make the rounds, chatting up everyone with cheerful ease. I'm okay, I'm fine, really, I tell them.

Candie's eyes track me across the room, and my heart does a tiny flip each time I catch her looking at me.

I sail through the first hour of recording. In the comforting, dim light of the recording booth, headphones over my head, I'm grounded, energized, in my element. Eyes closed, lips against the mesh of the pop filter, the song spools out of me, effortless, each note pitch-perfect, precise darts sinking into bull's-eyes. No strain, all confidence.

Just like I said. I'm totally fine.

Five minutes later, our producer stops me to give feedback. I glance up at the glass pane of the control room, and suddenly, there's a man in a baseball cap and gray sweatshirt in the back corner. He wasn't there when we started the session.

My whole body locks up. Terror stomps down like a foot on my throat, and I let out a strangled noise that's half gasp, half sob.

"It's him! *It's him!*" I sputter and point.

Mina and Candie burst into the booth, rushing to my side. The producers follow, and they're reassuring me that the man is just an assistant, showing me his ID badge, proof that he isn't dangerous, but it doesn't work, all I see are vengeful eyes beneath the brim of his cap, the ringing echo of the gun firing in my ears.

Their words smear into incoherent noise; I can't make out anything over the violent rush of blood pounding on my eardrums. *Please, back up, I need space*, I try to say, but the adults keep crowding around me, their faces looming too close, hands reaching and grabbing; they're just trying to help, but it's making it worse and I push at them. *Stop, don't touch me—!*

"Sunny." Candie's voice calling my name cuts through the jumble of sound. Her hand lands on my arm, a sturdy beam of support holding me up just as I'm about to topple and shatter. Instead of recoiling from her touch, the tension gripping my body relents for a second, and I slump forward, my head knocking against her shoulder.

"Let's get you outside, okay?" Candie guides me out of the booth like that, my face tucked into the crook of her neck, her arm braced around me, a protective barrier between the world and me. "Mina, go grab some water."

The hallway outside is short, nothing like the expansive corridor where the gunman attacked us, but all I can think is *There's someone hiding just around the corner*, and I can't stop thinking it, the fear is so real, a physical force clamping down around my chest, squeezing tighter and tighter.

"Here, sit down." Candie leads me to a bench and lowers me onto it.

I sink down, shutting my eyes against a surge of nausea. "I think I'm going to throw up."

Candie's hand moves to the center of my back, the pressure gentle but firm. "Breathe. Everything is all right. You're safe."

She rubs her hand in slow circles as I struggle to take in even breaths.

"Look at me." Candie tilts my chin up until our gazes meet. "You're safe here. I won't let anything happen to you."

The second she says it, it becomes fact. Like air, like gravity, I believe it without question. Relief is almost instantaneous. I release a trembling exhale and try my best to focus on the timbre of her voice, the weight of her palm, the sureness in her.

"Breathe in," she says.

I inhale deeply.

"Now hold it."

I do, feeling the pressure build in my lungs.

"Now breathe out."

I exhale.

"Good. Just like that. Again."

I don't know how long we do this, but when I look up again Mina is standing in front of us with three bottles of Evian cradled in her arms, her whole face scrunched in worry. Candie takes one of the waters and cracks open the cap, handing it to me, and I gulp down half the bottle in a matter of seconds.

"Feel better?" Candie asks.

I do. In fact, I'm completely relaxed, my heart sedated, my breaths coming out even.

As Candie rubs soothing circles on my back, I lock eyes with Mina. The conversation we had last night replays in my mind.

Powers.

Could Candie really do something like that? Did she make me calm down? Did she order my pulse to slow? Will my lungs to ease? The same way she got the stalker to drop the gun and get on the floor?

"Sunday, are you all right?" Ms. Tao steps up to the three of us. She glances at Candie, and Candie's hand falls as she backs away from me, giving Ms. Tao a wide berth.

"I think I'm okay now," I tell her, my mouth bone-dry, even after all that water.

"Maybe you should take the rest of the day off," Ms. Tao says.

"Yeah, you should definitely go home," Mina agrees.

"*No,*" I say, fighting back. "I'm staying."

"Don't push yourself," Candie says.

"If I quit now, then he wins," I tell them. "I'm *not* going to let him win."

I spend the next half hour convincing Ms. Tao that, yes, I freaked out a little, but I've got my shit together now. Eventually I'm allowed back into the studio, but I'm barred from singing, and spend the rest of the day sitting by the mixing console, watching Candie and Mina from the other side of the glass. Every so often I catch Candie's eyes, and that deep sense of calm cascades from the top of my head down through my limbs.

You're safe. I won't let anything happen to you.

At the end of the day, Mina and I approach Candie, just like we planned.

"Are you free this weekend, Candie? We never got to do that movie night," I ask with a hopeful smile.

"I think it'd be nice for us to spend some time to check in with one another," Mina says. "After . . . what we've been through."

Turns out, we didn't need all that strategizing ahead of time.

Candie nods, her expression slightly resigned, like she knows the conversation she's been avoiding has finally arrived. "Sure, what time?"

Chapter 13

THEN

Three years ago

On the Saturday that Mina and Candie are coming over, I spend the entire afternoon rearranging and organizing all the half-packed moving boxes so that my house isn't such a disaster zone. Mina and I decided the meeting should take place at my house because my mom won't be home, and if we had gone to Mina's we would have had to deal with her mother ambushing us with refreshments every fifteen minutes.

I clean for hours—and I *hate* cleaning—because I don't want Candie to think Mama and I live like hoarders.

I spend a lot of energy trying to impress Candie in general. When I'm in a scene, I consider how she would deliver a line. I think about what musical choices she'd make when performing a song. When I'm shopping, I question if Candie would approve of my fashion choices. I wonder where she goes after she leaves the studio, who she's with, what she's doing, and if she'd rather be doing those things with me.

I wonder if she thinks about me as often as I think of her.

Mina and Candie show up promptly at seven. We celebrate this inaugural event on my bedroom floor, a large pizza and a two-liter bottle of soda shared between us. We chat about how recording went this first week back, about our thoughts on the new script we just received for season two, and read some heartwarming messages sent to us by fans, now filtered by our social media manager.

Every time there's a lull in the discussion, Mina and I share glances, gauging when we should broach the subject.

"So . . . my mom's thinking about hiring extra security for me after my meltdown on Monday," I say, trying to work my way up to the elephant in the room.

"Like a bodyguard? Can you request a cute one?" Mina grins.

"It's probably going to be a very not cute fifty-year-old divorced ex-cop," I lament. "Besides. I think we already have a bodyguard."

I glance at Candie meaningfully. Mina gives me a nod of solidarity. Candie's eyes are lowered and she seems to be deeply contemplating her soda as she turns the plastic cup around and around in her hands. Before we can launch into the questions we've been preparing to ask all night, Candie speaks first.

"I'm sorry." Her voice is fraught with remorse. "For what you've both had to go through because of me."

"Stop," Mina hurriedly consoles her. "Please don't blame yourself!"

"None of what happened is your fault," I emphasize.

"I just wanted to make sure you both know how sorry I am." Candie sets the cup in her hand aside. When she looks back at us, there's a sense of resolution in her tone. "And there's something else I need to tell you."

We watch as Candie reaches for her bag and pulls out a small ornate metal canister no bigger than her palm. Candie draws in a breath and asks, "Have you ever heard of the celestial maiden?"

I lean forward a little, peering at the tin curiously. "I think so. It's a folktale, right?"

"Is it that myth about the female sky spirit whose robe is stolen, and she has to marry the man who took her clothes?" Mina asks, brimming with interest. "Sort of like the selkie myth?"

Candie nods. Then she says in a quiet, reverent voice, "It's not just a folktale."

Mina and I go still, our eyes widening as Candie's statement reverberates in my room.

"I can show you," Candie says, her eyes moving slowly between me and Mina. "Do you trust me?"

We nod. Of course we do. We trust her with our lives.

She opens the lid of the tin. The contents inside are brownish-red, like clay. Candie dips her fingers into the canister, scooping out a bit of it, then reaches for my face. Her fingertips touch my forehead—soft, so soft—applying the balm across the arc of my eyebrows, drawing down the bridge my nose, and over my cheeks. It feels like I'm being anointed. Chosen.

"My family originated from a remote fishing village on an island in the East China Sea," Candie begins. "A thousand years ago, a miracle took place on that island."

She repeats the process on Mina's face, spreading the clay carefully over her features. Then she asks us to join hands. Mina takes Candie's left hand, and I take her right, our grips forming a bond of energy.

"Close your eyes," Candie requests.

Mina and I shut our eyes. The world dims and all that's left is the feeling of Candie's hand in mine, the sound of her gentle, even breaths.

Candie begins to sing. Her lovely voice pools out then curls in to form a melodic chant in a dialect I don't recognize. It sounds like an incantation, a hymn. It's so beautiful. The unfamiliar words caress my skin, sink into my pores, and I wait in suspended anticipation for what Candie will show us.

"You can open your eyes now," Candie's voice says.

I open my eyes to an endless expanse of green.

There are trees in every direction, reaching skyward.

Sky. I look up at the sound of birdcalls as the fluttering shadows of wings sail overhead against thin wisps of clouds. We're outdoors. In the woods.

This isn't possible. We were just in my room a few seconds ago.

A cool mist settles against my arms. When I breathe in, the air is heavy with the scent of fresh earth. Instead of my bedroom carpet, I'm sitting on a patch of grass.

Candie releases our hands and rises to her feet, motioning for us to stand.

Mina pushes up eagerly, spinning on her heels as she takes in the surroundings with stunned excitement. I skim my hands over the blades of grass, and my fingers come away wet with dew. It feels *real*. At the same time, there's an eerie dreamlike quality to the environment, where everything seems to blur at the edge of my periphery.

I open my mouth to ask Candie where we are, how we got here, and a hundred other burning questions, but my voice sputters out as muffled bubbles of sound, like I'm trying to talk underwater. Mina's saying something as well, her lips moving rapidly, but her voice is dimmed, too.

"It's all right. You're safe in this place."

Candie's voice is the only one we can hear. She gestures for Mina and me to follow her, and the three of us head into the dense forest.

The trees are endless, the canopy expanding far into the distance. Finally, the greenery grows sparse, and we emerge from the wilderness onto a bright white beach. I shield my eyes from the sudden harsh light. Jagged cliffs cradle the shoreline, and I smell the salt spray from the waves.

"During the autumn solstice moon, a celestial maiden descended from the heavens onto the island. While she was bathing in the ocean, a fisherman spotted her from the shore," Candie tells us. She points to the water.

A beautiful woman stands in the shallows.

The woman is nude, her skin wet and glistening, long hair clinging to the soft swell of her hips, the backs of her thighs.

A man is watching her from the beach. He wears a simple robe, his hair gathered back in a traditional topknot. Slowly, the man makes his way across the sand toward her. She doesn't turn away to hide her body, standing bold and bare, unashamed in her nakedness, the tide lapping at her calves.

Slowly, the man approaches her, as though in a trance. In his arms, the man carries a bundle of shimmering robes. He holds the garments out to the maiden, his eyes brimming with devotion as vast as the sea, and the maiden accepts the robes.

"He fell in love with her, and the celestial maiden returned his feelings," Candie tells us. "She decided not to go back to the heavenly realm, and to remain with her beloved. The island became her home. The villagers, her family."

After the maiden dresses herself, the two venture up the beach, hand in hand.

We follow them back into the trees, twisting and curving through the forest. When we exit the woods this time, we're standing at the entrance of a village. Behind the simple wooden gate sits a collection of huts made of mud bricks and thatched roofs.

There seems to be a public celebration taking place. Firecrackers are going off, gongs and drums pounding along to the joyful blare of a suona. We enter through the gates, passing by throngs of excited villagers.

Two people stand in the center of the village, in the middle of a crowd. They're dressed in red robes, and I recognize the man as the one we saw earlier. In front of him is a woman, a red veil draped over her head. Between them, they hold a strip of red fabric tied together at the center in an elaborate knot. The two turn to face each other and bow deeply.

A wedding ceremony.

When the celestial maiden and her new husband finish their bows, the townspeople rush forward, parading them through the street. We follow behind them, walking down a path paved with flower petals—pink plum, creamy magnolias, violet orchids—a fragrant carpet snaking through the village.

The path ends, and we look up to see the celestial maiden performing a dance up on a dais. The dance is beautiful, hypnotic; I'm captivated by the curling shape of her hands, the toss of her arms, the elegant leaps and bends of her body.

"The celestial maiden loved her new family very much," Candie continues. "She blessed the entire village with good fortune and talents beyond their dreams. She sang to the heavens so the rains would come, the fields overflowing during each harvest. She danced in the tides, and the fishermen returned safely from every storm, their nets full."

We follow the maiden as she makes her way through the village, watch as she is met with nothing but adoration and worship. Everywhere the maiden goes in the village, she is surrounded by people vying for her attention. Men and woman bow to her, some fully prostrating themselves at her feet when she passes. I lose all sense of time and space in this strange illusion of a village. Every corner we turn, we see the maiden engaging in a different act of service. We see her teaching the children to read and write. We watch her tend to the elderly and the ill. We see her demonstrate her dance to a cohort of young women dressed in white robes.

"The residents of the island were devoted to her. To further cement their bond, the celestial maiden handpicked girls from the village to be her personal disciples. She taught them the divine songs and dances of the heavenly realm, granted them the ability to charm and enchant the mind," Candie says.

The young women in white robes encircle the celestial maiden, dancing in unison, their long, loose sleeves billowing outward.

The women leap and spin and turn, faster and faster, and suddenly it feels like the world around me is moving, like I'm spinning along with them. I shut my eyes for only a second to reorient myself.

When I open my eyes again, I'm back in my bedroom.

The three of us are still sitting in a circle on the floor, our hands linked. I blink at Mina, and she blinks back at me. We both turn to Candie.

"My family members are descendants of her chosen disciples," Candie reveals, her voice calm and quiet. "I am under the maiden's divine protection. That's how I was able to stop that man from hurting us. In moments of duress, I can call upon her powers and affect the actions of others."

"Holy shit," I mutter. "Holy *shit*."

"That's . . . oh my god, that's . . ." Mina can't seem to summon the words she needs.

"The clay on your faces comes from the shoreline where the maiden first emerged from the ocean. We use it in our blessings ceremonies," Candie explains.

The world as I understand it shifts and collapses, washing clean away as a shocking new universe is revealed underneath. I've never believed in anything remotely occult; everything from astrology to mediums to feng shui to tarot readings had seemed equally made-up to me. But I can't deny what we just experienced, the fact that I was standing in an ancient fishing village, watching an ancient legend play out before my eyes.

"What I just shared with you are the maiden's memories. Through the blessings ritual, the maiden's time with us has been passed down through the generations, a piece of her that her disciples can treasure forever. I wanted you both to experience the ritual, so that you could both see it. See me. Because I consider you family."

Heat rises to my cheeks, my heart fluttering fast. Candie not only thinks of us as friends but considers us even closer than that. The kind of closeness I've been seeking from her since the very beginning. Now she's bestowed the honor on me in a ritualized ceremony.

"I know it'll take time to process all this. And I'm sorry if it's frightening, or strange," Candie says, uncharacteristically demure. "But know that the maiden will watch over you both. Nothing like that will ever happen again."

"Candie, this story, this power you have, it's *incredible.*" Mina's voice is full of awe. "There's nothing frightening or strange about it."

"There's nothing frightening or strange about *you*," I emphasize.

Candie's eyes soften with relief, like she had been afraid that Mina and I would reject her after finally allowing us to see who she really is. I slide my arms around Candie's neck and pull her into an embrace. Mina leans in as well, our bodies curving against Candie like a pair of folding wings.

"We love you," I say. "Everything about you. Thank you for sharing this with us."

Candie's frame sinks into ours as she lets out a deep exhale. After a moment, she murmurs against our shoulders, "Promise to keep this between the three of us?"

"We promise," Mina and I say together.

And with that vow, a new bond between us is forged.

We hold her tight, anchoring her, reassuring her that we have heard her truth, accepted it, and are prepared to guard it. We are no longer the individuals we were before. We are a unit now, three against the world, come hell or high water, from this day till the very end.

Chapter 14

NOW

Candie doesn't return to our room until right before the curfew. I sit up in my bed immediately, firing off questions at her the second she closes the door.

"How's Blake? What happened? Is she going to be okay?"

Candie tosses her bag onto the chair and sits down on her bed. "It was an allergic reaction," she says, echoing Faye's theory from dinner. "Ms. Tao is going room-to-room to let everyone know. They haven't determined what caused it yet, but they're going to be changing out the cafeteria menu tomorrow. Blake's okay now, but she'll be going home."

Candie looks tired. Her defenses temporarily lowered, that iron shield dropping. This is a side of her she doesn't readily show to others.

"Candie . . . You can be honest with me," I tell her. *I already know your secrets.*

I search her face for a sign, a hint, any indication that she might be ready to open herself up to me again. That there's a chance we might be able to talk truthfully about what may or may not be happening here.

But she turns away, the fortress walls going back up, an impenetrable barrier pushing me back. "I'm exhausted. I need to lie down."

The blatant rejection hurts more than the threats she threw down last night. Defeat crashes over me. I switch off my night-stand light and lie down, rolling onto my side so my back is facing her. Hefting the blankets up to my chin, I stare at the wall, stubbornly holding in the tears until my vision starts to dim.

I don't know when I fell asleep, but when I stir from a restlessly short sleep cycle, the room is pitch-black. In the dark, I hear the sighing creak of the room door opening.

I bolt up into a sitting position, my body alert and tense, remembering the nightmare from the other night, the feeling of that icy phantom hand snatching me. I catch just a quick glimpse of Candie's silhouette as the door latches shut behind her with a gentle thud.

Where is she going in the middle of the night?

The creeping, uneasy dread roiling in my gut all day solidifies into a singular, compulsory thought: *Go after her.*

I scramble out of bed and into my shoes, cross the floor and push open the door. The still, silent hallway greets me, free of all the bustling bodies darting in and out of the dorm rooms during the day.

I crane my neck out and look down the hall to see flowing long hair disappearing around the corner and down the stairwell. Without giving myself time to think, I slide out from behind the door and follow after her, taking care to make my steps as soft as possible, trying my best to stay back and out of view while not losing sight of Candie as we circle down the stairwell.

Once we hit the first-floor landing, I peer out from around the staircase. Candie's shadow continues moving into the darkened halls, and I sneak forward quickly. Past the lounge, past the gym, she makes a sharp turn to the right and vanishes. I rush to catch up with her.

When I come around the corner, I'm standing at the entrance to the cafeteria. All the lights are off, the barren chairs and tables in the dining area blanketed in a muted glow of moonlight shining in from the windows.

No Candice. I lost her.

I lift a hand to my mouth and chew feverishly on a hangnail. I can turn back, go upstairs and lie in wait until she returns, then spring an interrogation session on her.

Or keep searching—and find out the truth for myself.

I turn on my heels and head to the practice rooms. Across from the cafeteria, and into the corridor that hosts the smaller studios and sound booths. Only a few of the larger rooms have viewing windows. I look in each one as I pass by, squinting to make out the shapes inside the unlit interiors.

Empty, empty, empty.

Most of the rooms are private with no way of seeing inside. Just as I'm contemplating whether I should open the rooms one by one, a shadow moves across the windowpane of the practice room near the back of the hall.

There's someone in there.

Cold fingers of fear wind up my core and around my throat. I swallow down the sandpaper dryness inside my mouth and force myself to continue forward. Candie is there. I know she is. The answers I want are right there in front of me.

Step by step, I edge closer to the room. Through the window, I see the shape of the person inside, spinning and dipping. Dancing. My hand lands on the handle. I suck in a breath through my teeth, and without giving myself any more time to hesitate, I yank open the door and flip on the lights in the room.

A shock of fluorescent white floods the space. The dancing figure jumps back and releases an earsplitting shriek.

"Jesus fucking Christ!" Eugenia Xin glares at me from inside the room, hands pressed to her heaving chest.

There's nobody else besides her in the studio.

"What are you doing here?" I demand, baffled.

"What are *you* doing here?" she snaps back.

It takes a brief moment for the realization to hit, that I'm not facing some unearthly horror, just a real-life flesh and blood menace. The tight squeeze of fear loosens a little. I shoot her a pointed look.

"Someone made a huge deal yesterday about how important it was to sign up for these practice rooms. And I'm pretty sure one A.M. is not an available time slot."

"Look. Just." Eugenia shifts her gaze around as if she's seeking escape routes out of this corner where I've trapped her. Finally, she glances at me in unwilling defeat. "Please don't tell Ms. Tao."

My mind shuffles gleefully through an array of proverbs about karma and turning tables. I let Eugenia sweat it out for a few more seconds before relenting.

"Relax. I'm not going to snitch on you. I'm breaking curfew, too."

She looks incredibly relieved while also trying really hard not to show any gratitude on her face.

"By the way, I meant to tell you earlier." Slowly, I extend the olive branch. "I thought you did a really good job leading the group. Yuna was way too harsh on you."

Eugenia stares at me in disbelief, then mutters with considerably less bite in her voice, "Thanks, but I don't need your approval. I'm here to win, and I'm going to wipe the floor with you next time."

She sounds dead serious, but I can't help the chortle that escapes.

"Are you challenging me to a dance-off? What do you think this is, a Channing Tatum movie?"

"Did you miss the part where this entire workshop is a dance-off or are you that desperate for a comeback that you didn't even read the contract before signing up?"

"Okay, *what* exactly is your problem with me?"

I'm pretty sure I know what it is, but seeing as we're potentially stuck in the same group for god knows how long, I'd rather clear the air right now.

"My 'problem' is that while the rest of us are breaking our backs trying to get our foot in the industry, you already *had* your chance." Eugenia doesn't sidestep the question. "You're coming in here with a huge advantage; you've got a producer mom and the program director backing you up. Why are you even here? To steal a spot from those of us who actually have to work for this?"

There it is. The thoughts I assume everyone is thinking, finally spoken aloud to my face. As much as it hurts, part of me appreciates Eugenia's unabashed bluntness. And her indictment isn't untrue.

"If it makes you feel any better, I haven't had a real conversation with my mom in months. And I actually haven't seen Ms. Tao in years," I say.

Eugenia says nothing, and a heavy quiet settles between us.

"The accident this morning was pretty crazy, huh?" I say.

"Accident, sabotage, who knows what that was." Eugenia scoffs.

"Wait. You think someone *sabotaged* Blake?" The alarms in my head start ringing. "Do you know something? Did you see anything? Was it Candie?"

I step up to her in my eagerness, and she moves back from me, grimacing.

"God, get out of my face, you have stank breath!" Then she blinks. "Candie? Candice Tsai?" Her eyes narrow. "Why, is she a backstabber? Should I be watching out for her?"

"I—Never mind. Forget I asked." I backtrack out the door. "Um, carry on with your dance party."

Eugenia doesn't let it go, following me out of the practice room into the darkened corridor. "Get back here; you can't just throw out something like that and then try to ditch—"

I don't hear the rest of her sentence.

My attention is fixed away from her, past the windows and doors of the practice rooms.

There's a girl at the other end of the hall. She's drenched in darkness, the contour of her body outlined by the ambient light coming from the cafeteria behind her. As my eyes adjust, I make out the shape of ruffled, puffy skirts. My hands start to tremble.

The girl's shoulders are hunched forward, as if her spine can't sustain her weight. Arms twist unnaturally at the elbows, legs bend at awkward angles. Her limbs look stuck on, like they don't belong on the torso they're attached to.

My chest seizes. Fear drowns out all rational thought.

What am I looking at? Is this real? Am I dreaming? Am I awake?

"Who is that?" Eugenia's question cuts through the spiraling panic.

"Y-you see her, too?"

"Who the fuck *is that*?"

"I'm not imagining it?" I whisper, as if speaking quietly will keep whoever—*what*ever—it is from hearing us.

We stare, breathless, as the figure starts to move. Jerky, stuttering at first, like her broken legs won't obey her command. Then she gains momentum, lurching forward, and starts striding toward us.

Someone screams; I don't know if it's me or Eugenia. We turn and bolt, full sprint, in the opposite direction down the hall. Behind us, thumping steps are closing in, but I don't dare look back. The end of the hallway rapidly approaches, and the horrible realization dawns that we might be running straight into a dead end.

Please let there be a fire escape, please let there be a fire escape—

An exit sign wedged against the ceiling glows with red salvation in the back corner. An out. I reach the door first and throw my entire body weight against the push bar. The door swings outward with a metallic squeal.

"In here!" I shout.

Eugenia barrels in after me. The door doesn't lead outside into the parking lot like I hoped. We're in another stairwell, with steps that only lead down. I had no idea there was a basement level beneath the ground floor. We tear down the stairs as fast as we can, thundering footsteps booming against the walls, and burst out through another fire-escape door.

We emerge in a barren hallway with unpainted walls and concrete floors that looks like it might be used for building maintenance. This floor was definitely not part of the tour. Low-wattage fluorescent lights blink above us, and unmarked doors line the halls.

The hallway splits off into several smaller corridors that all seem to be identical to the one we're running down. As we pass by another hallway intersection, a flash of brown in the sea of gray catches my attention. I skid to a stop, my eyes darting to the left.

At the far end of the corridor is a wooden door, its unfinished and aged surface incongruent with the metal and concrete environment.

There's something painted all over the surface of the door; symbols from a language I don't recognize. A sick feeling curdles in my stomach, a primal voice from deep within screams that I'm not supposed to be here. That I'm not supposed to see this.

That there's something locked behind that door.

"There's the stairs!"

Eugenia's fingers clamp down around my wrist, and she drags me along down the hall. She pushes open another set of double doors at the end of the hall, and we're back in a stairwell. We scramble upward, our breathing ragged, our steps growing sluggish, but we don't stop; we climb up flight after flight until we see exit doors again. Bursting out of the stairwell, we nearly slam face-first into someone standing on the other side of the doors. The world spins in a messy crash of limbs and hair and screeches.

"What are you two doing out here?"

I shake off the shock from the impact and take in my surroundings. We're back on the dormitory floor. Though it seems we had run up far too many flights of stairs to only make it to the third floor. Or is this actually the fourth floor? The fifth?

A supremely annoyed Candie folds her arms and glares back at me.

"I should report you both for breaking curfew," she says harshly.

Eugenia and I glance at each other. No words come. All we can do is pant and gasp, sweaty and breathless, hearts pounding out of control from panic and adrenaline and confusion.

"Sorry," Eugenia manages to choke out. "I'm going back to my room right now."

I watch as Eugenia takes slow, swaying steps down the hall like she's intoxicated and her legs are about to fail her. She pulls open the door to her room and slips inside.

Candie turns to me. "Well?" she prompts, waiting for an explanation.

My thoughts are an unintelligible mess. How am I supposed

to explain what just happened? What I saw? The thing chasing us in the hallway. The basement level with all those cell-like rooms. That strange door.

I turn back to the stairwell. There's nobody coming up the stairs, nothing chasing after me.

"I—" My voice returns in a dry rasp. "I followed you out here."

"Sunny, what are you talking about?" Candie snaps. "*You* were the one who got up in the middle of the night and left the room. I chased you down to the first floor and then you disappeared. I followed *you* out here."

Chapter 15

NOW

The next morning, I snap awake at the sound of my alarm.

Despite that fever dream of a night, I'm alert the second my eyes slide open, and I roll over to check Candie's side of the room.

She's there. Still asleep, burrowed deep inside her blankets. I shove my sheets aside and pad across the floor to her bedside. We didn't talk after we came back to the room last night. Just went to lie back down in the suffocating silence. I think I spent most of the night staring at the ceiling. I probably only got two hours of actual sleep.

"Candie." I shake her shoulders gently. "Wake up."

She stirs and turns at the sound of my voice. "Hmm?"

"I need to talk to you."

Candie combs a hand through her bedraggled hair and yawns. "What is it?" she murmurs, sleep soft, the defensive barbed wire wrapped around her unraveled overnight. Something in my gut clenches into an aching ball.

"Last night, when I left the room . . . I saw her."

"Who?"

I breathe deep, then let her name fall from my lips for the first time since the funeral. "I think it was Mina."

At that, Candie sits up, fully awake. She stares at me, waiting for me to elaborate. I can't read her emotions; her face is blank, no wide eyes or slacked jaw, and it makes me feel so foolish that I end up retracting it.

"It might have been someone trying to scare me. I don't know. We also got lost in the building and saw some weird stuff. Did you know there was a whole basement level beneath the first floor?"

"Sunny." Candie's lapsing into her placating tone again, the way she used to talk to me when I was spiraling. "Being in this environment is probably triggering a lot of negative emotions and memories." Her hand lands like a brief breeze on my shoulder. "I really think you should consider going home."

Her words are a bucket of ice water splashed into my face. I push her hand aside, heat rising in my chest. "Why are you trying so hard to get rid of me? You really want me to fail that badly?"

"That's not what I said."

"Then what *are* you saying? That you think I made my bed and deserve to sleep in it? That I should just vanish into obscurity forever?"

Cold fury ignites in Candie's eyes. "Name *one* time where I haven't stood up for you."

I look away from her, avoiding the searing truth in her gaze. She's right. Candie brought us into the fold, shared her secrets, her powers. Shielded me and protected me. Avenged me.

"Is there any way . . ." I stumble through the question, not sure exactly what I'm asking. "Is there any chance at all that Mina might still be . . ."

"Of course not," Candie says, pushing out of her bed and brushing past me to the dresser. Her shadow shifts between us, dark at her feet. "Mina is gone."

Eugenia is a lot less nasty during the morning group rehearsals. She's still terse and impatient as she doles out directions, but the majority of her frustration is clearly directed at herself.

"Looks like that evaluation finally knocked her off the Clydesdale she rode in on," Alexis says, winking at me.

"She's probably freaking out about getting eliminated," Hannah adds, a smidge of schadenfreude in her tiny smile.

I don't breathe a word to Alexis and Hannah about last night. I promised I wouldn't rat out Eugenia, and promises matter to me, even if it means giving the competition a leg up. For now. My gaze flickers across the practice room to where Eugenia is fiddling with the speaker system. She pointedly evades eye contact. I guess we're just going to pretend we weren't chased down the halls screaming last night. That's fine. Avoidance I can do. I am the *queen* of avoidance.

"Let's go from the first chorus again!" Eugenia spins around, shouting at us like a carnival barker.

I don't know how she's so amped right now. After two consecutive nights of no sleep, all I want to do is lie down in the very spot I'm standing and nap. But hers is the exact kind of all-consuming, whatever-it-takes dedication the industry expects. If you're not willing to wring your soul dry, there are a thousand, a million girls right behind you ready to step up and shove you off the stage. Eugenia is giving it her all, everyone is, and despite securing an early win, my old nemeses—insecurity, anxiety, and guilt—rear their ugly Hydra heads.

Do I really still have what it takes? Or was yesterday just a fluke? After retreating from the public eye in disgrace and hiding from the world for two years, can I really just strap my gloves back on and climb in the ring with these girls, all of them bursting with talent and hunger, fighting as hard as they can for a shot at their dreams? The dream that I was handed—and ended up squandering and destroying with my bare hands?

"Five, six, seven, eight!" Eugenia counts.

The music booms, and my overwrought brain switches off, my body going into autopilot mode. The exhaustion and pain vanish. No soreness, no cramping. The song powers me, that thrumming bass line looping around my joints like muscle memory, carrying me through each transition with ease. I remember all the steps. I don't make any mistakes. The doubts fade, and suddenly I feel so wonderfully strong, ready to impress the judges and earn my spot in the finals. I shut my eyes; I can already feel the heat of the spotlight, the expansion of my chest as the crowd screams my name.

After the session, I head to the lockers to pick up my things before lunch. When I open the cabinet door and reach in, my fingers brush against several loose sheets of paper scattered on top of my bag. I pull them out.

Mina's face is splashed across dozens of printed pages. They're all printouts of news articles. Articles about Mina.

Teen star Mina Park's death ruled a suicide.

The truth behind Mina Park's tragic death.

Sweet Cadence *cast mourns the passing of beloved costar.*

My hands cramp up. The papers sift through my fingers and scatter to the floor. Cold panic threatens to overtake my system, before a flash flood of rage washes away the fear.

Someone *is* trying to scare me.

I slam the locker door shut and bend to scoop up all the dropped papers, gripping them in a tight fist. I turn and storm past the practice rooms, down the corridor, calling out when I spot the person I'm looking for.

"Eugenia!"

Eugenia turns at the sound of her name, only to clam up when she sees me.

I march right up to her. "We need to talk."

Her eyes shift around the busy atrium. "Why?"

A few curious heads turn to us. My hand lashes out and I grab Eugenia's wrist, dragging her down a side hall by the cafeteria where there's no foot traffic.

"What the hell do you want?" Eugenia snaps once we're alone, yanking her hand away from me.

I shove the papers at her.

"What's this?" She glares at me but takes the crumpled sheets.

"You tell me."

Eugenia sifts through them with irritation and disinterest at first, before realization gradually settles on her face. Her throat bobs as she swallows.

"Someone put these in my locker," I say.

Eugenia's expression grows more disturbed as her eyes move across the bold headlines. Then she abruptly thrusts all the printouts back at me, like she can't get them out of her hands fast enough. "Well, it wasn't me!"

"And you have no idea who it might be?"

"Why would I?" she snaps.

"Because *you* were the one who trashed me and brought up my past on day one? And we were together last night when the ghost from *Ju-On* tried to run us down? In legal terms, I think that's what they call *suspicious as fuck*."

Eugenia steps toward me, shooting me a haughty look that I assume she practices often in front of a mirror. "When I come for you, you'll *know* it's me. I have nothing to do with this."

I'm about to shoot back a retort when I suddenly realize where we're standing. This is the hallway that leads down to the practice rooms. The hallway we were chased down last night by the "ghost." Except, all I see at the end of the hallway is a solid expanse of white wall. There is no red exit sign, no emergency exit door.

I turn, pointing a finger down the hall. ". . . Wasn't there a door there last night? The one with the stairs that went down to the basement with all those rooms?"

Eugenia's sharp gaze follows the path of my finger. She squints. A brief confusion clouds her eyes, before she blinks it away. "I don't know. It was dark. I wasn't paying attention."

"Yeah, you were busy screaming directly in my ear."

"When I find out who the fuck that was last night, they'll be the ones screaming." She sneers. "I'm a tae kwon do black belt."

"You'll definitely get sent home if you start roundhouse kicking people into submission."

Eugenia's glare reaches new levels of incineration, but it produces the opposite intended effect in me. The rigid tension in my shoulders relaxes. She's probably telling the truth.

"If you want to find the culprit, wanna join forces? As fellow victims," I offer in a just-kidding-but-not-really sort of way.

Eugenia gives me a look like I just suggested we do the Tour de France together on a tandem bike, before she turns away and starts back down the hall.

"Eugenia, wait—" I reach out a hand to—what? Warn her? Calm her? Make sure she's real, too, not just an apparition, or a manifestation of my guilt?

Eugenia shoots a harsh look over her shoulder, and I retract my hand. ". . . Be careful," I say.

That afternoon after sessions end, I walk down every hallway on the first floor, open every emergency door I come across. All the doors open to the outside, or to a stairwell with steps going up to the second floor.

There's no door with a stairway that leads down to the basement.

"Who would do something like that?" Faye gasps when I tell her about my locker surprise on our way to dinner.

"I thought it might have been Eugenia so I confronted her. But it's not."

"Are you sure? She could be lying..." Faye drops her voice to a fearful whisper, as though she's expecting that the mere insinuation will cause Eugenia to burst out from behind a pillar.

"I don't think so. She was just as freaked out by it as I was."

I feel worse about keeping last night a secret from Faye than I did hiding it from Alexis and Hannah. Even though Eugenia seems convinced that it was a prank, something about that encounter feels completely different from the printouts in my locker. My palms grow clammy just thinking about that shadowy broken figure in the hall, and that strange wooden door in the basement.

But... can I really rely on my mind when it's been trapped inside a horror fun house on a loop for two years, my memories waging constant psychological warfare on me?

No. I didn't imagine it. Eugenia was there. She saw the same things I did.

My anxiety must be showing because Faye's hand lands against my shoulder, her knuckles brushing lightly against my jaw.

"Sunny? Are you okay?"

I turn to her and force a reassuring smile. "I'll be fine. I'm used to this. If someone's targeting me this hard, it just means they feel threatened."

"Exactly!" Faye says, pumping her fists in the air, miming the cheerleading moves I was known for on *Sweet Cadence*. "Don't back down!"

Watching those old moves reenacted didn't trigger the cringe of shame I thought I'd feel. Whether she realizes it or not, Faye's been steadily repairing the gouges and tears in my self-esteem.

Commotion echoes from farther up the hall in the atrium.

At first, it sounds like the usual hustle of girls traveling up and down the corridors, but the muffled voices become louder, followed by thundering footsteps. Faye and I shoot a quick look at each other before we break out into a sprint until we hit the congestion of bodies crowded around the base of the stairs. I strain to see over the tops of everyone's bobbing heads.

A girl is splayed on the bottom step of the staircase. She's crying, leaning over to hold her leg. I only catch a fleeting glimpse, but it's enough to see—her leg is turned below the knee at an unnatural angle, twisted to the side.

The crooked, bent limbs of the apparition from last night flash across my mind, and my hand flies up to cover my mouth.

"What did you see?" Faye strains on tiptoe, trying to look. "What's going on?"

"Jessica fell on the stairs; I think she really hurt herself!" a girl to our left answers.

"What happened? Did anyone see?" More voices join the chorus.

"Back up; give us some space! Everyone, please clear the hallway!" Yuna and two other trainers show up and start pushing their way upstream to Jessica.

I draw in a gasp as the crowds part. Candie is there, at the center of it all, crouched next to Jessica on the stairs. Goose bumps burst along the length of my arm and race up the back of my neck. When Yuna approaches, Candie aids the instructors as they heft Jessica up from the floor and maneuver her down the hall.

"Did you see it? Is she okay? Sunny?" Faye is speaking to me, but it barely registers over my careening thoughts.

This is the second time Candie's been right there when disaster struck. Regardless of what explanation we'll be given this time, I can't ignore it anymore.

I've seen this exact kind of grisly accident before.

I grab Faye's arm and pull her away from the crowd, heading straight for the outdoor patio. When we're outside, away from everyone's eyes and ears, I turn her to me solemnly.

"Faye, listen. I think there might be some bad players here that are trying to hurt other competitors."

"What?" Faye's eyes pop wide. "You mean, you don't think that was just an accident?"

I shake my head. "The printouts in my locker weren't an accident. What happened to Blake probably wasn't an accident, either. And last night, I"—I stop myself before I let the information slip—"saw something really strange, too. There are so many idol programs out there that you can audition for. I have a really bad feeling about this place. I know it's hard to believe, but you have to trust me. I think you should drop out."

"That's—!" As expected, she's completely taken aback. "It's only the first week, I can't leave now! I haven't gotten a chance to prove myself yet!"

The slight tremble of her sad mouth makes me realize the utter hypocrisy in my request. Here I am asking her to leave, when I blew up at Candie for asking me to do the same. "Maybe it's my grief speaking. I just don't want to see anyone else get hurt."

"What about you?" Faye reaches out and catches my arm, concern etching deep into her face. "You're already being targeted; what if this person tries to hurt you next?"

"You want to know the truth?" It feels awful and embarrassing having to admit it aloud to another person, but the confession is already poised to leap out of me, having hit the threshold after weeks of pressure and buildup. "One of the main reasons I'm here . . . maybe *the* reason, is because of Candie."

Faye blinks, her wide eyes growing even more owlish.

"I saw her post a video about entering this program, and before I knew it, I was sending in an audition. She hasn't spoken to me in two years. This feels like the last chance for me to . . . fix things."

Faye's hand on my arm tightens reassuringly. "You still really care about her, don't you?"

I place my hand over hers and squeeze. "Please just think about what I said. And if anything else happens, promise me you'll consider leaving?"

Faye purses her lips and after what looks like heavy internal deliberation with herself, she finally nods. "Okay."

An update comes half an hour later, and the explanation for Jessica's incident is similar to Blake's: an extremely unfortunate accident. Jessica had apparently injured her ankle earlier in the day and lost her footing on the stairs.

Two "accidents" in three days.

I don't think I've had a single moment's rest since I got here. These first few days have honestly felt like two weeks.

Curfew's not for another hour or so, but the halls outside my room are conspicuously quiet. There were no instructions for everyone to return to their rooms early, yet there's a distinct lack of the usual last-minute activity frenzy as the entire floor tries to squeeze in that final bit of social interaction before lights-out.

Candie hasn't returned. It's like she's deliberately trying to spend as little time alone with me as possible. Or there's something she's trying to hide. I glance over to her side of the room, my eyes roaming over her desk and dresser as I consider the ethics of snooping through her things.

Several persistent knocks pull me away from my wild speculations. I cross the room to answer the door, expecting Faye again, and instead find Eugenia standing in the hallway, looking for all the world like someone had forced her at gunpoint to knock on my door. She glances over her left shoulder, then her right, as if checking to make sure the coast is clear.

"Well? You going to let me in?"

I step back, blinking, as she waltzes into my room, planting herself firmly in the center of it, her overbearing energy sucking up all the oxygen in the space. She waits for me to shut the door before folding her arms across her chest.

"All right. I want to find out who's behind all this weird shit that's happening."

Chapter 16

THEN

Three years ago

I've already experienced the wild thrill of being launched into another world from our sudden celebrity. There are still plenty of days when I'm reduced to a baby bird blinking into the foreign chaos of my new life, everything too bright, too loud, too much. But being gifted the history of Candie's lineage is like transcending another plane.

Walking around with this kind of earth-shattering information feels like transporting live explosives that I am in no way qualified to handle. I can't stop wondering if every ordinary stranger I pass on the street wields unthinkable power, if there are secret societies or covens of witches, if even the most obscure of urban legends have merit.

As weighty of a burden as it is to hide something this massive, I break out in a smile whenever I think about being the keeper of Candie's secrets. More than the TV show and the record deal and the fans, the fact that Candie chose me as one of only two people to entrust with this knowledge is the one thing that has made me feel truly *special*.

Mina's going through a similar revelation. Before landing the role on *Sweet Cadence*, she was living in Seoul, taking part in a trainee program for a major entertainment agency. She was eliminated from the program after nearly a year of punishing training, and had told us how crushing it was, how her confidence was obliterated and she was completely ready to give up on her dreams, until she auditioned for *Sweet Cadence* on a whim.

Now Mina's completely convinced that the celestial maiden had brought the three of us together, that there's fate and magic circulating between us whenever we step onstage, that with Candie's power and the maiden's blessing we'll be able to reach the kind of success only few can ever hope for.

I'm starting to believe it, too.

Filming for season two of *Sweet Cadence* just wrapped, and Ms. Tao tells us that the network is already discussing renewals ahead of schedule. The show's music is being streamed everywhere, and doll versions of ourselves sit on shelves in toy aisles across the country. Plans for a national tour this summer are underway. I'm backstage in a VIP dressing room getting ready to rehearse our first award-show performance with my two best friends, and I don't think I'll ever be as happy as I am right now.

"Here. You've barely eaten anything all day."

A massive muffin from the complimentary basket appears in my field of view, and I blink at the pastry in my face. Candie

holds it out to me in offering. She's right: I've been too preoccu-
pied with rehearsing the choreography in my head.

"You're going to do fine," Candie assures me.

I realize that Candie can read my moods now like they're
projected on a teleprompter. She always notices when I'm worried or stressed out, and depending on the situation, she either
offers me a swift kick in the butt or makes sure that I'm fed.

"Or I'm going to embarrass us on live TV and get us laughed
out of the industry," I groan.

"Negativity is a self-fulfilling prophecy!" Mina reminds me,
leaning over from her chair to flick my forehead playfully.

"Besides, nobody actually eats those muffins. That thing's
probably recycled from another gift basket. I bet it's rock-solid
in the middle." I scowl at the calorie-laden offering. "I shouldn't
have carbs, anyway."

I thought I was prepared for it, ready to girl power it up, put
my "fight the system" boots on and reject the way girls on TV
need to be thin *thin* thin. And yet here I am, cowering in the
presence of a blueberry muffin. Lately, the multitude of ways my
body gets openly commented on, judged, debated, and mocked
has me sweating with dread whenever I even think about stepping on a scale. And every morning when I look at myself in the
mirror, I uncover new things about my face that I've never con-
sidered before but now adamantly dislike—the undainty angle
of my jaw, the lack of volume in my eyebrows, the dull color of
my lips, the slack shape of my earlobes.

"You should eat something," Candie insists. "Here, I'll split
it with you."

She pulls apart the muffin and hands half to me.

When I finally give in and take it, Candie smiles brightly. I change my mind on the spot and decide that I'm willing to shove the entire basket of pastries into my mouth just to keep that smile on her face.

Before I can take a bite, our dressing room door flies open. A frantic PA comes rushing in, adjusting her headset and scrutinizing the clipboard in her hands, saying, "I—I really do apologize for this."

Mina lets out a tiny excited gasp. I glance over to see that the PA is not speaking to us, but to the five glamorous members of VIXEN filling the doorway. I nearly drop the muffin in my hand from delighted shock.

After the music video for their last single went viral, VIXEN shot to the top of the pop-music charts. They're led by Soomin Yeom, and as one of the first all–Asian American girl groups, it's not a stretch to say they threw the doors open for many of us. We've been in the industry for more than a year now, and we've amassed a decent fan base for ourselves, but it's still nearly impossible to act casual during surprise encounters with artists we admire.

VIXEN's aesthetic matches their group name—each of them is model gorgeous, sporting shiny embroidered jackets, metallic lipstick, aggressive haircuts, leather boots, and unapologetic sex appeal at seven in the morning. By contrast, Candie, Mina, and I, with our network-approved family-friendly image, look like our moms just dropped us off for a VIXEN fan event.

Mina immediately stands and bows, greeting Soomin in Korean, formal and polite in the presence of a girl with seniority. Candie and I quickly follow her lead, dipping our heads.

Soomin doesn't look at us.

"Explain to me again why these children are getting our usual dressing room when we specifically requested that it be reserved for us?" Soomin poses the question loudly at the PA and the rest of VIXEN, as if we're not standing right there.

"I'm not sure where the miscommunication was, but it won't happen again," the PA assures, looking very much like someone who is terrified that they're about to lose their job.

"I'm so sorry," Mina says, bowing her apology, "has there been some kind of mix-up?"

Soomin's silver-lined eyes slide sideways. She gives Mina an uninterested once-over, then looks away again like she's seen enough and won't ever need to take a second glance again.

"Sit down, sweetie, the adults are speaking."

The insult is a collective slap across all our faces.

This isn't the first time this has happened, but each time is just as awful as the last. We've met actors and singers we loved, and had all our expectations shattered by nasty attitudes and unkind comments. It's a constant reminder for me to be my absolute best self when interacting with fans. I can't live with any of them thinking of me the way I do some of my old faves. But it cuts far deeper coming from someone like Soomin, who should be standing with us as we push back against an industry built to exclude us.

Mina doesn't defend herself. She doesn't even frown. She just bows again. "We'd be happy to switch rooms if you'd like."

I know in traditional East Asian cultures, it's a grave social transgression to talk back to people older than you. But it's hard to stand by and watch Mina lower her head to someone who's treating her with so much disrespect. I feel enraged. Helpless. Beside me, Candie's face is cold and inscrutable. I know she must be angry, too. There's nothing we can do except stand back as Mina works her people skills.

Suddenly, another member of VIXEN gets Soomin's attention, gesturing outside while speaking feverishly in Korean. Soomin turns toward the door at once. The girls clear out of the dressing room in a hurry, the haughty looks on their faces wiped free and replaced by adoring smiles.

As they move away from us, I lean forward to see that the girls of VIXEN are talking to a boy. A very familiar-looking boy. My hand shoots out to grab Mina's arm in excitement.

It's Jin-hwan.

Jin-hwan Woo.

My idol obsession for the past two years.

I've proudly stated this fact in at least five separate interviews, and often jokingly refer to Jin-hwan as my "husband" when I'm gushing about him in private to Mina and Candie. I've spent so much money on his merch that my mother has threatened to cut off access to her credit card.

Since his debut, he's risen to become a full-fledged globe-trotting sensation. I've been secretly hoping that we might run across him at an event for a long time now, but I'm pretty certain he's not one of the performers for this award show.

Jin-hwan is in casual wear and sporting a baseball cap, but even the plainest of street clothes can't contain his devastating charm. My fingers clench down against Mina's arm as I repress an excited scream when he lets out a full and easy laugh at something Soomin says. Jin-hwan doesn't look like he's getting ready to hit the stage for rehearsals. And that's when I realize. His girlfriend, pop star Brailey Corbyn, is one of the headlining acts.

Jin-hwan Woo and Brailey Corbyn are *the* current It couple, on the covers of every weekly tabloid, K-pop prince and America's sweetheart, a union straight out of a romantic comedy. Dating bans are standard in a K-pop idol's contract, but Jin-hwan was born and raised in New York, and he refused to let the entertainment agency control his private life. He made international news by going public with Brailey onstage at his own concert. Not that I've spent an unhealthy amount of time inserting myself into that scenario or anything.

Soomin seems to have forgotten all about us as she giggles and fawns over Jin-hwan. For a split second, Jin-hwan looks in through the doorway in our direction, and I swear that he locks eyes with me. He smiles a little and nods. Most of his hair is tucked beneath a hat, but that single perfect lock of his bangs still grazes his lashes when he tips his head.

Before I can determine if I imagined the look, he's already moving down the hall with Soomin and VIXEN in tow, all of them chatting blithely to him in Korean. The poor PA tosses out a quick apology to us and rushes after them.

I let go of Mina and finally let out that squeal I've been suppressing. "Did that really happen? My husband just swooped in out of nowhere and rescued us!"

Neither of them look remotely happy or relieved.

Mina's face is red, and I recognize all-too-familiar emotions on her face.

Humiliation. Defeat.

"He didn't do anything." Candie's voice is frosty. Unimpressed. "He just happened to walk by and distracted them."

Faced with their deep lack of enthusiasm, I swallow and rein in my inner fangirl. Now is clearly not the time.

"Well, that was nostalgic," Mina mumbles. "Reminds me of my trainee days. People like that always think they can throw their weight around just because they're more 'successful.' What they don't realize is that, eventually, they'll mess with the wrong person."

Mina glances to Candie. There's a harshness in her eyes, a complete about-face from the penitent, submissive performance she just put on.

All at once, I realize what Mina's suggesting. Deviousness brews inside me as I look to Candie as well. "You can get them back, right, Candie?"

"If they're treating us this way, they're probably doing it to other acts, too," Mina adds. "We'd basically be performing a public service."

Candie is quiet for a while, considering our request for retribution. We crowd in around her, waiting for the verdict. Finally, Candie takes Mina's hand in her left, and my hand in her right, the three of us standing in that symbolic closed circle.

A slow, vindictive smile spreads across Candie's face. "She definitely messed with the wrong person."

The three of us seek out our manager and the producers backstage.

"We have some time before our segment; we'd love it if we

could watch a bit of VIXEN's performance," Candie requests, her face awash with an excitement so convincing it deserves acting awards. "We're big fans of theirs."

We're given the okay, and a producer allows us backstage. We watch from the monitors as VIXEN takes their positions onstage.

The pounding intro beats of their latest single kick in, the stage lights blast, and massive neon letters flare behind them, spelling out their group name. The five of them weave in and out of intricate, elaborate formations that we could never pull off as a trio. Soomin's stage presence is indisputable. She's absolutely killing it. Her performance is so dazzling it has me reverting back to fan mode and nearly forgetting how awfully she had just treated us.

I force myself to look away from VIXEN and back to Candie.

She's staring at Soomin with frightening intensity. An electric thrill crackles through me like a bushfire, knowing that Candie is about to drop the guillotine blade of revenge onto Soomin's unsuspecting neck.

All at once, the VIXEN performance takes a turn. Their perfect harmonies collapse, each of their voices pitching wildly, completely off-key. The members of VIXEN at first attempt to continue but soon begin to glance frantically at one another as they can't seem to hit any of their notes—and are also unable to stop the terrible-sounding performance.

Confusion mounts backstage as we start to hear bewildered chatter from the crew.

Mina's face twists as she tries to hold back a laugh. I bounce on my heels in delight at this absolutely hysterical display.

Candie's mouth moves, and I watch as her lips form a single silent word. *Fall.*

Soomin spins to the front of their formation. Then, right in front of our eyes, Soomin's left ankle twists. She flies forward, smashing into the stage with unnatural force, like an invisible hand rose up and shoved her down.

The crew erupts into waves of shocked gasps and exclamations. I clamp my hands over my mouth.

"My leg, *my leg!*" Soomin's cries ring out through the whole theater as the producers crowd around her, bombarding the stage, blocking her from view. All I can do is stare, frozen, like I've just witnessed a blatant hit-and-run, unsure of what to do next.

Candie tugs us both away from the unfolding commotion, rushing us back down the halls backstage, away from the scene as though we were never there. We don't utter a word to one another until we make it safely back inside our dressing room.

To my great surprise, Mina bursts into gleeful laughter once the door is shut. "You did it, Candie; you got her!"

"Soomin is going to be okay, though, right?" I ask, remembering how loud she was screaming.

"She'll be fine," Candie says breezily, without any remorse. "I only tripped her a little. The only thing that's hurt is her ego."

Soomin sounded like she had hurt more than her ego, but she clearly desires to be the center of attention, so maybe it's not nearly as bad as she was making it out to be. And now she got exactly what she wanted—utter infamy, forever. This incident will be trending within the hour and will probably end up on several live-performance fail compilations.

What Candie did to the gunman was self-defense. This time, her actions were premeditated. A deliberate attack, meant to inflict damage.

A few summers ago, I saw Mama do something similar.

Mama was on location in Hong Kong scouting for a film she was producing and had brought me along. It was the only time she tried to meet up with my father. I don't know how she got him to agree. Or maybe she misunderstood him, because we sat inside the restaurant of our hotel for hours before we realized he wasn't going to show up.

The next day was the one free day Mama had, but we weren't in the mood to do any of the sightseeing we had planned. We ended up walking the congested city streets aimlessly, until we passed by a row of little old ladies running booths that looked like makeshift shrines under a soaring overpass.

Banners advertising BLESSINGS HERE and VILLAIN HITTING hung above their stalls. Figurines of deities sat on the shrine shelves behind plates of fruit offerings and pots of burning incense. Every stall was busy, customers sitting on plastic stools, conferring in Cantonese with the older women. A loud racket of wood pounding against stone echoed across every booth.

To my surprise, my mother, who was in no way religious or superstitious, lined up to sit down at one of these stalls. When it was her turn, the older woman presented Mama with slips of paper—one with a drawing of a man, one with a woman. Mama wrote down the Chinese characters of my father's name onto the drawing of the man and handed it back to the lady, who then proceeded to bash the slips of paper against a slab of stone with a wooden shoe while reciting incantations. When the beating was done, the woman lit the tattered drawings and other paper offerings aflame on a large candle in the incense pot while muttering more prayers.

"It's called villain hitting," Mama said, explaining the ritual after she finished her session. "The paper drawings are supposed to represent bad people in your life, and the ladies 'hit' them to give them bad luck."

"Did you just pay money to put a curse on my father?" It was hard to imagine my shrewd and business-minded mother being taken in by something like this. "You don't actually believe that's real, do you?"

Mama only shrugged. "I'm sure it's all a hoax. But it made me feel better."

But what I just saw Candie do to Soomin was no hoax.

It was justice. It was power. Swift, vicious, and satisfying.

You're safe. I won't let anything happen to you.

I reach out to take Candie's hand in mine, clasping it tight, and a deep calm floods my veins as I'm cradled in the knowledge that the power contained in this one slender hand can keep the rest of the world at bay.

Chapter 17

NOW

Eugenia stares me down, waiting for my response to her offer.

It takes a few seconds to identify that the lightness in my chest is relief. An irrational urge to hug her strikes me out of nowhere, and I almost laugh out loud at the impulse.

"Have you gone to Ms. Tao about that stuff in your locker?" she asks.

I shake my head. "I didn't want to draw any more attention to myself. I threw it out."

"You *threw out* the evidence?" She takes a step in toward me. "Tell me again what you were doing out after curfew last night?"

"I . . ." The longer I hesitate to answer, the more suspicious her eyes grow. "I have insomnia and night terrors. I just wanted to get some fresh air."

That admission seems to put an end to her inquisition for now, even though she's still casting me a distrusting look, as though she could tell I was only telling a half-truth. I start ushering her back out the door. "Come on. There's still some time before curfew."

"To do what?" Eugenia asks.

"Somebody must have used the computer lab to print those articles. Maybe we can snoop around the browser histories and find an email or Twitter account or something."

Out in the hallway, a small group of girls pass by on the way to their rooms, chatting quietly among themselves, and I realize that I haven't learned most people's names, and I don't recognize most of their faces, especially with many of the girls wearing the same trendy style of makeup.

"Have you gotten to know any of the other girls?" I ask.

"There's not many people worth knowing," Eugenia says.

"I'll take that as a compliment, then," I say, turning down the stairwell.

After looping around through a series of different hallways, we still can't find the computer lab. I swear I was just there yesterday to send an email to my mother. Or was it the day before? Being in the studio for daylong stretches without a phone has made it entirely too easy to lose track of time.

"God, why don't any of these rooms have signs on the doors?" Eugenia complains, looking as lost as I feel.

We turn down another hallway and finally find a large room that looks like a hotel business center, full of sleek monitors sitting in orderly rows. I push open the heavy glass door and sit down at the first monitor I reach, jiggling the mouse to shake away the screen saver. Eugenia moves down the row to a different computer and sits down at the keyboard.

After a few long seconds of waiting, the web browser I

opened still sits blank. I try typing a couple of websites into the search bar. "Is your internet working?"

"No, nothing's loading." Eugenia rapidly clicks her mouse in frustration.

"I heard that the internet's pretty much been spotty since day one," a third voice says. "Some girls think they're throttling us on purpose to keep us offline."

I look up to see Alexis leaning her head into the doorway.

"Who said that? What else have you heard?" Eugenia questions sharply.

Alexis raises an unimpressed eyebrow. "Damn, girl, you really need to chill. Go do some yoga out on the lawn or something."

"We're just trying to look up some choreography ideas," I cover hastily.

Alexis glances from me to Eugenia and then back to me. "Is she forcing you to be her personal assistant or something? Blink twice if you need help."

I kick my office chair back and wheel over next to Eugenia, throwing a chummy arm over her shoulder. "Nope, we actually talked it out and agreed to bury the hatchet for the good of the group. Isn't that right, Genie?"

Eugenia's smile is rigid and 90 percent teeth. "You're so right, bestie."

Alexis looks like she wants to comment on this weird development but ultimately decides she doesn't want to get involved. "I snagged a few extras of those face-mask samples they were handing out at orientation; you want some?" she offers me.

"Sure, I'll stop by your room later?"

"'Kay." She gives us another curious look before leaning back out. "See you guys tomorrow."

After Alexis has walked sufficiently far away, I sigh. "Looks like we're going to have to get information the old-fashioned way. By talking to people."

"Take your arm off me." Eugenia shimmies her shoulders and tries to wheel her computer chair away from mine.

I pull the arm back and hold out my hand to her. "Partners? You can be the bad cop, obviously."

She stares down at my hand with reluctance and borderline distaste before taking it and giving me a half-hearted shake. "You really should go moisturize," she says. "You look haggard as hell."

During group sessions the next day, I watch Candie from behind the rows of dancing girls separating us, unable to stop the great swell of sadness.

Two years ago, I believed with absolute certainty that no matter what happened, Mina, Candie, and I would always be friends.

After Mina's funeral, I didn't know how I was going to go on without her. Without the constant pinging of texts that brightened my day, without anyone to turn to when something reminded me of our silly inside jokes, without the endless midnight conversations that would spontaneously erupt only after we'd said good night.

The idea of losing Candie, too, was unthinkable.

But the unthinkable happened. No matter how hard I tried to reach her, the distance just kept expanding, until I was standing on earth gazing up at the faraway galaxy Candie had drifted off to. Every message I sent out was a probe dropping into an unknowable black hole, and the replies I got back were fragments of data that were impossible to interpret or piece together. I couldn't piece *us* back together. Candie didn't want me in her life anymore. There was nothing I could do except watch our relationship die in slow motion.

Is she even the same person anymore? The person who protected me from harm, who showed me a world of things that aren't supposed to exist?

Celestial spirits. Magical incantations. The power to compel others against their will. Those things weren't real until I met Candie. Until I saw the impossible things she could do. I already brought up Candie once with Eugenia. Revealing more would mean divulging her secrets, and I've sworn to Candie that I'd take them to my grave.

And even if I did talk . . . would anyone believe me?

"—Addie Chu and Sunday Lee are the top scorers for today."

I look up just in time to catch the tail end of Yuna's announcement.

Me. At the top. Again. The other girls are clapping, but clearly out of pure obligation, the pretty faces around me forming a blank wall of indifference.

"And sadly, we'll be saying goodbye to Stella Heo and Viola Yang."

Even though there's only been a few rounds of eliminations,

the group already looks much smaller than it did a few days ago. My gaze unconsciously moves to seek out Candie in the crowd. On the other side of the room, she's chatting with the girl next to her.

She hasn't looked over at me once.

After we're dismissed, I meet Eugenia on the patio behind the building.

Beyond the floor-to-ceiling glass windows of the cafeteria is the outside seating area. It overlooks the back lawn that stretches onward until it meets the woods surrounding the complex. Nobody else is out here, but we still venture away from the patio, all the way across the grass lawn to the edge of the trees, where there's little chance someone will walk by and overhear our conversation.

"That's the second time you've made top scorer; you're practically a walking target at this point," Eugenia says.

"Story of my life," I grumble.

"So. Suspects," Eugenia starts without preamble. "I've narrowed it down to twelve."

"Twelve?"

"I started with nineteen this morning," she says. "First of all, both of Blake's roommates are automatically suspects, since they could have tampered with her skin-care products or makeup. Yuki's been talking shit about everyone since the day she got here, and Hyuna's family is totally bankrupt and on the verge of financial ruin, so she has a lot of incentive to debut. Ivy was next to Jessica when she 'tripped.' Turns out, nobody actually saw her fall. So there *is* a chance she was pushed. Sana is apparently a huge Brailey Corbyn fan, so she's got reason to be nasty to you. And the way Alexis just *happened* to be there to tell us the internet was out? Couldn't be shadier if she had wire cutters in her hands. And also there's—"

"Wait a minute, hold on." I raise a hand to pause her monologue even though I'm mildly impressed by her ability to gather this much intel in one day. "Do you actually have real proof or are you basing all this off speculation and vibes?"

She gives me a fiery glare, like she can't believe I would dare question her methods. "I'm a cheerleader; I can smell desperate losers who'd kill for fame and popularity from miles away."

"Of course you're a cheerleader." I nod in a sage that-explains-everything way. "Captain? No, wait, with how badly you wanted to be the leader, you must be the vice-captain?"

"There *is* no such thing as vice-captain. God, you'd think you would have done your research before auditioning."

"Just so you know, they didn't tell us anything about the parts beforehand," I tell her.

"Yeah, I *do* know," she snaps. "I was there."

"Wait. *You* auditioned for *Sweet Cadence*?" Suddenly, her hostility toward me is starting to make a whole lot of sense.

"I didn't make it past the first round. It's whatever." She dismisses the topic entirely and returns to the purpose of our meeting. "Back to suspects. Who do you have?"

"Um. Not as many as you."

Eugenia's eyes narrow again. "Are you about to pull a group project on me where I do all the research and you show up with three Google links and expect to collect an A?"

"I really only have one person I'm concerned about," I admit.

She frowns. "Candice?"

I nod.

"I guess Blake *was* in her group, and she was also right there to help Jessica, plus she's your roommate." Eugenia's brow furrows deeper in dismay. "But why target *you*? And using Mina . . ." Her eyes slide sideways to me. "Did you two actually hate each other's guts behind the scenes or something?"

"What? No!"

Eugenia doesn't look remotely convinced. I mull over my next words, then take a long breath.

"She's done something like this before."

Eugenia's eyes pop wide. "Like what?"

"Take people down. People who've wronged her."

People who've wronged me.

Eugenia's sharp gaze drills into me as she waits for me to elaborate.

"I'm just saying. She doesn't show her enemies any mercy."

"Is that what's going on?" Eugenia continues to pry. "You guys have a grudge or something? What happened between you two?"

"What do you think happened?" I snap. The question jabs like a needle against an exposed nerve. "Our best friend died, our show got canceled, and we haven't spoken since."

Eugenia's mouth pulls shut into a tight line. She's silent for several seconds before cocking her head.

"I'm just trying to understand. Why would Candice have any reason to do this? She's one of the strongest competitors, so she's basically guaranteed a spot." She casts another sidelong glance at me. "Unless you think she has another reason?"

"I don't know. She doesn't tell me anything." I glance back at the building where the bustling silhouettes of girls glide back and forth across the cafeteria windows. "We're not friends anymore."

Chapter 18

THEN

Two and a half years ago

"**Come on, Sunny, get** up. We're not finished yet," Candie says.

I'm on my back on the studio floor, arms and legs splayed like a limp, beached starfish. The music track blares onward, but I'm done, scooped clean of energy and motivation. Candie leans over me, hands on her hips, her breathing barely elevated, the shine on her skin amounting to only a "light misting" of moisture after nearly two straight hours of nonstop cardio. She looks glowing. Glowing and annoyed.

"Up." Candie nudges a foot against mine.

Since our national tour was announced, Candie's been going extra hard on me, like she's made it her life's sole purpose to ensure I'm as prepared as possible, adding extra practice sessions *on top* of regular rehearsals. I know she's only trying to keep her promise to me. The vow she made that we would thrive in an industry with the attention span of a blink. Usually I look forward all week to these sessions of ours, reveling in the one-on-one instruction, but knowing Mina's off camping with her family at Malibu Creek while I'm stuck in the studio all weekend makes me wish that Candie and I were there, too, or at a beach, or at the movies, or anywhere else where we could be having fun without utter physical exhaustion.

"I literally can't move anymore," I gasp at the ceiling.

"You can make it to the end of this song," Candie insists.

"But I'm in *sooo* much pain." I flop my limbs once helplessly. "Please, let me live!"

There's a strategic balance when it comes to negotiating with Candie, one that I've gradually perfected over the past year. The most effective method to soften her is to appeal to her carefully concealed tender and squishy heart by acting just a tiny bit wounded and pitiful.

Sure enough, Candie sighs and kneels down next to me. "Where does it hurt?"

I stick out my left foot petulantly, pointing at it.

Candie takes my ankle into her hands. Warm fingers slide up against my skin and start rubbing in firm circles, kneading into the tense muscle of my calf. I wince at the pressure bearing down on aching tendons, then sigh contentedly as the tightness is massaged out. It feels so good. I'm tempted to play up the pain a bit more, anything to keep her hands where they are.

When Candie pulls away, I let out a soft whine. She comes back a few seconds later with a roll of athletic tape and drops down next to me, taking my ankle back in her hands.

"So . . . I should probably take it easy, huh?" I hedge.

Candie gives me a flat sideways glance as she wraps the tape around my ankle. But silence usually means concession, so I decide to chance it, gently stretching out my luck like taffy.

"The LA County Fair is running," I comment, trying to float it as an offhand thought. "Mama used to take me every year, but I don't think I've gone since I was, like, ten. Maybe we could take the day off tomorrow and go together?"

"And how is walking around a fair 'taking it easy'?"

"That's—" True. I'm so exhausted my brain fully gives up on producing a good excuse. Somehow, I manage to slump farther into the floorboards, stewing in disappointment.

"Do you really want to go?" Candie asks, her hand resting lightly on my ankle.

My head snaps toward Candie, before pouncing on that faint whiff of compromise, nodding pleadingly.

"All right," Candie says under the onslaught of my puppy-dog eyes. "Let's do it."

I whoop in joy and launch myself from the floor, throwing my arms around her. She tries half-heartedly to unlatch my sweaty arms suctioned tight around her neck before eventually surrendering to my affections.

Standing beneath the towering rim of the Ferris wheel and the swinging arm of pendulum rides, surrounded by delighted screams and the salty-sweet smell of popcorn and fried dough, I feel like I'm eight years old again and my mother is holding my hand as we wait in line for the drop ride I demanded we go on but cried the whole way through. From across the fairground I spy the drop tower, and in a fit of masochistic nostalgia, I start dragging Candie toward it.

We're both incognito, wearing hats, sunglasses, and face masks. Despite the concealment, Candie manages to make the look work. She's wearing stylish oversize shades and a wide-brimmed hat, her long hair curled, hanging in loose waves over bare shoulders. The bodice of her dress hugs her frame, the ruffled skirt skimming the tops of her knees. She looks like she's dressed for a *Vogue* shoot instead of a casual day of fun at the fair.

When we get to the bottom of the intimidating tower, I turn to see Candie hanging back, her body language full of hesitation.

"Can it be? The fearless Candice Tsai can't do thrill rides?" I tease.

"I've never been on one," Candie says.

I'm aghast. *"Never?"*

Candie shakes her head. "I've never been allowed to come to places like this."

Her answer casts an abrupt shadow over my festive mood. Suddenly I have a million new questions about her life, about her childhood, her family, the types of restrictions she's under, about what it really means to be a follower of the celestial maiden.

She's already shown me things beyond comprehension, but there are still so many secrets she's clutching close to her chest, doors she won't allow Mina and me to look behind. The thought is thorny and sour on my tongue, hard to swallow. But this desire to be let in, to see and know *everything* about her even after she's already given so much . . . it's too greedy, too selfish. I furiously stomp down my intrusive curiosity.

"Maybe we don't start with this ride if it's your first time . . ."

I begin to walk away from the line. Candie catches my wrist.

"Let's go on. I want to," Candie says in the tone she uses when she's not interested in pushback.

"Okay." I laugh, getting back in the line. "If we die, we die together!" I grin and take just a tiny bit of childish glee in Candie finally being the one who looks weak in the knees.

I scream-laugh through every drop, while Candie stays dead silent next to me, clutching the safety bar like she might fly out of the seat if she doesn't. Afterward, I try taunting her into going on another thrill ride to see if she balks, but Candie simply smooths out her hair and tells me that she'll try anything I want. I let her off the hook and suggest we get cotton candy instead.

We pass by the carnival games, and when I spot a massive French bulldog plushie hanging from the rack of prizes, I step up to the balloon darts booth. I gathered from watching Candie's videos that she loved French bulldog–themed items, and I fork over a criminal amount of money for a dozen darts, hoping to add a new item to Candie's collection. My aim is shit and I lose miserably, pouting and complaining about how these games are all rigged, until Candie pays for a turn and easily wins the plushie for herself.

"You didn't cheat with your superpowers, did you?" I whisper, prodding her in the side with an accusing finger.

"No, but it's not like I'd need superpowers to beat your high score of two," she teases.

"Shut up." I laugh, elbowing her in the side.

Candie turns and holds the stuffed dog out to me. "Here. For you."

"Oh, so now you're trying to give me a consolation prize?" I push it back at her.

"It won't fit in my dorm room," she says, handing the plushie insistently to me with both hands. "And if I tried to give it to my cousins, they'll fight over it and there would be so much hair pulling and tears that my aunt will end up throwing it out."

"Are you sure you don't want it?" I question, finally accepting the offering. "It's really cute."

"I'm sure," she says. I can't see her expression behind the sunglasses and mask, but she sounds like she's smiling. "And every time you look at its cute face, you can remember how I cutely kicked your ass at darts."

"All right, that's it, I'm making you go on the ring of fire!"

I can't remember the last time I was able to do this. Spend time with someone in public, laughing together, having a good time, taking photos that aren't staged or carefully arranged so they can be uploaded for promo. It isn't until the sun starts to set that I notice Candie's brows are pinched, her steps unsteady, and I realize that she's been spending the entire day going on rides with me, not once turning anything down.

"Are you feeling okay? Here, let's sit down." I take Candie's arm, helping her over to a bench, and carefully lower us both down. Candie pulls off her sunglasses and leans her head against my shoulder. She seems exhausted.

"I'm so sorry. I shouldn't have made you go on all those rides back-to-back," I apologize.

"Did you have fun?" Candie's voice is muffled against my shirt.

"It was the best day I've had in a long time," I tell her.

She glances up at me, her long lashes lowering as she blinks slowly. "Me too."

The spinning ride beside us throws a cascade of blue and purple across Candie's face, the neon lights making her eyes shine. A comforting warmth spreads from where her cheek is pressed to my shoulder; the feeling flows into my chest and nestles down, a satiated, happy weight.

"It's almost the summer solstice," Candie says. "My aunt will be busy tomorrow preparing for the ceremonies. Would you . . . like to come over?"

I blink in delighted shock. Candie's inviting me to her home. She's finally opening that shut door and welcoming me inside. "I'd love to."

Overhead, the first vibrant burst of fireworks booms over the fairgrounds, and my heart bursts along with the colorful display in triumphant celebration.

Candie's aunt's home is a sprawling estate in Pasadena, one of those houses that looks stately enough to have its own name. Behind the iron gates, a long driveway shaded by low-hanging branches winds up to the two-story mansion. Massive columns line the grand front doors. I ring the doorbell cautiously, the opulent architecture making me feel like an unwanted solicitor despite Candie personally inviting me over just yesterday.

The door slides open a few inches, and I almost expect to see a butler in a waistcoat on the other side. Instead, a little girl who looks about nine or ten glances up at me from the crack.

"Hi there! You must be one of Candice's cousins?" I lean forward, hands on my knees. "I'm Sunny. Can you let Candice know I'm here?"

The girl tilts her face up to regard me, and I can see the faint familial resemblance in her delicate bone structure, in those stunning wide eyes.

"You shouldn't be here," the girl says.

"Um," I say.

"Go away." She points a finger down the driveway, like she's trying to shoo a stray dog. "And don't come back."

"Yingyi. Don't be rude," Candie's stern voice calls out from inside the house. The girl closes her mouth and steps aside, staring at me the whole time.

Candie pulls the door fully open and reaches out to catch my wrist, guiding me in. "I'm sorry about that. We're working on her social skills." She shoots her cousin a quick admonishing glance.

The girl—Yingyi—glances from Candie to me, then back to Candie warily. "You're going to get us in trouble," she says.

"Not if you don't say anything," Candie tells her. "And you won't, right?"

Yingyi purses her lips but doesn't object any further as Candie leads me past her into the house.

The interior of the home is shaded and cool, with most of the curtains drawn. There's a lot of marble and granite, all cold hard surfaces and sparse pieces of wood furniture. I try to sneakily search for family photos of any kind, but there are none. The only piece of information I've managed to wrangle out of Candie about her parents is that her mother is a socialite who works as an art dealer and constantly travels between Europe and Asia attending various high-society functions. Candie's never told me what her aunt does for a living to afford such a lavish home.

I suppose if one has the ability to make others submit to your will, money isn't likely to be an issue.

Candie leads me to the formal living room, and my attention is drawn to the large ink-wash painting hanging up over the mantel. The painting is of a female figure dancing. She's wreathed in ribbons of fabric, the long sleeves of her traditional Chinese garment thrown up in movement. The figure is lively and rendered with exquisite detail, but her face is left mostly blank, with only a few vague strokes to imply features.

"Is that—? Gah!" I turn to ask Candie if the woman in the painting is the celestial maiden and let out a small yelp when I'm caught off guard by two more little girls looking intently at me over the back of the couch. "She multiplied!"

"What did I say about staring at people, you two?" Candie lectures, before turning to me, apologetic once more. "You're the first person outside of the family who's been in this house, so they're curious." She points to the stairway. "Back to your rooms, both of you."

The girls hang their heads, but they don't try to argue with Candie. They slide off the couch wordlessly and begin shuffling toward the stairs.

"Aw, it's okay, Candie, let them hang out with us for a bit!"

The two girls immediately perk up, pausing in their steps to await the verdict.

Unable to withstand the onslaught of that many pairs of pleading eyes, Candie gives in. "Fine. You two behave yourselves, and don't bother Sunny too much. I'll be right back."

The minute Candie steps out of the living room, the two girls pull me down onto the couch and bombard me with one question after another.

"You're Candice's friend, right, the one on TV with her?"

"Yup, that's me."

"Are you here to play?"

"Sort of?"

"Can you take us to a playground?"

"Um, only if Candie says we can . . ."

"Don't talk to her!" Yingyi snaps at her sisters from the doorway.

When Candie comes back carrying a tray with round pastries that smell like sesame and honey, Yingyi wrinkles her nose in protest. "We're only supposed to eat those on special occasions."

"This *is* a special occasion," Candie says. "It's fine if you don't want any, that just means more for your sisters."

"We want them, we want them!" the other girls chime in, bouncing impatiently in their seats as Candie serves us each a plate and pours us cups of fragrant floral tea. Yingyi reluctantly joins us, accepting her portion and eating in huffy silence.

As reserved as Candie can be at times, it's undeniable how much of herself she gives to those around her. The respect and adoration on her little cousins' faces reflect the way I feel when

I'm with Candie. Like I'm deeply cared for, like even if the sky crashes down, she'd be there to prop it back up for me.

But as I watch Candie wipe crumbs from their chins, I start to wonder: Who, if anyone, is taking care of Candie?

After we clear the plates away, Candie brings me upstairs to her room, and I have to suppress a fangirlish squeal when I recognize the decor from her videos.

"I'm sorry for the way Yingyi spoke to you. We were raised to be very selective about who we befriend, and which outsiders we allow into our lives," Candie explains, sitting down next to me on her bed. "She's a good girl; this is just what we've been taught."

That's why Candie's always kept to herself and turned down our invitations, I realize.

"But I'm not an 'outsider' anymore, right?" I appeal.

"No," she affirms with a smile. "You're not."

"If your family is so strict, how come they let you enter the entertainment industry?"

"Because in doing so, I'm honoring the gifts I was given," Candie tells me. "Many descendants over the ages have become legendary performers. They were dancers in the imperial courts of emperors, actresses during the golden age of Shanghai cinema. By continuing that legacy, I'm bringing more blessings to our family. That's why I've been pushing us so hard. It's important to me that we succeed."

"But is it *your* dream?" I frown. "Do you actually want to be doing this? Or is it all for your family? For the celestial maiden?" It's a question I ask myself sometimes. Is everything I'm working for truly because of my own desires, or my mother's?

Candie takes a few seconds to think over her answer.

"Yes," she says finally. "It feels like I'm where I'm supposed to be, doing what I was born to do. But what I'm most grateful for"—she reaches out, resting a hand on top of mine—"is getting to meet you and Mina. And I want to keep doing this with you two for as long as possible."

Her skin against mine makes my chest thrum, happiness ballooning against my ribs, expanding outward until it becomes a little hard to breathe.

"I never properly thanked you, for what you did," Candie says.

"Huh?"

"When that stalker pulled the gun on us . . . you protected me." Her hand squeezes down around mine. "Thank you."

I blink, a little flabbergasted. "I didn't do anything! *You* were the one who saved us!"

Candie shakes her head. "I hesitated. You didn't."

"You know, you really don't need to be this hard-core Teflon warrior all the time and shoulder every responsibility yourself," I chide. It feels strange being the one to chastise her. "Whenever you're tired, I want you to lean on me, okay? Family's supposed to take care of each other, right?"

Candie stares quietly at me for a moment. Then a gentle smile returns to her face. "I want to show you something."

She stands and crosses the floor to the piano in the corner of the room. "I've been working on this on and off." She sits down and places her hands on the keys. I lean back on my palms to listen as Candie begins to play.

Music fills the space between us, envelops us. It's still a

rudimentary composition, a musical sketch, but I can hear the shape of a song forming around the unique harmonic intervals I recognize from Candie's chanting incantation during the blessings ritual she held with us on my bedroom floor. The chord progression is lovingly sweet at first, then tumultuous and wild, before turning deeply melancholic, the notes swelling with longing.

"That's beautiful . . . ," I exclaim. "You wrote it?"

Candie's hands halt, the music pausing as she nods.

"You need to play this for Mr. Kim on Monday; he's going to flip and want to lay down the track immediately. I'm serious; it could be our next single, it's *that* good."

"I'm not ready to play it for anyone else yet." Candie looks over her shoulder at me. "Just you."

Something about her confession draws me toward her.

I stand from the bed, walking over to join her on the piano bench. She shifts to make room for me. Our hips and shoulders slide against each other's when I sit down beside her. I'm close enough to smell her favorite citrus fragrance, tart and inviting. I imagine Candie getting ready in this room, tilting her head, stretching the milky column of her throat as she sprays the mist at the nape of her neck.

"Candie . . ."

Her curved hands pause over the keys. She turns to me. "Yes?"

My cheeks heat under the intensity of her waiting gaze. My heart stutters, then begins to race. I can't think with her face so close, can't concentrate with her knees touching mine beneath the piano.

What *was* it that I wanted to tell her?

That I think about her all the time? That I often space out when she's speaking because I can't stop staring at her mouth? That whenever she wears a backless dress all I want to do is run my fingertips along the line of her spine down to the dip of her lower back?

I glance back down at the piano before I can say anything stupid. "What if you tried something like this?"

I play back what she just showed me with a few chords adjusted. Even against the backdrop of music, the hard beating of my pulse is astonishingly loud in my ears.

"Hmm." Candie leans against me, her body a warm, insistent weight. "I like that."

Two hands become four as Candie's fingers join mine on the piano. Together, we wander the black and white keys in discovery. I shut my eyes, humming quietly along, a loose improvisation building and receding, mimicking the ebb and flow of our playing.

We do this for hours, side by side, humming and playing the piano. At one point there's pen and paper in front of us and we're scribbling down notations and snippets of lyrics, our ideas and voices layering over each other's until it feels like we've sunk into the music together, becoming one.

Chapter 19

NOW

One week ends, and another begins.

I'm completely entrenched in the routine now, spending all day inside the studio and practice rooms. I can hardly tell what time it is, can barely remember what day of the week it is. I keep trying to remind myself to call Mama and check in but always forget at the end of each exhausting day. Several more girls have been eliminated, and those who remain seem more determined and focused than ever. Each morning the tension grows; any performance could be our last, any second another elimination could take place.

At dinner break, Eugenia and I carry our food trays out onto the patio and sit down at one of the outdoor dining tables so we can talk without being overheard. Despite the sweltering temperature, there's a merciful breeze and a miraculous lack of mosquitoes. There haven't been any new incidents in the past few days, and all the "suspects" who we've managed to corner and ask questions about seem to accept the "freak accident" explanation. Nobody's response had seemed especially suspicious, but Eugenia and I are not ready to let down our guards.

"Do you know if they fixed the internet yet?" I ask as I pop the lid off my premade salad. "I wanted to FaceTime my mom tonight."

"No idea." Eugenia's head is down, examining the sushi on her tray like she's a food critic grading the presentation.

"You haven't talked to your family?"

"Why?" she rebuffs, as if it's an utterly asinine question. "They know where I am."

"Ooh, interesting. I sense tension there. Tell me more." I tuck a hand under my chin and lean forward. Eugenia pointedly ignores me as she mixes wasabi into her soy sauce.

"I'm going to take a wild guess and say your family doesn't support your idol dreams?" I ask.

"Honestly? I'm past the point of caring. It's my life. I'm not going to let them dictate it for me," she snaps, and I can practically see that ferocious aura radiating off her. Looks like I've hit the nail right on the disapproving parents' head. "They already have two other accomplished doctor daughters to fawn over and brag about to all their friends. I'm going to do what I want, whether they like it or not."

As much of an unlikable bully as she can be sometimes, I can't help but be a little envious of Eugenia's resolve.

"I'm sorry your parents aren't supportive," I tell her. "My mother's been dragging me around to auditions all my life, and it was only recently that I realized she was doing all that for her, not for me. And when my career ended, it was like she lost interest in me. She works fifty-hour weeks, and whenever I try to talk to her about things, she just books an extra therapy session for me so she doesn't have to deal with my feelings." I stare down at the plate of food in front of me, my fork hovering. "I don't know how to forgive her for it."

"You don't have to. We're not required to forgive people who treat us like shit, even if they are family," Eugenia says.

I turn to her slowly. "You know, every once in a while you say something so shockingly nice to me that it makes me reconsider this whole nemesis thing."

"I'm just stating facts. It's not that deep." She places a roll in her mouth and immediately recoils. "Ugh, gross, this isn't even made with sushi rice!"

Out of the corner of my eye, I catch a dot of pink moving toward our table. Faye makes her way across the dining terrace and approaches us with a nervous, flighty look in her eyes, holding her tray in front of her with all the awkward stiffness of an outcast approaching the popular girls in a cafeteria. ". . . Can I sit with you guys?"

"Of course!" I motion to the empty chair next to me.

Faye hesitates, glancing at Eugenia.

Eugenia stands, brings her tray over to the trash can, and empties the whole thing in. "I'm going to go find something actually edible." She turns and heads back into the cafeteria without looking at Faye once.

I roll my eyes. "Ignore her. God forbid the food here isn't Michelin rated."

Faye sits down then, and I can almost hear her physically

relax. She waits for the patio door to close behind Eugenia before asking, "Sunny, are you . . . mad at me about something?"

"What? Of course not! Why would you think that?"

"It's just, you've been spending a lot of time with Eugenia. I always see you two talking. Are you guys, like, friends now?"

"Oh. Um." I struggle to come up with a simple explanation. "Kind of? We've more or less agreed to a truce."

I don't blame Faye for asking. When I first got here, Eugenia and I were on a collision course, and now we're commiserating over our emotionally unavailable parents. In a tense competition where I don't know who to trust, I appreciate the way Eugenia doesn't put any effort into concealing who she is. She shows all her aggression up front instead of hiding it behind a smile like everyone else. She's utterly unapologetic in her awfulness, and that, strangely enough, has become a weird comfort.

Ever since I was targeted, I've been keeping my distance from Faye. She's obviously picked up on it. I know it might have the unintended consequence of hurting her feelings, but I don't want anything to happen to her, and it's safer for her to stay uninvolved.

Faye shakes her head, pink curls tossing. "I'm sorry; I sound like such a needy stalker."

"No, it's my fault," I tell her. "You're the first friend I've made in years. Don't worry, I'm not going to ditch you for Eugenia, okay?" I lean in toward her for emphasis. *"Okay?"*

"Okay." She smiles, finally.

The conversation flows easily and just when I thought I had

successfully dispelled any discomfort, Faye looks up from her food and says, "How are things going with Candice?"

I tense involuntarily, then school my expression into something I hope looks neutral. "I'm still working on it."

"I'm sad to hear you two had drifted apart . . . You seemed to have such a genuine friendship; it didn't look like just an act for the cameras . . ." She stops herself. "Sorry, I didn't mean to bring it up."

"It's all right. I'm fine talking about it," I tell her. "After what happened, there was just so much grief and guilt that we didn't know how to communicate anymore. That, and she never forgave me for what happened with Jin-hwan."

Faye's eyes grow round. "So all those rumors about you and him were true?"

"Some of it was. Some of it was completely made up by the tabloids. I knew it was wrong, but I didn't care. I was so insecure and desperate for love back then that I let him pressure me into things I wasn't really comfortable with."

"I'm so sorry for what he put you through," Faye says quietly.

"Thank you," I say, even though it still doesn't feel like I deserve any sympathy. "I've learned my lesson. A piece of industry advice—be careful who you open yourself up to. Just one mistake and it could all be over." I gesture to myself with my fork. "May my fall from grace be a cautionary tale."

"I understand." She nods and adds, "But it just seems so exhausting to have your guard up all the time. I don't want to think the worst of everyone I meet."

"You remind me of Mina sometimes. That's totally something she would say."

The idealistic glow in Faye's eyes is so familiar that I can't help but smile.

"Actually, you know what? I take it back," I tell her. "Forget everything I just said. Don't let cynical bitches like me crush your spirit. The world needs more optimistic people like you."

Faye's smile spreads wider, and for one peaceful moment it eases all the stress of the competition and the paranoid intrusive thoughts gnawing at the back of my mind.

The glass door to the patio pushes open again. I glance up to see Hannah carrying a food tray, heading out into the courtyard. Faye waves at her, and I take a few more absent bites of my food. As Hannah shuffles closer, I notice that something's off.

She's moving like she's in a trance, swaying slightly from side to side, dragging her feet. Her lips are moving, like she's talking to us.

"What's that?" Faye calls out.

Hannah's arms go limp and her entire tray crashes to the ground, splattering her dinner everywhere. I throw my chair back and stand.

"It's not right . . . ," Hannah mumbles faintly.

My body goes tense at those horribly familiar words. Did she say what I think she did?

"Hannah, what's wrong?!" Faye grows alarmed, too, as we both start moving toward her.

Hannah doesn't respond. Doesn't even seem to see us. She turns to stare at her own reflection in the wall of windowpanes.

"It's not right," she moans, grinding the heel of her palm into her cheeks. She's still holding a knife in her other hand.

Suddenly, her loose fingers curl into a tight fist around the handle, and she raises the knife up to her face.

"Hannah!" My eyes shoot wide and I dash forward, but I don't make it to her in time.

Hannah carves the knife hard into the side of her face, dragging the blade down from her temple to her chin. Behind me, Faye's horrified scream pierces the courtyard.

"This isn't my face! *This isn't my face!*" Hannah wails as she digs the blade in, opening up jagged red cuts in her skin.

The temperature of my blood plummets. My heart slams up into my throat.

It's the same.

The same thing Mina said before she fell from her balcony.

I grab Hannah's wrist when I reach her, forcing her to stop the assault on herself. The bloody knife falls onto the grass. "Go get help!" I yell as I wrestle with Hannah's limbs, fighting to restrain her. Faye stands petrified at my side.

"Faye! Go, *now!*" I scream at her.

She blinks, startling, then breaks into a sprint across the patio, weaving madly through the obstacle course of chairs and tables before diving back inside the building.

Hannah crumples to her knees and I drop down with her, gathering her trembling body into a tight bear hug, terrified that she's going to hurt herself again. Hannah squirms and writhes, blood spilling from the gashes in thick glossy ribbons, staining the front of my shirt. Now that I'm looking at her up close, I see that her eyes are so wide, much wider than they should be, crowded with spidery veins. Her cheeks look higher, her chin sharper.

I look up in a panic to check if Faye's managed to flag anyone down, but I can't see into the cafeteria windows from my position on the ground.

A shadow shifts on the other side of the vast lawn. A person. "Help!" I scream out. "I need help!"

The lights of the patio don't reach that far into the dark. The glow illuminates just enough for me to see that the person in the trees is a girl. Clad in that familiar pink-and-white dress. Short hair, her face hidden in shadow. Hannah groans weakly against my chest.

". . . Minnie?" My voice trickles out in a shaking, terrified whisper. "Is that you?"

The ghostly figure doesn't move. It stares back at me from across the courtyard. Then it turns, crooked legs moving unnaturally, the same way it did when it chased me and Eugenia down the hallway.

It crosses the lawn and ambles up to the building. Stretching out one long, thin arm, it pulls open the glass door and walks inside.

In my arms, Hannah mumbles, "I want to go home."

Chapter 20

THEN

Two and a half years ago

The biggest perk of being a celebrity, by far, is getting invited to other celebrities' parties.

We're at fellow teen star Ava Kwan's sweet sixteen inside a nightclub that she's rented out for the occasion, and even though most of the partygoers look around our age, there is definitely rum in this virgin daiquiri I'm sipping, spicy and syrupy, scorching down my throat in hot trails.

The music is loud enough to feel, a tornado of sound shaking my insides like a maniacal rattle. Strobe lights and lasers ignite above, shooting streams of neon. Tidal waves of people leap and dance while the DJ onstage pumps his fist and manipulates the breakneck track. I've been to plenty of concerts, but this is the first time I've been inside a real adult club, even if it's technically for another teen's birthday party. The booming energy is a lit stick of dynamite flaring in my chest, threatening to splatter me into pieces at any minute.

Candie's sitting next to me at the bar, a glass in her hand, the shimmering trails of her earrings gliding over her shoulder with each shift of her head. She crosses her legs, the cut of her skirt sliding dangerously high on her thighs. She dips in close to speak to me over the roar of the party, dark smoky eyes blinking languidly, and all the other flashy, exciting things happening around us cease to attract my attention.

We lost track of Mina a while ago, when the lead singer of an indie band who looked a good ten years older than us absconded with her to the dance floor. And a part of me thinks that we should probably go find Mina, but I can't focus on anything other than Candie's glossy smile behind the rim of her glass, so easy and uninhibited, like she's finally free from all the expectations weighing her down. We take ambitious sips of our colorful drinks, then exchange glasses to taste each other's. Candie presses in again to speak, her bare arm sliding against mine.

"What?" I shout back.

She gestures behind herself at the crowd before reaching out to grab my hand and pull me off the barstool, our drinks abandoned. We squeeze through the compression of grinding, sweaty bodies until we're at the center of it all, the music an unstoppable pressure pushing down on my skull, rumbling my chest, making my ears ring. Together, we free-fall into the beat, letting the swell of noise toss us in its wake, laughing and shouting along with the crowd.

In between flashes of strobe lighting, a boy slides up behind

Candie. To my shock, instead of pushing him away, Candie allows him to put his hands on her, lets him dance up against her.

Suddenly, I have no idea what to do with myself. I stop dancing, a stationary statue while the walls of flesh continue to surge around me. The boy lowers his face into the curve of Candie's neck, and she tosses her head back, her eyes fluttering shut.

My face burns. I'm not sure if I'm scandalized, embarrassed, upset, or my brain is just overheating from the dancing and the alcohol and getting cooked alive inside this human furnace. The guy's palm on Candie's thigh starts to drift, boldly heading for the hem of her skirt. Rage erupts in me, fierce and volcanic. I reach out and yank Candie away from him.

"Get your hands off her!" I scream over the thundering music.

"The fuck? We were just dancing!" he yells back.

"You were trying to put your hand up her skirt, you fucking creep!" I shove at him, hard enough to knock him off-balance and make him collide into the person behind him.

"It's fine! Sunny, *Sunny*." Candie tugs me back by my elbow. "I'm fine; I've got it under control."

She slides up to the boy again, and this time, she leans in to say something in his ear. When Candie steps back, the boy starts dancing with even more enthusiasm, his body moving wildly, like a puppet being jerked along by the music.

"What did you say to him?" I ask.

"I told him to dance as hard as he could, and not stop, for the next three hours." Candie laughs like she had merely played a casual, harmless prank.

I gape at her, but before I can ask her to maybe consider

undoing that command, she steps in close to me and drapes her loose-jointed arms around my neck. "See? All under control."

Candie leans down until our foreheads meet, her long lashes brushing my bangs with each blink. "I've never seen you snap at someone like that," she notes. A pause, before she smiles and adds, "Are you jealous?"

"I—*What?!*" I squawk, bristling with embarrassment. "I just didn't want you to get groped!"

Candie's laughing again, and I realize then that there's a possibility that she's totally wasted.

"If you want to dry hump randos, we should at least come up with a signal or a code or something," I tell her. Lecturing her is hardly effective when she's towering over me. Stupid stilettos, making her so damn tall.

She leans down, past my cheek, and presses her mouth to my ear. "If I'm ever in trouble again, you'll come to my rescue, right?"

Each huff of her breath sends an electric spark jolting through my system. "Speaking of trouble, should we go find Mina?" I attempt to gather my thoughts, which seem to have all melted into a sweltering, soupy mess. "Make sure she's okay?"

"After this song," Candie says. "Now shut up and dance with me."

Candie's arms tighten around my neck.

My hands slide around her waist.

She starts moving against me, slow at first, despite the racing beat of the music. The crowd rushes in against us, and Candie pulls our bodies flush. We rock against each other, our hips swaying, thighs slotting together. Her hands start to roam, curling against my nape, stroking along my shoulder blades, gliding down my sides, and the heat rises so quickly that my head feels like it's going to ignite.

I realize that what she said earlier was right.

I don't want Candie to dance with anyone else like this.

I don't want her to touch anyone else like this.

I want . . .

Candie's fingers seek out mine. She links our hands together, raising our arms up into the crisscrossing streams of lights cascading from the ceiling. We dance until our legs turn to jelly, until we can barely hold ourselves up, our limbs scaffolded against each other to keep from collapsing.

I don't know what time it is when the rideshare drops us off at my building. The security guard casts us a slightly dismayed look as we traipse through the lobby barefoot, heels in our hands, makeup runny from sweat, laughing maniacally at nothing and everything. Mina's dangled between Candie and me, one arm around my shoulders and the other around Candie's. She goes from laughing along with us to passed out from the time it takes the elevator to get from the ground floor to the penthouse.

Mama's not home, probably out at a different Hollywood party, working hard on finding her next ex-boyfriend. Candie and I maneuver Mina through the front hall and living room to my bedroom, tucking her in on the collection of beanbags on the floor, before crashing into my bed together, trying and failing to keep quiet.

"Shh, shh!" Candie slaps a hand over my mouth. "We don't want to wake Mina!"

"Shh, yourself!" I laugh into the warm press of Candie's palm.

It's funny because both of our voices are blown from shouting all night and we can barely speak above a raspy whisper, anyway. We can't seem to stop laughing, our shoulders shaking from the effort to keep ourselves contained. Gradually, we float down from our high, laughter subsiding to giggles, fading into deep, calm breaths.

"Sometimes I feel like this is all just a dream," I say in the dark. "Like I'm going to wake up tomorrow and just be a nobody again."

"We're going to be so famous that you'll never be a nobody," Candie says. "After the national tour, we'll go on a global one. We'll be everywhere. We'll conquer the world."

"Will that make you happy?" I whisper.

"I'm happiest when I'm with you," she whispers back.

We're not in a crowded club anymore. Whatever effects that half a daiquiri had on me have surely worn off. The air in my bedroom is cool, and I'm wearing a tiny cocktail dress that leaves most of my skin exposed, but I'm burning up, worse than before, heat flaring up my neck, singeing my cheeks. I'm staring at Candie's mouth again, wanting to reach out and brush a thumb against the fullness of her bottom lip. I want to press my hand to her heart and feel if her pulse is racing as fast as mine.

She is so achingly beautiful.

Candie's hand shifts against the sheets, reaching up to my face. I melt into her touch as her fingers travel along my jaw down to my chin.

She tips my face up, leans in, and touches her lips to mine.

Enormous, wild feelings erupt inside me. Before I can

identify any of them, I'm already pressing back into the kiss. Her arm loops around my waist, pulling our bodies together, the fingers on my face sifting into my hair. It feels like I'm being dropped from a great height, falling toward her, an inevitable gravity, faster and faster—

Down on the floor, Mina lets out a sudden low groan and sits up.

We break away from each other abruptly, scrambling to put an appropriate amount of space between us, gasping for air.

"I don't feel good . . . ," Mina grumbles.

We both turn to Mina, unsure of what she did or didn't see. Mina's shoulders convulse. Her face contorts painfully. She clamps a hand over her mouth and struggles to push herself up, and it takes me longer than it should to recognize the emergency.

"Oh, shit! Hold on, Minnie!"

Candie and I dart out of bed, and we're barely able to get Mina across the hall to the bathroom in time. The second I lift up the toilet lid Mina drops to her knees and hurls her guts out into the toilet.

We spend the rest of the night taking turns rubbing Mina's back on the cold tiled floor, neither of us bringing up what we were doing before Mina's untimely interruption.

We don't speak about the kiss the day after. Or the day after that.

The weekend comes and goes without a single call or text from Candie.

When we return to the studio the following week, Candie is her usual work-mode self, professional and focused. She doesn't act differently around me, but every time our eyes meet for too long, she glances away first. After a week of us both dancing wide avoidant circles around it, anxious and fearful questions invade my thoughts.

How is Candie feeling?

Is she upset?

Does she regret it?

Did it even happen, or was the kiss a drunken hallucination?

Every time I want to bring it up, I lose my nerve. In moments of uncertainty, I look to Candie for guidance. Candie always takes time to thoroughly process her thoughts before voicing an opinion. And so that's what I do. I don't push. I give her time. I give her space. I follow her lead and don't say a word, even though it's all I can think about.

The entire week I can barely concentrate at work or during rehearsals for our tour. When Candie and I are in a scene together, I have to do everything I can to push back the flashes of being pressed up against her, the lingering sensation of her fingers in my hair, the memory of that single small sigh slipping from her lips before the soft heat of her mouth covered mine.

I didn't imagine it. It definitely happened.

I want it to happen again.

But Candie is still not ready to discuss it, and so I continue to stay quiet. Finally, two more excruciating days later, Candie comes to me.

"Sunny, can we talk?"

There's a stillness in her eyes that unnerves me.

"Yeah, of course." I nod.

I've been waiting for us to have this conversation for so long, but now that the moment has arrived, all I feel is panic and an overwhelming urge to bolt and run.

We find a small unoccupied side room, and Candie shuts the door behind us. She gestures to the chairs, but I stand stiffly, unable to bring myself to sit down.

"I want to apologize," she begins. "I've been thinking a lot, and there are some things I think I need to let you know."

"Oh," I say, blinking. "Okay."

The panic in my chest begins to tighten.

"We shouldn't have been drinking. I should have stopped us. I'm sorry I let you down."

The tightness sharpens into a lance, driving inward.

"I shouldn't have . . ." She pauses to gather herself. "I think drinking impaired our judgment."

The sharpness gouges all the way in and begins to twist. It hurts. It really hurts.

"There's something I haven't told you about the maiden's blessings." The way she says "blessings" is ominous, nothing like the romantic tale she had shared with us before. "Her gifts can charm others, and they can also draw people in. Sometimes, that draw can grow to become a dangerous fixation, an obsession . . ."

The shock on my face from her putting me in the same category as the stalker who tried to murder her must have derailed her from finishing that sentence.

Is that what she thinks of me?

That I'm the same as that man, that I'm just a mindless, hyp-notized fan?

That the feelings I have for her aren't genuine?

"It's best that we don't cross any lines we shouldn't," she concludes with a sense of finality. "Our careers are just getting started; it's not worth the risk. You understand, right?"

I don't understand.

I don't understand how she can be so composed as she shoves me backward off a cliff. I don't understand how she can think that none of it is real, that I was just being pulled in by some supernatural force of attraction when she was right there with me, feeling the same things.

Wasn't she?

She sounds so certain of her decision. She's made up her mind. Candie is smarter than me, more mature; she considers situations carefully while I simply barrel ahead. If she thinks having feelings for each other is crossing the line, then it is. If she's concerned that it will impact our careers, then it probably will. If she believes that what happened was a mistake, then it must have been.

"I . . ." I can't think of a single thing to say in defense of myself. "I guess."

"I'm sorry, Sunny," she apologizes again. "I don't want you to feel like anything has changed." With every word, her voice sounds farther away. "You're still very important to me."

But not important enough.

No matter how much I work, how hard I try, it's not enough. Why am I never enough?

You're safe. I won't let anything happen to you.

I believed her blindly. I didn't realize that the promise didn't apply if the harm came from Candie herself. As we step out of the room together and walk back to the set in silence, the hurt is swallowed up by a chasm of numbness.

The pain is gone.

I feel nothing.

I'm nothing.

Chapter 21

THEN

Two years ago

"Are you ready? You better sit down for this news," Ms. Tao announces, smiling at me like she's got the world's best surprise behind her back and can't wait to pull it out.

We're already sitting on the studio floor, too tired to stand after the grueling rehearsals for our upcoming national tour. I wipe at the sweat on my collarbone with a towel and gulp from my water bottle, expecting to hear that our single just went platinum, or maybe a *Sweet Cadence* movie is being developed.

"Remember that special cameo I've been teasing?" Ms. Tao says. "Jin-hwan Woo's team just confirmed. He'll be guest starring in the season finale."

I shoot up off the floor to screech in Ms. Tao's face. "You're not messing with me, are you?!"

"They just signed the contract this morning," she says. "I knew you'd be especially excited about it."

"My vision boards really came through in a big way." I pretend to wipe a fake tear from my eye.

"Wow, I can't believe you literally manifested this," Mina mutters in amazement.

"Doesn't he have a girlfriend?" Candie comments mildly.

I shoot her a sideways glance. For the most part, things between us have returned to a tenuous "pre-incident" normalcy. As in, Candie pretends that none of it ever happened, and I vehemently avoid thinking about it. But the fact of the matter is that the bitter aftertaste of her complete rejection of me still remains, and every once in a while, it bubbles up and seeps into our interactions.

"It's not like she has a ring on her finger," I retort.

Jin-hwan and Brailey are still together, but taking into consideration the average length of celebrity-couple relationships, he might become single any day now.

"You should be mindful of how you interact with him," Candie says. "You never know how the gossip mags will spin it."

"Not everything needs to be about our reputation, Candie," I shoot back. Then, a little vindictively, I ask, "Also, would you prefer a pink or purple bridesmaid dress for my pending nuptials?"

Candie gives me a chilly, unamused stare before turning away. I ignore her attitude and continue to discuss the pros and cons of a spring versus summer wedding with Mina.

She was the one who pushed me away and told me to keep my distance.

And that's exactly what I'm going to do.

I fully expected a superstar of Jin-hwan's caliber to show up at the studio with a presidential motorcade, for there to be wall-to-wall security, and fans screaming for him as he dodges them and the paparazzi to make it inside the studio.

But Jin-hwan arrives without an entourage, with only a single assistant and his manager. He's personable and humble, exactly the same as he appears on-screen. He greets everyone with impeccable manners, not a hint of arrogant celebrity or the famed attitude of his native New York.

Jin-hwan was scouted by an entertainment agency on a visit back to Seoul when he was thirteen. It's the norm for trainees to toil for years within a company in hopes of being selected to become part of a group, but Jin-hwan debuted quickly and became a solo sensation practically overnight. And, sure, he's in a highly publicized relationship, but I can't help but stare at his chiseled face, the same one featured in the posters of him hanging on my bedroom wall, and *oh god* he caught me looking, he's coming over—

"It's so nice to meet you, Sunday." Jin-hwan is taking my hand to shake. I don't know how I'm going to survive this conversation, let alone film a whole scene with him.

"Sunny is fine." I squeeze out what I hope is a casual smile.

Candie's warning rings in my head. *Be mindful of how you interact with him.*

I clasp my hand a little tighter around his petulantly.

"My little sister loves you," Jin-hwan says. "Do you mind if we get a picture so I can send it to her?"

I can't believe those are real words that came out of his actual mouth.

International superstar Jin-hwan Woo just asked for a picture with *me*.

"Yes, sure, of course!" I give him three rapid affirmatives in a row in case he changes his mind.

He slides his arm around me and lifts his phone up to the optimal selfie angle, tucking his face close to mine, and casually snaps a few pictures. I'm shocked my legs haven't collapsed out from under me by this point.

"Here, give me your number, I'll text you the pictures."

With slightly trembling fingers, I tap my number into his phone.

On the way home from the studio that night, I check my phone to see that Jin-hwan has followed me on all my accounts and liked several of my posts. Close to midnight, I get a text from him with the pictures of us attached, my smile incredibly forced in all of them.

Can't wait to get to know you better! :)

Jin-hwan's only on set for two days, and somehow, I manage to get through filming without letting my raging celebrity crush on him make all our scenes unbearably awkward. Or maybe he was just gracious enough not to mention it. By the end of the second day, we've shared a few laughs at the craft table and even bonded over the fact that we both love cats but our severe allergies prevent us from owning any. I was prepared for that to be the end of this brief fairy tale. The two of us will be immortalized on film together; my dreams have been thoroughly realized.

I didn't expect a text from him the very next day telling me what a great time he had on set.

Or for him to text me again the following day to ask if I have any suggestions for donut shops in LA.

Two days later, he texts me again to ask my opinion of the latest Fast & Furious movie, and we end up having an unexpectedly heated debate on the definitive ranking of every movie in the franchise.

Before I realize it, we're texting nearly every day.

He's always traveling, so the messages arrive at random intervals, from unpredictable time zones. Every text I receive is a direct hit of adrenaline, sending my heart rate soaring and keeping me light-headed and vibrating for hours at a time. Whenever there is a lull in responses I sink into a mild depression, convinced I've said something too stupid to recover from and that he's blocked my number.

But he always texts back.

He tells me about the events he attends, shares the silly pranks that his roadies play on him, sends me pictures of the massive bowls of noodles he consumes at midnight in defiance of his company-issued diet plan. And when we're discussing the irony of how we're both playing high schoolers while missing out on having an actual high school experience, I forget that I'm talking to the object of my obsession. Until I'm engaging in my new nightly ritual of rereading our entire text chain from beginning to end and see his name labeled at the top.

Then a text arrives at 1:03 A.M. on a Tuesday, a message that changes everything.

> I'll be in LA next week. Can I come visit you on set? Miss you.

I read the message over and over until the letters bleed together.

I consider showing the text to Mina for a second opinion. We've shared almost all our secrets with each other. The only thing I never told her was what happened between Candie and me.

I read over Jin-hwan's message again, lingering on the last two words. *Miss you.*

The fear of rejection strikes me, and I begin to doubt the meaning of his words.

Friends say that to one another, right?

A set visit between industry pals is normal, isn't it?

I'm reading too much into this, *aren't I?*

As much as I've tried to ignore her existence, and as Candie so kindly reminded me, Brailey is Jin-hwan's girlfriend. His beautiful, talented, incredibly famous girlfriend whose fan base is known to be viciously protective and prone to mass co-ordinated online attacks whenever they believe Brailey's been slighted.

But when Jin-hwan shows up at the studio and presents me with a box of donuts from the bakery I recommended to him, I invite him back to my trailer without a second thought.

He leans in and kisses me the minute my trailer door swings shut.

When I don't respond immediately, too stunned by what's happening, Jin-hwan hesitates, pulling back to give me a questioning look.

"I'm sorry; I thought we—"

I lean up and press my mouth to his, burying his half apology in another kiss.

It doesn't matter if this makes me the lowest of the low, the worst kind of girl, the kind who other girls write hate songs about, the kind who'll get dragged through the dirt and never recover if anyone ever finds out about what I'm doing.

He chose me. He wants me. Nothing else matters.

He trails his mouth away from mine and dips his head in against the crook of my neck. He kisses a wet trail upward, then nips at my ear with his teeth.

Several knocks sound on my trailer door. We barely register it in time to step back from each other before the door opens.

Candie leans her head inside. "Break's over; director's calling us back," she says.

"Y-yup, I'll be right there," I answer.

She doesn't ask why we're alone, why the atmosphere is so tense, why Jin-hwan's hair is considerably messier than it was when he first arrived, why I've suddenly developed a nervous stutter.

But when Candie turns away without another word and shuts the door, the first stab of guilt cuts its way through the rose-tinted layers of delusion as I realize what I've done.

Mina and I are tucked away in a private booth inside an exclusive izakaya restaurant, the table in front of us filled edge to edge with little ceramic dishes—plump gyoza dumplings, glistening sticks of yakitori, golden brown karaage, delicate slices of sashimi.

We've ordered way too much food for two people, but it's our first night off in forever. Candie didn't come with us; she's been declining our invitations to hang out again, insisting that she needs to do tour prep, even though we've been rehearsing nonstop for months now.

I finally broke down and told Mina everything a few weeks ago. She was shocked at first, but as expected, she accepted all my bad decisions without any condemnation or judgment, and it made me feel a little less like an absolute garbage human being.

"So," Mina leans in and whispers, even though we're alone in the booth and the dining room noise is loud enough to drown out anything we say within these walls. "You stayed over at his place on Friday, right? What happened?"

"Well. Things . . ." I'm suddenly hyperaware of the fact that we're in public, and that I haven't fully processed it all yet. Heat spreads across my cheeks, and I finish vaguely, ". . . happened."

Mina's eyes stretch wide. "Did you guys . . . ?"

I fiddle with the curly straw in my drink and nod.

Mina blinks a few times and carefully asks, "How was it? Are you feeling okay?"

Sudden. Was how it was.

Between our packed schedules, Jin-hwan and I have only managed to hang out a few times. And to avoid being photographed together, we only meet in the middle of the night. For as often as I had joked about my romantic future with him, it's a lot less romantic in reality.

Last Friday he called me at 11:40 P.M. and asked if I could come over to his apartment.

One minute we were watching a movie, the next we were making out, and then he was pulling my shirt up, and I didn't stop him.

It's what I wanted. I'm living the ultimate fantasy.

That's what I told myself the next day when it hurt to pee and there was pink blood in the toilet and no messages on my phone from him. But with Mina's large expectant eyes pinning me down, I can't bring myself to lie anymore.

"It happened really fast. I think I was in shock." The nervous laughter that bursts out of me is unattractive and loud.

I thought Mina would be quick to comfort, or be upset on my behalf, but her answer stuns me a bit.

"Yeah." Mina stares down at her plate. "My first time wasn't that great, either."

I bolt up straight from my slouch. In the two plus years I've known her, Mina's never mentioned anything about having a boyfriend or even a fling.

"Who was it with?" I ask eagerly.

"Just some boy from the same training program I was in," she answers quickly. "We were breaking the rules, meeting up in secret. After I was cut from the program and came back to the states, he ghosted me."

"Shit, I'm so sorry, Minnie."

"It's okay. I'm over it now. We were never a real couple, anyway," Mina says, but I can see the sadness she's trying to cover up with her reassuring smile. "Sunny, Jin-hwan *is* going to break up with Brailey, right? You . . ." Mina bites her lip. "You should make sure that he . . . really cares about you."

I nod, prodding at the agedashi tofu, making the bonito flakes jiggle. "Don't worry. He says things with Brailey have been rocky for a while. They're mostly keeping it up for appearances and their fans. He's pretty sure she's hooking up with the guitarist of her touring band."

It all sounded perfectly reasonable when he explained it to me.

"He told me he definitely wants to be with me, but he needs to figure out the best way to end things with her so that it won't blow up in their faces. Did I tell you Brailey just started following me? It's so awkward; I don't know what I'm going to do if she starts talking to me."

I try not to go down the hellish rabbit hole of comparison,

but it's inevitable when I get notifications that Brailey's liked my posts and end up losing hours scrolling through her entire feed. Or when I see that Jin-hwan's phone wallpaper is still a picture of them in Paris together. Or when her videos are top trending again, when she's receiving another award or featured on another magazine, those blond curls and snowy limbs, just constant reminders of how she's the ideal embodiment of wholesome Americana pop in ways I will never be.

Mina listens quietly, then looks down. Everything I've told her seems to finally be sinking in, and she looks conflicted. Worried. But as usual, Mina takes the compassionate path. ". . . I just don't want you to get hurt, Sunny."

Too late for that. And the person who hurt me wasn't Jin-hwan.

He's the one who's taking huge risks to be with me.

Candie would rather sacrifice me to save her own career.

"I know."

"Have you told Candie about any of this yet?" Mina lobs the question gently across the table.

Mina's asked me a few times if things were okay between me and Candie; she's noticed the strain in our exchanges, seen how we are quick to snap at each other now in ways we never were. I told her that it's just the pre-tour stress getting to us, and me having trouble meeting Candie's drill-sergeant expectations.

It's strange, and maybe a little despicable, that the only times I experience flushes of shame and guilt are not the times when I'm kissing someone else's boyfriend but when I think about how I'm hiding all of it from Candie. It feels like I'm being unfaithful the same way Jin-hwan is, even though Candie has made it perfectly clear she doesn't want to ever "cross that line."

Candie's been acting distant again. She's walled off and withdrawn like she used to be, before we cracked her defenses. She's taken her self-appointed role as team commander to insufferable new heights, demanding we push ourselves harder, longer, making us watch recordings of our own performances over and over just so she can unearth every opportunity for improvement. Pretty much anything sets her off these days, and I'm tired of getting micromanaged and raked over the coals for tiny mistakes.

I already know I'm not good enough for her; I don't need her to point out every single way I'm inadequate.

"I'll talk to her as soon as the tour is over," I tell Mina. "Promise."

"Maybe Candie can ask the celestial maiden to help speed up Jin-hwan and Brailey's break up," Mina offers with a mischievous grin.

"Don't give me any ideas," I say with a cackle. "Now tell me everything that happened with that boy. From the beginning. Spare no details."

I'm texting with Jin-hwan again during rehearsals.

It's the week before our tour, the precious final moments when we should be pouring all our attention into perfecting our set, but I just can't stay focused. I know I shouldn't be texting with him out in the open, but we've both been so busy that we haven't had time to call each other. I have no idea when we'll even be in the same city next. I need to take advantage of every minute I'm able to reach him, every second.

Out of nowhere, a hand reaches down in front of my face and snatches the phone out of my hands.

"Hey!" My head snaps up.

Candie's got my phone captive in her grasp, her eyes moving across the screen as she reads our text messages. The inevitable moment I've been putting off for months slams without warning into my chest, knocking the air from my lungs.

"I keep waiting for you to come clean, but I'm tired of turning a blind eye," Candie says.

No excuses or explanations will save me now. My thoughts crash into one another in a blazing pileup. "I was going to tell you after the tour."

"Not only are you hooking up with a cheater, you're letting him talk you into sending dirty pictures? I thought you were smarter than this." Candie shoves my phone back at me.

It takes me another second to remember what Jin-hwan and I were just talking about.

"We're in a long-distance relationship; it's normal!" The disgust on Candie's face sends a hot burst of embarrassment flaring up in me.

"Do you realize how easily pictures of you can leak?" Candie bites back. "Is it really too much to ask that you *think* things through before you do them?"

"This is why I didn't tell you!" The defensiveness grows into anger as my voice rises. "I knew you'd react like this. You're not even mad that I hid it from you; you're just mad that it might fuck up our reputation! *Your* reputation!"

"Calm down, please, both of you!" Mina steps in valiantly, but her usual soothing waters don't even come close to putting out this fire.

"You need to stop seeing him," Candie orders.

"Why should I?" I snap.

"Because he has an *actual* girlfriend! The press would murder you, and then her army of fans would pick apart your carcass."

"He's going to leave her. He wants to be with me," I declare with full conviction, like I've been called to a witness stand.

"Is that what he told you?" Candie chortles, the sound of it derisive and mocking, nothing like her usual tinkling laughter. "How stupid can you possibly be?"

I shake my head. "I've done everything you've ever asked me to do. I've pushed myself to the breaking point for you. Don't ask me to do this."

"He doesn't love you," she tells me coldly.

The way she says it as if it's an absolute concrete fact—as if it's preposterous that someone like him could possibly love me—hurts more than anything else she's said.

"Please, can we all just step back and take a deep breath?" Mina begs. But instead of placating Candie, Mina only draws her ire.

"You knew about this, too, didn't you?" Candie rounds on Mina.

"I—well—um," Mina stammers.

"Of course you did. I bet you encouraged it," Candie accuses.

"Are you really just going to stand by and enable her to selfishly throw away everything we've worked so hard for these last two years?"

"That's really unfair, Candie." Mina's demeanor crumbles. She looks deeply wounded. "You know how much *Sweet Cadence* means to me."

"Right. I'm the bad guy. I'm always the bad guy." Candie steps back from both of us, isolating herself. "If this blows up in our faces, we're done. Brailey and Jin-hwan will walk away unscathed, but *we* won't be able to recover from a scandal like this. Don't you two get that?"

"Because that's all you care about now, isn't it?!" I yell at her, the dam breaking. All the anger and hurt I've been bottling up rushes out in a furious torrent. "When was the last time you even asked us how we were doing? Do you know that Mina's grandmother's cancer came back and she's in the hospital again? You're such an egotistical glory hound that all you care about now are ratings and how we're doing on the charts! You don't give a shit about anything else; you only care about being fucking famous!"

"I care about you!" Candie shouts, finally losing her composure.

I turn away from her and head for the door before the tears can fall.

"*Stop!*" Candie orders.

The command hits my ears, sinks into my body, and I'm frozen in the doorway, completely still, one foot over the threshold. Even the breath in my lungs seizes. I can't breathe.

It lasts for only two, three seconds.

All at once, my body is released, air comes rushing through my nose, and I let out a loud gasp. Mina hurries over immediately, rubbing my back as I cough.

I glance up at Candie in disbelief. That terrible feeling in my gut, all those fearful questions and dark doubts I've dismissed and ignored since the VIXEN incident flood back.

If Candie can hurt Soomin like that, can make people's bodies turn against them . . .

Would she one day do it to us?

"I—I'm sorry," Candie stammers. "That wasn't what I . . . I wasn't trying to—"

I take Mina by the wrist and flee from the studio, leaving a shaken Candie behind to watch us go.

Chapter 22

NOW

After the ambulance leaves, Faye and I find ourselves sitting side by side across from Ms. Tao in her office, like a couple of poorly behaved schoolgirls about to be admonished by the headmistress. Like we didn't just watch a girl try to slice off her own face.

Ms. Tao folds one hand neatly on top of the other and leans forward in her chair, shutting her eyes.

"Sadly, this isn't the first time I've witnessed this type of stress-induced behavior. We've reached out to Hannah's family, and her mother informed us that Hannah has been struggling for quite some time." She sighs deeply. "Our goal has always been to challenge you girls without sacrificing your mental health, but we've clearly failed Hannah. On behalf of myself and all of the instructors here at SKN, I want to apologize to the both of you as well. Thanks to your swift response, we were able to get Hannah the help she needed in time."

"I'm glad she's with her family now," I say.

I've changed into a new outfit, but when I look down I swear I can still see the red spread of Hannah's blood across my chest. Faye stays quiet, like she has been since we first walked in.

Ms. Tao spares us a doleful smile. "I absolutely understand if you need to take some time to process. And please know that you have my full support if you decide to withdraw from the program."

I drink in her words and let them sink deep. And I consider it. Leaving. Giving up.

I picture myself going back to my room and packing my belongings into my suitcase. I imagine calling my mother and telling her I failed, again. I envision waiting outside in the parking lot for Mama to pick me up, the long silent ride home. I think about how easy it would be to go up into my room, shut the door, and hide away from the world again, plugging my ears and covering my eyes. Just like I did last time.

Hannah's face layers over Blake's face, which layers over Mina's face.

I see Mina's body falling backward off that balcony, again and again.

My hands clench and unclench in my lap, the crescent press of nails cutting into the inside of my palms. It's connected. All of it. It must be.

And all of it leads back to Candie.

Once we're back out in the hallway, I take Faye's arm and lead her into the stairwell, glancing around carefully to make sure no one's nearby. Then I turn her to face me.

"You promised me, Faye." I need to get her out of here, and

I will resort to emotional blackmail if I have to. "You promised that if anything else happened, you would leave. I think it's safer if you did."

"But I don't want to!" She shakes her head, her voice fraught with despair. "I've come so far!"

"Trust me, this won't be your only shot. You'll have another chance. You're so talented and full of heart, you're definitely going to make it. Just not here. Not this time."

I rest both hands on her small shoulders.

"Please," I beg. "I couldn't save Mina, and I—" My voice starts to wobble, and I fight to keep it even. "I need you to be okay. I won't forgive myself if anything happens to you. Please do this for me."

Finally, Faye's shoulders begin to sag under the weight of my hands.

"Okay." She nods. "I'll let Ms. Tao know that I'm leaving."

I exhale a long, deep sigh of relief.

"If it's not safe, why are you choosing to stay?" Faye asks, her eyes full of worry.

"Whatever is going on here, I think Candie might be involved," I tell her. "I need to find out the truth from her myself."

Faye wraps her arms around me and pulls me into a long hug, as if she's convinced that this is goodbye forever. "Please be careful, Sunny."

Small embers of determination gather in the pit of my stomach, growing brighter and hotter until flames rise.

Tonight. I need to speak with Candie tonight.

I won't let her avoid the conversation any longer.

What is happening to the girls in this workshop is tied to

Mina, somehow. To the celestial maiden. I can't stand by and let another tragedy like that happen again.

I'm going straight to the source, and I'm going to find out exactly what's behind the hidden corners of this building.

At the end of the day, I sit at the table in my room battling with my hair.

I've googled my father only a few times when I was young, and the search results showed me photos of a tall, thin-faced man with messy curly hair. He somewhat reflects the person I picture in my mind: a chain-smoking, caffeine-chugging auteur who doesn't give a damn about the illegitimate children he's sired. I don't look like him at all. The only thing I've inherited from him is my head of thick, wavy hair.

The brush in my hand snags on a stubborn tangle at the back of my head, and I wince, hissing back the pain.

"You're going to damage your hair pulling at it like that," Candie's voice says from across the room.

I jolt slightly in my chair, turning from the table to glance at her. Candie sets her bag of toiletries down on her nightstand. I didn't even hear her come into the room.

She walks over to me and lifts a hand in offering. I hesitate for a second before dropping the brush into her open palm. She moves to stand behind my chair and starts to gather my hair meticulously into her hands. Fingernails glide in tingling arcs against my scalp, sending a sharp wave of shivers rolling down my back. The brush runs from the top of my head downward in slow, even strokes, stirring memories lying just beneath the surface.

We used to do this all the time. Candie would comb my hair with a brush, sometimes with just her fingers. It was calming for us both. Therapeutic, on hard days. She'd do it at the foot of hotel beds, when we were traveling in cars between events, when we were waiting around on set, bored. She told me once that she loved my hair. It validated my opinion that my hair was my best physical feature.

My eyes are lulled shut by the soft whisper of bristles as they pass by my ear. I assume she's extending this familiar, soothing kindness because of what happened with Hannah and me. It works; it's almost frightening how fast I flash back to the only period of my life when I felt truly safe and secure, buffered between Mina's smiles and Candie's protection. A small, anxious voice reminds me to stay on guard, but I can't help but lean into her touch.

"I think about Minnie all the time," I say.

"I think about her, too," Candie says. "But I'm trying to focus on the future. She would have wanted that for us."

"What she wanted was to star in a Broadway show."

"And own an alpaca farm."

I can't see it, but I hear the small smile in Candie's voice.

"She wanted to do so many things." I stare at the white wall in front of me. "She'll never get the chance."

Candie is silent behind me. The brush strokes keep coming, continuous and rhythmic. She reaches for the hair products on my table and dabs some oil in my hair to tame the frizz.

"Is it you, Candie?" I ask her, point-blank. "Are you hurting the other girls? Forcing them out of the competition?"

All movement from Candie halts. We're plunged into silence for an excruciatingly long time.

"Why would you think that?" Candie asks finally.

"Because you've done it before," I say in a low voice, like I'm afraid someone might overhear.

"Everything I've done, I did for you and for Mina," she says.

The brush pulls away entirely. Her arm slides up to drop the brush back onto my desk. I reach out, my fingers catching her wrist. Her skin under my palm is hot and damp from the shower. I pull her in toward me, my thumb pressing against the round bump of bone.

"Has it been long enough now? Can we talk about us? Can we talk about what happened?"

I search her eyes for the answer. We're close enough for me to smell the fresh scent of soap rising from her body, the fragrance of her shampoo. Droplets of water fall from her bangs and land on my knee.

"There's nothing to talk about," Candie says. "What's done is done. We can't change anything. We can only move forward."

She pulls her wrist free, banishing me from the warmth of her contact, retreating to her side of the room. She slides on her headphones and settles down in her bed to read, making it abundantly clear she's not interested in anything else I have to say.

I'm unmoored again, bobbing helplessly out to sea, adrift in the pitch-black waters with all the horrible things swimming just below my feet, watching as Candie floats away.

I've spent so much time watching her walk away from me.

Always too afraid to chase after her, too afraid to express what I want, too afraid of rejection, of crossing boundaries, of pushing past the point of no return.

I have nothing left to lose now.

I get up from my table and cross the floor to her bed. I sit myself down on the edge of her mattress. When she glances up at me, I reach out with both hands and gently pull off her headphones.

"What are you doing?" She's stunned, clearly not expecting me to break from my pattern of following her lead in avoiding the unresolved mess of our relationship.

"There's something I've never told you," I say, taking the book out of her hands as well, setting it on the nightstand. "I didn't realize it at the time. I think I was so drawn in by Jin-hwan because I was heartbroken and he made me feel loved. And I wanted to spite you. I wanted to make you jealous."

Candie blinks rapidly, unable to hide her surprise.

"It worked, right? You were always watching me when I was flirting with him. And you were mad that time you caught us in the trailer. You tried to act like you weren't, but I knew you were furious."

I lean forward, drawing our faces near. "I can show you. What Jin-hwan and I were doing before you walked in . . ."

Candie is at her most formidable when she's backed into a corner. She doesn't like it when she's not the voice of authority, not the one calling the shots. I want to see what she does when I pull her off the throne of control.

I lean in on my palms, closer and closer, until my lips touch down against the side of her neck. Beneath me, Candie goes entirely still. I wonder if I listen at her chest if I'd hear a thundering rhythm echoing my own frantic heartbeat.

I brush my mouth lightly up along her pulse to her ear. When my teeth graze her earlobe, her breath hitches sharply. The sound makes my head swim with dizzying bursts of white heat. My hand curls against her waist, fingertips skimming the vulnerable patch of exposed skin under the hem of her sleep shirt. Candie's hands reach up and land against my shoulders, not drawing me closer, but not pushing me away, either.

I sit back from her slowly. There's a high flush on Candie's cheeks, the both of us trying and failing to regulate our breathing.

"You said that my feelings might have been influenced by the maiden. What else is the maiden capable of?"

The second I mention the maiden, Candie's expression shifts. The flustered look vanishes, replaced by something else entirely. She turns away from me to face the wall, her shoulders hunching inward. ". . . I can't talk about this."

Suddenly, she looks small and lost.

She looks scared.

The memory of Candie quietly sobbing in that bathroom flashes into sharp relief. Her reddened eyes. How hard she was trying to hide any sign of weakness.

The realization finally hits me. I've always been too slow on the pickup, too oblivious to hidden intentions, to the ways seemingly unrelated details fit together to form a larger picture.

I've been wrong this entire time.

Candie *wanted* me to think of her as a hostile presence. She's acting cold and removed for the express purpose of pushing me away from her, but it's exactly that—an act. She's trying to protect me from something. Something that terrifies her.

The pieces finally click into place.

The celestial maiden that Candie has described as a divine guardian spirit who grants wishes and blessings ... might not be so benevolent after all.

Chapter 23

NOW

Nobody is talking about Hannah.

In the days following her departure, the mood among the girls has been light. They bounce on the balls of their feet, singing to themselves as they sail down the hallways together. I start to question if it happened the way I remember it.

Was there really a knife? Did I really see her hurt herself? Was I really cradling Hannah in my arms, with those deep gashes down the side of her face? Faye was the only other person who was present, but she's gone now; there's no one else who can confirm my version of events.

This isn't my face.

I want to go home.

When I try to recall what happened, all I hear is Mina's voice saying those awful things, not Hannah's. I shut my eyes tight, fighting the encroaching headache.

"Maybe Hannah really did have a mental breakdown and it's unrelated to the other injuries?" Eugenia says.

When I open my eyes again, the world reorients. It's morning. I'm in Eugenia's room. She's taking an agonizingly long time getting ready. I've been waiting for what feels like hours now, and she hasn't moved from the chair, still gazing into the vanity mirror she's set up on her desk. Both of her roommates have already left for their morning session.

I glance at the clock on her nightstand. "It's almost eight thirty. What are you doing, counting pores?"

She pushes her fingertips against the edges of her eyes, rubs the apples of her cheeks, then smooths her hands down around her jawline. "My skin feels so fucking irritated," she laments. "Am I breaking out?"

I heave a massive sigh and walk over. "Let me see."

She swivels in her chair and I lean in to examine her skin for any signs of redness or the telltale bump of an erupting pimple. I don't see any suspicious patches, but as I inspect closer, the lines of her face suddenly take on a foreign quality. In the span of a blink, it's as if all of her features have shifted ever so slightly; her sharp, angled eyes seem larger, her strong nose is more tapered, the harsh corners of her jaw somehow rounder, softer.

When I blink again, her face looks the same once more. It must've been the angle of the lights casting weird shadows. I lean back and cross my arms impatiently. "You look fine. Stunning. The gods are weeping. Will you hurry up?"

"Is it just me, or are people getting less ugly around here?"

Eugenia comments as she digs through her makeup bag. She pulls out a small tin canister, flat and round in her palm.

I freeze. "What is that?"

"The clay mask samples they were handing out weeks ago. I thought you got some?" She opens the lid and goes to dip her fingers inside.

"No! *Don't use that!*" I surge forward, knocking the tin out of her hands and onto the floor.

"What the hell was that for?!" Eugenia squawks.

Some of the canister's contents spill on the floor. It's a deep, dark brown. I lean forward, trying to determine if there are hints of red, if it matches the color in my memory.

"Have you lost your mind?!" Eugenia stares incredulously at me.

I stare down at the tin on the floor, then back up to her. Slowly, I stumble backward toward the door. "I—I think I need some air."

I turn and rush out, leaving an irritated Eugenia behind.

Along the hallway, several room doors are left open, the spaces inside empty of occupants, the beds cleared of sheets. A while ago, I lost count of how many girls still remain in the program. Somewhere on this floor there should be an exit that leads out onto the balcony. I've been out there before.

Where is it? Why can't I remember?

As I turn a corner, I nearly crash into someone coming down the other end of the hall. "Sorry!"

"It's no problem at all, Sunday." The other girl beams at me.

For a few seconds I'm utterly confused. She knows my name, and she's wearing dance clothes. I should be acquainted with everyone now, and yet I'm drawing a blank on who this person is. There's a prescriptive quality to her prettiness—watery eyes framed by heavy lashes, thin nose, pointed chin, black hair that runs bone straight down to her waist.

"Are you all right?" the girl asks. "You seem a little tired."

I fall back in shock. I recognize her voice now. Alexis. This girl is Alexis.

"Your hair . . . ," I manage to get out.

"Yuna dyed it for me." She pushes a dark lock over her shoulder, her sunshine blond gone. "The natural look is much more on trend. Does it look good?"

"Yeah, it—it looks great . . . Did you, uh, change your makeup, too?" I ask.

"Just a little. It's hard to compete with all you heavyweights." She smiles, humble in a way she wasn't when I first met her. Her teeth are painfully white.

"Did you get a chance to say goodbye to Hannah?" I try asking. Alexis and Hannah had hit it off right away and became close over the last several weeks of us being in the same dance group. Surely she'll have a lot to say about what happened to her?

"Oh, yes. I hope she gets well soon" is all Alexis says.

Not only does she look different, her keen, vibrant personality and sardonic sense of humor seem to have been ironed flat into that syrupy idol voice that I employ to make myself more likable.

"Practice is about to start," she says cheerily. "We should head down."

"I'm, uh—" *I don't want to go anywhere with you.* "I'm actually waiting for Eugenia . . ."

"I'll see you there, then. Hurry up; you don't want to be late."

She turns and walks past me down the hall, silken hair flowing with the motion, the bottom edge fanning out in a perfect semicircle, precise as if it was drawn with a protractor.

The minute she's fully out of view, I'm gripped by the instinct to run, to get as far away from this spot as possible. Instead of going down to the dance hall, I think about running for the lobby, out the front doors, through the parking lot, and just continuing to run and run and run.

A plume of pink snags at the edge of my peripheral vision, and I turn just in time to see what I'm almost certain is pink hair disappearing around the corner. My throat closes up, breath stifling. Faye. That was Faye.

But she left days ago. We said goodbye. I helped her pack. I saw her leave.

Didn't I?

I chase after that flash of pink down the hall. When I turn the corner, I find myself in a windowless side hall.

There's a door at the other end of the short corridor. The door is made out of dark wood, standing in harsh contrast against the pristine white walls. There are symbols and pictographic characters painted across the surface.

Where have I seen that door before?

Without giving myself a chance to turn back, I walk up to it and pull the handle.

The door swings wide to reveal a dark recess. The light from the hallway doesn't penetrate the shadows. I can't see anything inside.

"Faye! Are you in there?" I call out, taking a few hesitant steps in past the doorway.

My voice echoes back at me. It seems the space stretches far deeper than I expected. I venture a few more steps in. "Don't worry; I'm coming for you—"

Slam. I jump when the door shuts heavily behind me, plunging me into pitch-black darkness.

I put my hands out in panic, but I can't see my fingers in front of me. I turn in the disorienting space, trying to feel for the door.

Just as I'm about to open my mouth to cry out for help, something cold encircles my ankle.

Fingers. A hand. It starts to pull me backward.

I kick frantically, throwing my body forward until I hit the solid wooden surface of the door. I scrabble for the knob, but it won't turn; the door is locked. I throw my fists against the door, pounding and shouting. No words come out of my mouth, only incoherent, terrified sounds.

In the darkness, a pair of hands rest on my shoulders. There's someone standing right behind me, breathing into my ear. I'm petrified in place. The hands move up, fingers crawling along my neck. They make a terrible sound, *creaaaak*, like the grinding of splintered bones. The hands are on my face now. Jagged nails press into my skin, dragging down the side of my cheeks.

I scream and scream.

The door flies open. Blinding fluorescent lights shine into my eyes.

"Sunny! Sunny, calm down!"

I barely register that someone's shouting my name. Hands, more hands, trying to hold me down. I buck and twist violently. Don't touch me. *Don't touch me!*

"Sunday! It's me!"

Through the blur of tears, I finally see Candie's face.

"Candie?"

"What were you doing in there?" she demands.

When I glance behind us, all I see is the open door to a storage closet. Cleaning supplies and cardboard boxes line the metal shelves.

"I thought . . . I saw Faye . . . a-and I followed her . . . I was worried that . . . ," I whimper, clutching at the front of Candie's shirt with both hands, shaking her as if I could rattle the truth out of her. "I didn't imagine it, right? What's behind that door, Candie? Tell me what's behind there!"

Candie steps in close, pressing her voice low. "Sunny, listen to me very carefully—"

"Morning session is about to begin, girls."

Candie stops speaking abruptly. I turn to see Ms. Tao walking toward us, her plum-red smile curving neatly. She comes up to me and gazes deeply into my eyes.

"You're all right, Sunday," Ms. Tao tells me.

"I'm all right," I repeat.

"When you get your body moving, you'll feel much better," she says.

"I'll feel much better." I nod.

"Candice, make sure Sunday comes along. It's time for practice."

Practice. That's right. I need to go to practice. It's the reason I'm here.

"I feel fine now," I tell Candie. "Come on. Let's go."

We follow Ms. Tao downstairs, joining the other girls as they file into the studio one after another. Candie walks beside me, guiding me, her grip on my arm tight the entire way.

Chapter 24

NOW

The days blend together.

In the studio, we twist and form our bodies to the unrelenting music, the steps second nature now. The song is a live thing threading under my skin, pulling my spine taut, extending my limbs. All the pain and feelings of discomfort are gone. I'm gripped by a singular, all-encompassing focus.

The hours fly by.

I'm constantly humming the music, the melody slipping from my lips in an unbroken stream, like exhaling. When I'm not humming, my foot compulsively taps the rhythm, my hands drumming against my thighs.

There's no more acting and stage-presence training. We dance all day, from morning until night, without stopping. But I'm not fatigued at all, fueled by a ceaseless energy that won't let me rest.

The girls around me are starting to blend together, too.

Everyone's changed their hair and makeup to a unified look. Glistening saucer eyes blink at me from around every corner. Rosy lips plump and full. Faces look sharper, cheekbones more defined.

It seems like just yesterday there was something important that I needed to do.

But now nothing feels as important as the dancing.

"Very good, everyone." Ms. Tao watches us from the front of the class. "You're nearly ready for the final evaluations tomorrow."

The finals are tomorrow?

Out of nowhere, a hit of clarity strikes through my skull like an ice pick, and I stop moving, a fixed boulder in the flowing stream of dancing bodies.

What day is it? What *week* is it?

I glance feverishly around the hall as if I could somehow spot a calendar hanging up somewhere. How long have I been here?

"Sunday? Are you all right?" someone to my right asks.

When was the last time I spoke to Mama?

"Why did you stop? Are you feeling tired?" someone to my left says.

I look side to side at nearly identical faces. I force my mouth to form a smile. "I'm fine," I assure them.

I can't tell them apart from one another, or from the rest of the girls behind them closing in on me.

At night, I rush through the hallways toward the computer lab. Even though Mama's always kept me at arm's length emotionally, in moments of crisis, I still feel an innate urge to run to her and cling like I did when the trick-or-treaters' scary outfits terrified me during my first Halloween.

I go up the stairs and search the second floor. I turn down corner after corner, walk past the row of administrative offices and empty meeting rooms only to end up back at the staircase after scouring the entire floor. Maybe it wasn't on the second floor after all? I shake my head and go back down to the first level. I trace the layout of the first floor and turn down a few hallways that aren't in the well-trod daily route of the dance hall, lockers, cafeteria, and practice rooms.

It's not here.

I go back to the stairwell and circle up to the second floor again. I do another sweep through the white corridors and end up going in a full circle, back at the stairs.

My heart chills. I can't find it. I can't find the computer lab.

Why can't I remember where it is?

Even though I know only dormitory rooms are on the third floor, I head up there anyway and start the search over.

A group of girls approaches from the other end of the hallway, the sound of their laughter both melodious and shrill. I turn and duck into the bathrooms, suddenly fearful of their eyelash-laden gaze and those smiles splitting over rows of stark white teeth.

The bathroom is humid, the mirrors foggy with condensation. The spray of the communal showers is going off behind me. I lean against the sink, gripping the edge of the counter, and hold my breath until the unnerving laughter and skipping footsteps pass by outside.

I reach out a hand to wipe the water droplets off the mirror, and stare into my reflection.

"Calm down," I tell myself. "You need to calm down."

But the longer I stare into the mirror, the more I start to notice inconsistencies in the topography of my face.

I run my fingers along the hill of my brow bone. Do my wider-set eyes seem a little bit closer together? I pinch my fingers against the sides of my nose. Does the bridge feel a little higher, more sculpted? I push the palms of my hands into the hollow of my cheeks. Have I lost weight? Or does my face look—

Different?

The shower turns off then, cheerful humming drifting out from the stalls over the steam. It's the same song we dance to—the only song—and my fingers automatically start tapping out the rhythm against the sink counter in response.

A girl comes up next to me, wrapped in a towel. There's a clay mask applied to her face, a thick layer of brown coating on her skin leaving only large circles around her eyes and mouth.

"Hello, Sunny," she says blithely.

It's Alexis. With her face covered like that, I'm not distracted by her features, and I recognize her voice instantly.

"Isn't it such a lovely night?" She sighs contentedly.

"Alexis, what happened to you? Why are you acting so different?" I can't understand it.

She doesn't answer, only turns to the mirror and starts humming again, fingers curling around the edge of the mask as she starts to remove it. The clay adheres stubbornly to her skin, and she digs her nails against its brown borders and *pulls*. A crescent-shaped red line begins to grow on her hairline, gradually widening as she pulls.

"Alexis, that's—" My voice dies in my throat.

There's a sickening squelch as the mask comes off, taking her skin along with it. Bit by bit, her face is pulled down—her eyebrows, her temples—sloughing off like the peel of an overripe fruit. Her forehead is an exposed globe of red flesh, shiny and glistening under the lights. She hums the whole time.

"Stop it; you're hurting yourself!" I choke out.

She turns to me, her face half gone. Her eyes are two blinking islands of pale skin in a gory sea, her nose nearly skinned. She smiles that blinding white smile.

"Are you all right? You look really tired."

Bile lurches up from my stomach.

I bolt out of the bathroom, the frantic momentum sending me careening into the wall on the opposite side of the hallway. I lean over, dry heaving against the carpet. My stomach flips and my throat tenses in agony. Nothing comes out. Panic swells, an imminent flood looming on the horizon. Beads of cold sweat gather across my forehead; my tongue is a thick, viscous slug filling up my mouth, my heart thundering in irregular spurts.

"Are you okay, Sunday?" A girl is suddenly at my side.

My eyes water, blurring my vision.

"Are you all right, Sunday?" another girl asks, close to my ear, her hand landing on my shoulder.

"*Don't touch me!*" I scream, shaking off the hands and launching myself forward.

Through the tidal waves of fear, I manage to pick out the numbers of Eugenia's dorm room in front of me like a beacon. Her door isn't latched. I scramble forward and fling myself in.

Eugenia is sitting at her table, staring into her vanity mirror with her back to me.

"Eugenia, I—I just . . . saw . . ."

I don't know how to explain what I witnessed in the bathroom, grasping for words through the panic. That's when I notice Eugenia's hair. Her hair, that only fell to the middle of her back a week ago, is now pooling down past her waist. She's in a white robe I've never seen her wear before.

I start walking to her but pause at the humming. She's humming the song, the same song. Slowly, Eugenia turns in her chair to me.

I let out a strangled sob. Her face is not Eugenia's face. Her eyes are far too large. Her cheeks too thin. Her smile too wide.

"Are you all right, Sunday?" The girl who looks like Alexis, like Hannah, like Mina, asks in Eugenia's voice. From behind me, that phrase is echoed and multiplied by many smacking mouths.

"Are you okay, Sunday?"

"Are you all right?"

"You look tired."

When I turn, the door is crowded with identical smiling faces. Elongated white hands stretch forward. They're dressed in white, too—floor-length robes with wide sleeves that hang loose, hems swishing against bare feet. The girls I saw in the hallway earlier, were they all wearing white, too?

"You should lie down, Sunday," Eugenia's voice says. I turn back to see her standing right in front of me, that beautifully horrible face leaning in. "You look a little tired."

"Get away from me!" I scream, lashing out, shoving and kicking at the canopy of hands until a gap is created. I dash out of Eugenia's room and run down the hallway of doors, straight for the stairwell. My survival impulse takes over entirely, and I tear down the stairs toward the first floor, pure terror propelling me forward.

I need to get away from these people.

I need to get out of here.

I reach the bottom of the stairs and scramble onto the landing, turning left toward the front of the building. The overhead lights have been switched off, leaving only moonlight to guide my way. I race past room after empty room. Turning the corner, I end up in another dark hallway.

It looks like the same hallway we just went down.

This isn't right.

I should be on the first floor. Where's the lobby? Where's the exit?

I turn on my heels and head back in the other direction, down the opposite hallway. I wind up at the same junction. An implausible loop.

This isn't the first floor. This doesn't look like any of the floors.

You're losing it, Sunday.

I cradle my head in my palms. "Stop saying that; I'm *not!*" I shout into the empty hallways.

From somewhere behind me comes a chorus of high-pitched humming, like air blowing across the rim of a glass. The girls. They're humming the song. That same song.

They're coming for me.

My back hits the wall, and I slide down, sinking to the floor onto my haunches. The panic sweeps in, and I'm powerless against the onslaught, my spine curling, forehead pressing into my knees, my chest racked by wild breaths.

A gentle hand rests on my arm, the comforting weight of it so, so familiar.

My head snaps up. Candie is kneeling in front of me.

She's backlit by the moon, but I can see that her face is still hers, those steely eyes, that determined mouth, my anchor, my protector. I reach for her, desperate fingers grabbing at her arms, her shirt collar, her hair, anything to keep from falling over the ledge.

"Breathe," Candie says. *"Breathe."*

I do as she tells me, taking in one shaky breath after another.

"Am I dreaming?" I gasp, when I can finally form words again. "What's happening, Candie?"

Candie's hands slip around my arms and she drags me to my feet. "Come on," she says, pulling me forward. "Hurry."

Sensation returns to my numb legs, and I force myself to move—left or right, I can't tell anymore, I've lost all sense of space. Another hallway, another turn, and suddenly there is another staircase, the two of us flying down the steps in a dizzying spiral.

We emerge in the atrium. I recognize where I am now. The front doors are just ahead of us.

We're almost there. We're almost out.

We race down the front corridor to the reception area, my eyes fixed on the open sea of asphalt, the black night sky, the freedom just beyond the glass. As we get closer to the door, Candie starts to fall behind me. I turn around, grasping for her.

She pushes me forward. "Go!"

"What about you?!" I shout back.

The humming grows closer, floating up to the reception hall

from the other end of the corridor. Long, distorted shadows of tall bodies stretch across the walls. There are so many of them. It sounds like they're just around the corner.

"I said *go!*"

Candie's hand shoots out, and I'm shoved backward out of the front doors.

The moist night wind hits my face as I crash into the grass of the front lawn. The building's glass doors swing shut—and stay shut. Candie doesn't come out.

I launch to my feet and rush back toward the building without a second thought. I stop dead when my feet pass through the threshold.

Where there was just a reception area two seconds ago is now a massive empty space. The reception desk is gone. The mural on the wall is gone. The chairs in the waiting area are gone.

There's no Candie. There's nothing at all.

Only the vacant lobby of an abandoned building.

Chapter 25

THEN

Two years ago

The *Sweet Cadence* national tour is supposed to be the highlight of our careers. It's everything we've been working for. But our fight and what Candie did loom like angry shadows over this monumental accomplishment.

Candie apologizes to me over and over.

She vows to never use her power around us again.

I know she didn't mean it. I believe her when she says it was an accident.

But I don't have time to dissect all the conflicting feelings and the fallout of the awful things we said to each other during that argument. We leave to go on tour in two days. And so we agree to patch the gaping wounds in our relationship with as many Band-Aids as we can before heading out on the road.

The cheering on opening night is so astonishingly loud that I can barely hear my voice in the earpiece. I panic and lose my footing during the very first number. Instead of carrying on as if I hadn't stumbled, Candie steps in close to me and takes my hand. Mina follows her lead and takes my other hand, the three of us abandoning the choreography, striding forward together into the flashing streams of multicolored stage lights.

And it feels like everything is right in the world, again.

The stadium goes wild, and the shouts of my name remind me that all these people are here for me, they support me, *they love me.* My voice bursts from my chest, bright and soaring and alive.

In Phoenix, an eight-year-old fan's encouraging words to me at the meet and greet backstage reduce me to tears. In Mina's hometown of Boston, we celebrate her birthday during the show, showering the audience with balloons and confetti as thousands of people sing happy birthday in unison. Each night, we step onstage to outstretched hands and thunderous screams. There are no more mishaps after the first night; we nail the harmonies and fly through the tricky choreography, closing out each show to standing ovations.

Onstage, our bond looks stronger than ever.

But once we're back on the tour bus, we don't speak to one another, each of us scrolling separately on our phones, or staring out the window as the highway markers go by.

I check my messages whenever I can. Jin-hwan hasn't texted me since the beginning of the tour. I send him lonely selfies in front of state landmarks complete with lame postcard captions like *Really wish you were here with me.*

The day after we get back from being on the road for two months, Jin-hwan answers me.

> I'm sorry, Sunny. Brailey and I are going to try to make it work, so we can't see each other anymore.

When Ms. Tao calls my mother and me to her office for a meeting, and I notice that Candie and Mina have not been invited, I know.

I prepare myself to come clean about Jin-hwan—it was only a matter of time. Turns out, she didn't call us in for an emergency PR meeting.

It's much, much worse.

She tells us with a grave expression that there's been a large-scale leak of a private celebrity group chat consisting of several prominent male K-pop stars and boy banders. The group was sharing photos with one another—intimate photos—of the girls they have been involved with.

The pictures I took for him, the ones of me in poses that I copied from cam girls, are among those leaked.

Ms. Tao assures us that the situation is under control, that those involved are cooperating fully with authorities. She promises that all the leaked photos have been removed from the internet and that there will be harsh disciplinary action from the boys' management companies.

My mother doesn't accept this. She is hysterical. She yells at

Ms. Tao, gets right up in her face and threatens to fire her on the spot, declares that she will be suing every person involved in this grave violation of my privacy. But I can't seem to summon up any sort of response, and I sit there in silence as my mother rages on my behalf.

"Someone has to be held responsible!" my mother shouts.

She doesn't know. *I* am the one responsible for all this. I fell for Jin-hwan's lovely lies. And now I've been carved empty. I have nothing left to give to anyone.

Jin-hwan's camp has already released a statement asking for privacy. He declines to comment on the nature of his relationship with me.

Over the next week, the headlines declare that Jin-hwan, Brailey, and I are this summer's most dramatic love triangle, pouring oil onto the flames of the photo-leak scandal. Fans dredge up candid shots and videos of all our past interactions, constructing time lines, analyzing our body language—it's all anyone can talk about—and suddenly I'm not Sunday Lee from *Sweet Cadence* anymore, I'm—

The other girl.

The boyfriend stealer.

The dirty skank who sent nudes of herself to Jin-hwan in an attempt to seduce him away from poor, unsuspecting Brailey.

The backlash against me is so intense that our agency cancels all our upcoming appearances and the studio goes into crisis management mode.

I hide away in my bedroom for days. I don't answer my phone, don't answer my mother as she pleads for me to speak to the PR coach she's hired.

Throughout the onslaught of this media storm, Brailey stands by Jin-hwan. She doesn't release any statements, only a cryptic post saying *You always receive what you put out into the universe* before unfollowing me. The Brailey Brigade takes that as a signal to declare war, and soon, every single one of our social media pages is flooded with hate.

Your career is OVER!!

Those nudes are so ugly lol

You've set such a bad example for all the little Asian American girls who looked up to you

Cancel the show already it's trash

Justice4Brailey!

I don't know how many days pass before I hear Mina and Candie outside my bedroom door, knocking gently, asking to be let in.

The fire-and-brimstone judgment I expected doesn't come. There is no "You should've known" or "I told you so." Candie and Mina hold me tightly in a protective embrace. Something in me thaws, and I finally, finally let it out.

I cry so hard and for so long that my entire face hurts and a migraine starts hammering on my skull. Mina and Candie hold me until the heavy sobs die down into quiet sniffles and fitful hiccups.

"The news cycle will move on; it always does. This'll all be over soon." Mina hands me tissues, drawing from her boundless well of optimism.

I doubt it.

"Stay off the internet. Don't look at anything." Candie rubs my back.

Impossible. I haven't.

I can't even look at Candie. She knew this would happen. She tried to warn me. I'm sure what she really wants to do right now is yell at me, tell me just how badly I fucked up, how selfish, how stupid, how pathetic—

"I deserve this, don't I?" I ask. My eyes are so swollen it's painful to blink.

"No." Candie reaches out and cups my face, forcing me to look up at her. "You've made mistakes, but this is not your fault. You don't deserve any of this."

"It's *his* fault," Mina grits out. She takes my hand in hers, squeezing it tight. "I need to admit something to you, Sunny."

"What is it?" I blink up at Mina, rubbing my sore eyes.

"I'm sorry I haven't been honest. But you deserve to know. Jin-hwan . . . was the boy that I told you about," Mina confesses. She turns to Candie, who looks confused about the admission. Mina adds, "I . . . hooked up with Jin-hwan before he debuted. When we were both trainees in Korea."

Her voice is small and weighed down with heavy guilt. She looks so ashamed. Candie's eyes widen, but she elects to stay silent.

At first, I think I misheard her. Mina and Jin-hwan hooked up? That *can't* be what she said.

But then it hits me.

The sad, slightly tortured looks she gave when I was recounting my exploits.

The way she was trying to warn me.

Mina continues on, her voice growing quieter. "My pictures

were in the leaks, too. You can't see my face in them, but . . .
it's me."

It takes me several shocked seconds to process the information.

"*What?*" Candie's clipped tone breaks the silence.

"Mina . . . why didn't you say anything?" I ask finally. "This
whole time . . ."

"I should have. I'm so, *so* sorry, Sunny." Mina's voice breaks.
"I should have told you the truth. But I was afraid. I knew how
much you liked him, I-I didn't want to upset you. I didn't want
something like that . . . someone like *him*, to affect our friendship. I didn't want you to hate me."

I *am* upset.

But not at Mina.

I'm furious at myself. For not seeing through all his lies sooner.
For going on and on about my affair when Mina had already been
hurt by him. For expecting Mina to comfort me while she was
suffering through the exact same betrayal of trust.

I feel like the worst friend in the world.

". . . I could never hate you. Ever," I tell Mina, pulling her into
another crushing hug.

Mina turns to Candie. For the first time, the perpetual warm
glow that lights Mina up from the inside has been snuffed out
and replaced with a vengeful fire. "We have to do something,"
Mina says to Candie. "We can't just let him walk away from this.
We have to make him pay for what he did."

The unspoken implication is clear. She wants *Candie* to
make him pay.

Candie remains quiet as she considers what's being asked of her. She turns to me. "What do you want, Sunny? What do you want me to do?"

"I want him to hurt." My voice is a strange rasp in my own ears, bitter and ugly. "I want him to hurt like I did."

A menacing darkness surfaces in Candie's eyes. "Then he will."

Candie finds out that Jin-hwan is lying low in a luxury condo in the Hollywood Hills. I don't know if she got this information through normal networking means or through coercion. I don't really care how.

All I care about is revenge.

When Candie, Mina, and I show up at his building, Candie tells the door attendant to let us in. He steps aside right away, welcoming us inside as if we're actual residents arriving home.

All three of us are dressed in mourner's black—black coats, black jeans, black heels. The end of this relationship does feel like a death. The once-cherished memories of Jin-hwan now cover my body like vicious, malignant growths.

Tonight, we're exorcising those tumors.

We take the elevator up to his floor, and we march, shoulder to shoulder, down the hall, like we're about to take to the stage, but this time to deliver a very different kind of show.

Candie rings the doorbell.

The unpleasant surprise on Jin-hwan's face when he opens the door brings a rush of spiteful glee. He glances warily at

Candie, and Mina, then finally me, and pulls off the gaming headset he's wearing.

"How did you get up here?" he demands.

"Let us in, Jin-hwan," Candie says.

Jin-hwan steps aside, out of the doorway, blinking in shock at having done something he clearly had no intention of doing.

Candie strides into the suite like she owns not only the unit but the entire building. Mina and I follow her, through the entryway, past the wet bar, and straight into the living room. Jin-hwan trails behind us, unable to wipe the utter confusion from his face.

Candie sits herself down on the massive leather sectional. I fold my arms across my chest and take a stance to Jin-hwan's right, while Mina glares at him from the left, the two of us boxing him in. Candie scans the marble coffee table in front of us— stubbed-out cigarettes in a large stone ashtray, open bags of snack foods, weed vape pen, and a bottle of alcohol.

"We just wanted to have a little chat," Candie says. "Sunny told me you've been hard to get ahold of, so we thought we'd come to you."

"Look, Sunday." Jin-hwan puts up his hands. "I've already said everything I had to say."

"I'm not here to try to get back together with you," I snap. "I just have one question."

"What is it?" he says impatiently.

"Are you sorry for what you did?" I ask him. "To me? To Mina? You do realize that spreading illicit pictures of a minor is a federal offense, right?"

He doesn't seem surprised that I included Mina in his rap sheet. Maybe he assumed I knew about them all along. He eyes me like I'm some shrieking banshee trying to drum up drama over nothing.

"You're acting like I'm some crazy sex predator. It was *my* privacy that was invaded." He turns to Mina then. "We were *both* minors, and we agreed we couldn't date seriously. You both offered to take those pictures for me. I didn't force you to do anything."

It's shocking how easily he clears himself of all responsibility. I can't reconcile this jarring dissonance. The Jin-hwan I knew—sweet, charming, who spoke to me about the tropical vacations he wanted to take me on, who mused about introducing me to his family over Christmas—has vanished, and in his place stands a cruel and dismissive usurper.

Or maybe, this is who he really is. I'm so, so stupid. How did I not see it? Tears leap into my eyes, but I clench my hands into fists and fight with everything I have to keep them from falling.

"I basically did you a favor, okay?" he tells me. "Hyun-bin from JunkLand asked me if he could shoot his shot, and Alex Zhao from H-I-T asked for your number, too. You'll be on someone else's arm walking down a red carpet next week. Plus, my company's already docked my pay and suspended a bunch of my appearances, so I think we're even."

"Not even close!" Mina snaps at him. "We're giving you a chance to apologize, and you don't even have the decency to do that!"

Jin-hwan narrows his eyes at us and sneers, "That's it. Get the fuck out of my apartment before I call security."

Candie makes no move to get up from the sofa. "I don't like the way you're speaking to us," she says. "You should go put some soap in your mouth."

At that, Jin-hwan turns and walks over to the kitchen. Just as Candie commands, he picks up the dishwashing detergent on the sink, opens his mouth, and starts pumping detergent onto his tongue.

"Swallow it," Candie says.

His eyes screw shut, choking and gagging on the liquid, Adam's apple bobbing with effort as he swallows the detergent.

A wide, vindictive grin spreads on my face. Mina watches on with satisfaction in her eyes.

"You took a lot from Sunny, and from Mina," Candie says. "We're here to collect."

From inside her satchel, Candie takes out a single incense stick, a small incense dish, and the ornate tin can that I instantly recognize. She opens the tin and scoops out some of the reddish-brown dirt into the dish, before lighting the incense, the fragrant smoke reaching upward in thin white curls.

"First, I need you to give me your hair," Candie tells him. "Get some scissors."

Jin-hwan obeys. He has no choice. He opens one of the kitchen drawers and returns to the living room with a pair of food shears.

"Cut," Candie says.

Instead of simply snipping off a piece of hair, Jin-hwan opens the shears wide and hacks at the side of his head viciously. I flinch. Mina recoils. Tears fill Jin-hwan's eyes as he attacks himself with the scissor blades, opening and closing them against his scalp. Gashes open quickly, thin rivers of red running down his hairline, onto his shirt collar. He only stops when Candie holds out a hand. Reaching up into the patchy red wounds on his head, Jin-hwan yanks out two handfuls of his hair and deposits them on Candie's outstretched palm.

Candie puts the hair into the dish, covering it with the dirt.

"Now pick up the ashtray," she tells him.

Jin-hwan reaches for the ashtray on the coffee table, raising the heavy black thing high into the air. He's a prisoner in his body, utterly powerless against her compulsion, the only indication that he's still in there is the raging panic trapped behind wide, unblinking eyes.

"I want you to loosen one of your teeth."

Jin-hwan brings the ashtray down on his face, smashing it full force into his mouth.

Mina lets out a harsh gasp and turns her head, unable to keep watching.

I don't look away. I force myself to stare at the gory display, as Jin-hwan pulls his arm back again and bludgeons himself over and over. Something cracks in his mouth. There are bits of white fragments mixed into the red slobber pooling out from his split lips.

"It won't come out that way," Candie instructs calmly, almost clinically. "Cut it out with the scissors."

Jin-hwan opens his mouth wide without hesitation and puts the scissors into his mouth.

It feels like I'm watching a stage production; there's something so far removed from reality, almost theatrical about the self-mutilation playing out before my eyes. The blood on his face is such a bright shade it could be red paint. He moans pitifully, digging the blade around his swollen gums and broken teeth.

Mina's covering her face with her hands, her shoulders shaking, but she doesn't ask Candie to stop.

Finally, Jin-hwan lowers the shears. He walks over to Candie and drops a bloody, half-broken tooth into the incense dish.

"Candie, I—I think we've made our point . . . ," I mutter. The sight of so much blood is starting to eclipse the joy of revenge.

"What do you think, Jin-hwan?" Candie asks. "Have we made our point? Are you sorry for what you did?"

Jin-hwan spits out a glob of blood in Candie's direction and screams, "Somebody *help me!*"

Candie shakes her head. "I don't think you're sorry at all."

Jin-hwan's lips close shut again like they've been sealed with tape, allowing only strained, muffled groans to escape. Candie rises to her feet, and I can tell Jin-hwan wants to inch back, but he's glued to his spot, unable to run, unable to scream.

"You seem to make a lot of decisions using what's in your pants. Maybe you'll think more clearly without it," Candie tells him.

Jin-hwan reaches for the scissors again.

With his other hand, he loosens his belt and unzips his pants. He moves the food shears down to the opening in his fly.

"Candie, *stop!*" I lunge forward and grab her arm, fingernails digging in. "That's enough!"

Candie finally turns to look at me. Her eyes are clear, her expression unconcerned.

"That's enough," I repeat, pulling at her. "We have what we need from him, right?"

Candie turns back to glance at Jin-hwan, battered and broken, blood pouring from his head, from his mouth, the shears hovering just above his crotch.

". . . Go lie down on your bed," Candie orders him, her voice devoid of emotion. "When you wake up, you won't remember that we were here. You'll believe that your weed was laced with another drug, and you had a bad trip. That's where your injuries came from."

Mina lowers her hands from her face then and breathes a shaky sigh of relief when Jin-hwan ambles away, closing the door to his bedroom behind him.

Candie reaches into her bag again. This time, she pulls out three masks. The surface of the masks is a brownish-red; they must have been made out of the same clay that Candie carries around in that tin of hers. The masks are painted, simplified representations of female faces. The large eyeholes and little lips are lined with red, and there are dots on the cheeks to represent rouge.

"Now that we have the offerings, we'll summon the maiden's spirit to avenge us. She'll bring him many ill fortunes for what he did." She hands us each a mask. "Do you both still want to go through with it?"

Mina nods slowly.

I nod as well. ". . . I'm ready."

"These masks are worn by the maiden's disciples during rituals," Candie explains. "When we put them on, we become members of her sacred inner circle."

Together, we fit the masks over our faces. Candie puts the incense dish and its contents down on the floor, and we sit cross-legged around it.

"Don't open your eyes until I say," Candie reminds us, like

last time. "We'll join hands to complete the bond. The circle cannot be broken until the ritual is finished."

Mina and I take her left and right hands respectively, and then hold hands with each other, closing the circle. Then we shut our eyes.

In the darkness, Candie chants in a low voice in that same language she used before. The temperature in the room seems to drop by several degrees, sending a shocking chill shuddering through my limbs. Candie continues to chant, her voice an anchor in the dark. My fingers curl tighter around her and Mina's hands.

A strong stench invades my nose. Like lifting the lid off a dumpster that's been sitting in the sun. Rotten eggs and fish guts and sulfur. I instinctively try to pull my hand back to cover my nose. Candie squeezes my hand, nails biting into my skin, reminding me to maintain the connection.

The smell grows stronger, pushing tears out of the tightly sealed edges of my eyelids. I hear Mina coughing to the right of me.

Candie continues chanting, undeterred, her voice rising, growing more fervent. A breeze blows past my shoulders, even though there are no open windows in the room.

Then I feel it. A presence.

There's something else with us in this room.

Something angry.

The heavy odor rolls over me in thick fumes, and I gag, stomach wrenching painfully. An urge I can't identify rises from the pit of my gut, claws up the walls of my throat, and slides itself over my tongue, pouring out my mouth in an unending stream. Words. I'm regurgitating words, words that I don't understand but that are somehow flowing fluently from my lips.

Next to me, I hear Mina reciting the words, too, all three of our voices now chanting in perfect unison.

Something brushes up against my leg. Hot breath blows across my neck. My whole body is trembling, but I cling to Candie's and Mina's hands no matter how weak my arms are growing.

"Oh god!" Mina screeches suddenly.

"Don't let go!" Candie's voice shouts from my left.

The reflexive need to open my eyes burns, but Candie's warning burns deeper. And I'm too terrified to actually look, to see exactly what we've summoned into this enclosed space with us.

"It's in my mouth!" Mina screams. *"It's in my eyes!"*

"Candie, we need to stop!" I yell. "I take it back; I don't want to do this anymore!"

"No, *don't!*" Candie commands. "Don't break the circle!"

It's too late. Mina's hand wrenches free from mine.

A shattering, unearthly screech reverberates through the space.

When I open my eyes, I see that the sound is coming from Mina. She's screaming. Candie reaches for Mina, trying to soothe her, but it doesn't work. Mina continues to scream, and when I see the petrified expression on Candie's face, I know.

The ritual has gone very wrong.

Chapter 26

NOW

Everything has disappeared. The furniture. The decor. The light fixtures.

The dance hall has vanished.

"Candie!" I scream into the darkness.

My voice bounces back at me in echoing waves. Even the tiles on the ground are gone. There's nothing but unfinished subfloor beneath my feet. No clean white paint, only drywall. The space is practically a construction zone, no sign of the beautiful performing arts center I first stepped into—how many weeks ago was it?

It's all an illusion.

I've experienced this once before, already. Candie showed me years ago, when she brought Mina and me into the celestial maiden's memories. Everything had felt so real there, the beach, the village, all those people . . .

How long have I been trapped in this mirage?

"Candie, where are you?!"

I step farther into the empty husk of the building. I have no idea what's inside. All I know is that Candie is still here.

"You need to get out of here," a hollow, frail voice says behind me.

I spin. The speaker shuffles out from the darkened corridor. Her shoulders are hunched, and when she steps closer I see the strings of pink hair clinging to her sallow face.

"Faye?" I gasp out.

Faye's wearing a white robe as well, with long broad sleeves, the heavy fabric hanging down to her ankles. Her feet are bare, too.

The answer comes together in a horrifying flash.

She's one of them.

"You, Ms. Tao, the other instructors . . . you're all in on it," I mutter in disbelief. "This workshop, you trying to be my friend, everything is a lie!"

"Run." Her voice is dry and coarse, with none of the bubbly quality that had reminded me so much of what I'd lost. "Before they realize you're gone."

Everything about Faye is different. This dour, gray stranger is nothing like the bright, optimistic Faye I had spent my days with, who smiled at me in a crowd of indifference, looked at me with those admiring eyes, the first person I've opened up to, the first real friend I've made since . . .

"I tried to warn you years ago," Faye says. "I told you to stay away. But you didn't listen."

With that, I finally realize why Faye seemed so familiar from the first day we met.

I've already met her once before.

"Are you . . . Yingyi?" I ask. "Candie's cousin?"

She stares back at me steadily, before giving a small nod.

The persona she'd been performing for me was a carefully concocted blend of my younger self's cheery naivete and Mina's supportive positivity. But now that she's shed that false outer coat, all I see is a little girl with wary eyes and a harsh scowl.

She's scared, too.

"Where's Candie?" I demand.

"You need to go while you still can," she says. "Candice asked me to keep you safe. It was her final request—she made me promise."

I grab Faye—Yingyi—by the shoulders, the fear in my body suddenly reshaping itself into protective fury. "What do you mean final? Is she in danger?"

Faye stays silent.

"I'm not walking out of here without her," I say. "Please. If you've been helping her this entire time, help me get to her."

Faye's head hangs in defeat. "I can't. I can't defy my family. I'm not strong enough."

"There's some sort of ritual happening, isn't there? Something to do with the celestial maiden?" I try to meet her gaze, but she refuses to look at me. "They'll punish you if they find out you helped me escape, right?"

Faye's shoulders tremble under my grasp.

"The safest thing for you to do is to keep me here," I tell her.

Finally, Faye glances up at me, a frown carving itself deep into the pallor of her forehead. "If I bring you in there, how will you get out?"

"I'll figure that out once I find Candie. She'll know what to do."

Faye is quiet again, and I bite down on my lip anxiously, waiting for a reply.

After a long minute, Faye reaches a hand into the billowing mouth of her sleeve and pulls out something sharp and glinting. A dagger. I suck in a quick breath and take a wide step back.

Faye holds the blade out in front of her as she starts down the darkened hallway. "Stay quiet," she says over her shoulder. "And if I tell you to run, *run.*"

I nod, quickly following as the shadows swallow up her small frame.

The layout of the dark and empty hallways is different, curving and turning in ways I don't recall. I try to keep my thoughts focused on Candie, rather than what we might be locked in here with.

Faye comes to a sudden stop. There's an opening in the wall, an arched doorway. I lean forward and peer into the cavity. A single, long flight of stairs leads straight down. I can't make out what's at the bottom. I've never come across this doorway and staircase before.

"This way," Faye says, stepping through the arch, down the stairs.

At the bottom of the staircase sits the mouth of a tunnel, a walkway that's only shoulder-width wide, forcing us to travel single file.

The air trapped in the passageway is clammy and moist. I hear liquid dripping from the other end. The tunnel grows narrower the farther we go, and it feels like I'm squeezing myself down a constricting throat toward an unimaginable end.

Just as the claustrophobia verges on suffocating, the passageway opens up. We stumble out into a long corridor. A banal, characterless interior that's vaguely reflective of the dormitory floor. Low-wattage fluorescent lights glow above, textureless beige tiles line the floors. There are identical doors on both sides of the hallway, running from one end to the other.

We're in the basement. Where Eugenia and I were chased down into all those nights before. Where I saw that wooden door painted with symbols.

Faye ushers me quickly into one of the rooms, shutting the door behind us. The chamber is small and windowless, with a line of metal storage cabinets along the back wall and a stainless-steel table in the center of the room. It looks like an operating table, and I can't stop myself from imagining what sorts of terrors might have been carried out on it.

"Were you the one who put those printouts in my locker?" I ask.

Faye doesn't deny it. "I told Candice that she should have just compelled you to leave from the start. But she wouldn't do it."

Guilt and relief slam into me at the same time. After the time she lost control during our fight, I used to fear that Candie would turn her power on me.

Now I know. Even in the worst of situations, Candie refuses to take away my free will.

I frown, glancing around the room once more. "What is the ritual for?"

Faye's dim eyes lift to meet mine. "Candice didn't tell you, after Mina?"

"No." I frown, digging deep, excavating old conversations, searching for this piece of information. I think back to the ritual. And I remember. The tufts of Jin-hwan's hair. The pieces of his broken teeth.

"Offerings," I realize. "The maiden wants live offerings?"

Defensiveness rises in her face when I speak of the maiden in a fearful tone, even as Faye defies her own beliefs to help me.

"The maiden gives to us from her own sacred body. We, as descendants of her first disciples, give back to her, to show our devotion. For centuries we've performed the blessings ceremony. Those who are deemed most worthy, who most embody the maiden's divine spirit, are chosen to accompany her in the next life." Faye says those harrowing words with serene affectation, as though she's reciting scripture.

All that practicing. The singing. The dancing. We've been preparing ourselves for our own slaughter.

"And their faces?" I ask. "Why do they all start to look the same?"

"Those who are touched by the maiden's spirit become one with her," Faye tells me. "Sometimes, her visage begins to physically manifest."

Eugenia. Alexis. Hannah. *Mina.*

I was looking right into the face of the maiden this entire time.

Nausea overtakes me. How many girls were sacrificed by the maiden's disciples in their rituals? And how many more will there be?

I wouldn't have even known about this workshop if I hadn't seen Candie's video about it. Candie, who maintains a large platform targeted at an audience of young, impressionable girls. Was she forced to make that announcement video? To attract unsuspecting victims? There will always be girls drawn in by these seductive promises, these irresistible dreams. Girls who will push themselves to the furthest limits, and then push beyond that if they believe there's an opportunity waiting on the other side. There's an unending supply chain of bodies.

A terrifying realization shoots through me.

"Is Candie the one chosen to 'accompany her'?" I ask Faye.

Suddenly, I feel it. The beat.

That deep, soothing rumble, vibrating inside my chest, syncing up with each pump of my heart. Every cell in my body buzzing, attuned and alert to the rhythm. It's the drums from the song we've been practicing to, on repeat, every day since I got here. The thrumming beckons me from the other side of the door, and my feet move in response. That ceaseless beat slides inside me, hooks itself in, and tugs at me with an irrefutable force.

"Do you feel that?" I say, pressing a hand to my chest.

Faye's voice cracks as she turns to face the door. "It's starting."

The thought hits me as the next drumbeats land. I turn to Faye. "If Candie is there, I need to get to that ceremony."

"That's your plan?" Faye asks, a little incredulous. "You're going to walk yourself right in?"

"Do you have any power?" I ask, hoping that she'll volunteer to aid me further. "Can you make people do what you want?"

Faye shakes her head. "Very few of us are granted with those blessings. Only those who are closest to the celestial maiden in spirit. The best I can do is probably create some kind of diversion. I can't help you much beyond that."

"That's good enough," I tell her.

"Are you sure about this?" Faye asks, the fear in her voice palpable.

"I told you. I'm not leaving without Candie," I repeat.

Faye is quiet for another moment before she turns. She takes out a white robe from the cabinets at the back of the room, handing it to me. I take off my shoes and clothes, hiding them away. After I pull on the robe, I see that Faye's holding a mask in her hands.

The same type of mask that Candie, Mina, and I put on during our botched ritual.

As I gingerly accept the mask, Faye pulls out her dagger. She steps forward and starts to secure and conceal the knife in the waist tie of my robe.

"It wasn't all a lie," she says.

"What wasn't?" I ask.

Faye looks up, her eyes dark with emotions I can't decipher.

"I did watch the show. It was one of the few things that made me happy. I used to send you messages, and you took the time to reply to every single one. You helped me feel less alone. I wasn't lying about how much that meant to me."

I don't know how to respond to her admission. Can't tell if it's another attempt to manipulate me, or if I genuinely made an impact on her. But before I can reply, before we can further discuss our plans, footsteps sound on the other side of the door.

Faye hurriedly fits the ritual mask over my face.

The door to the chamber swings open. Yuna stands in the doorway, also dressed in the same pristine white robes.

"Why aren't you at the ceremonial hall?" Yuna asks. "The ritual is about to begin."

Faye bows her head. "I've prepared the final dancer," she says, gesturing to me. "She's dressed and ready."

Yuna turns to me, eyes traveling from my masked face down to my bare feet. I hold my breath.

"Good," Yuna says curtly. "I'll take her from here."

Faye keeps her head bowed.

"Come," Yuna says, extending an elegant hand to me, motioning for me to follow.

And I do as I'm told.

Chapter 27

NOW

There is a row of masked girls in white robes waiting outside in the hall.

Yuna orders me to the back of the line. As I walk past the masked faces, I can't help but wonder who is in this line. Is Eugenia here? Hannah?

The drumbeats sound from the other end of the hall, and we walk, the beat guiding our procession through the winding corridors, footsteps in sync as we march to the rhythmic beacon. I want to look over my shoulder and check if Faye is with us, but I keep my eyes locked on the glossy heads of hair in front of me.

Yuna turns down into another thin tunnel, and we follow her in, shuffling forward in the humid channel.

There's light at the other end, a beckoning orange glow.

We're running now, bare feet slapping down against the ground in time with the drums. Sweet spikes of adrenaline slice through me, coiled springs of anticipation gather in my legs. I remember this feeling. The nervous yet joyful momentum that bubbles and boils in the moments before taking the stage. I realize that's exactly what we're about to do. We're about to present the fruits of our labor, to showcase what they've done to our minds and our bodies.

We're about to perform the ritual.

The tunnel ends, the ceiling opens up above us, and we burst onstage inside a darkened concert hall.

Sunny! Sunny! Sunny, we love you!

The theater is both cavernous and oppressive at the same time. The ceiling must be two, three stories tall—there was no hint of this type of structure existing beneath our feet. I realize that we might not be connected to the building at all. Seated in the audience are the women who run the workshop. The instructors, administrative assistants, receptionists, they're all here, dressed in white robes, watching us. The drums boom like applause.

At the center of the stage there is a raised wooden platform, surrounded by thick candles and burning incense, plates overflowing with vermillion flowers and the sliced-open bellies of ripened fruit.

This isn't a stage at all.

It's an offering table.

The music begins. Suddenly, I'm not afraid anymore. My body throws itself into motion and begins the sequence of steps that's become as natural as inhaling, as instinctive as thought. We perform the movements exactly as we've learned, memorized, and practiced repeatedly to the exclusion of food and rest, until all the days stretched and melded together, until we emptied ourselves of everything but the dancing. We leap and spin in graceful rotations, throwing the loose sleeves of our robes upward, each of us a spoke of this large wheel.

We begin to sing. Unfamiliar vowels and consonants collide and intertwine. I can't understand any of it, but I've heard this language before. We've been singing it in the practice rooms, singing it to ourselves as we walk down the halls. The same language Candie chanted in when she involved us in her rituals.

Even as I realize this, I can't stop; my feet continue to move, my arms extend, my voice rises, and the only thing I can focus on is how seamlessly I fit here, how I belong here, how I'm meant to be here.

Someone new ascends the stage.

Candie. It's Candie. We lean and part, allowing her to enter our circle.

Behind her, Ms. Tao follows, her heavy robe sweeping against her ankles. In her hands, she carries a bowl full of brownish-red clay and crushed flower petals.

"Go on," Ms. Tao says, and Candie walks forward to the center of the stage, standing before the platform. Red-orange light flickers from the candle flames, casting aberrant shadows across Candie's face. Slowly, like she's being guided by invisible hands, Candie climbs onto the platform, lying down flat on her back.

I join hands with my fellow dancers, and we form a full circle around Candie and Ms. Tao.

Ms. Tao dips her hand into the bowl, scooping a handful of clay, and applies it onto Candie's forehead and her cheeks. She pushes up the sleeves and hems of Candie's robe and smears it in wide swaths across Candie's arms and legs.

Our voices swell louder, the pounding beat rising.

There's a glint of light, before I see the dagger in Ms. Tao's hand.

The blade lowers, curving a crimson path along the edge of the brown clay on Candie's leg. Candie's face scrunches, but she doesn't make a sound.

"Don't fight it. Surrender yourself," Ms. Tao says. "There is no greater honor than offering your body to the maiden, to reside by her side for all eternity."

Candie's eyes are wild and furious under the sweat-drenched hair plastered against her furrowed brow. Blood pools from the deep cut running down the length of her leg, dripping along the sides of the platform.

You're safe. I won't let anything happen to you.

If I'm in trouble, you'll rescue me, right?

Something in me lets out a feral scream.

My body tenses and rebels against the soothing lull of the music.

Out of nowhere, a forceful wind sweeps across the stage. The flames of the candles are extinguished in an instant, plunging the performance hall into sudden darkness.

This is it. The diversion from Faye.

My body springs into movement. I break away from the formation. Lunging forward, I free the dagger from my sleeve. With both hands gripping the hilt, I plunge the blade down into Ms. Tao's back.

Chapter 28

NOW

The cover of darkness lasts only for a few seconds before the house lights of the theater switch on.

I let go of the hilt of the dagger and stumble back.

Ms. Tao's head turns, her eyes bulging as she takes in her assailant. The corner of her mouth twitches, and she lets out a gargled gasp. It takes me another second to see that I had sunk the dagger deep into the back side of Ms. Tao's neck. Blood spurts, spraying down onto the white of Ms. Tao's robe, and she collapses forward onto her knees.

The circle of masked dancers sways blithely. The women in the audience shoot to their feet.

I dash toward the platform. "Candie, it's me!"

I wrap an arm around her shoulder, tugging her up. She's shaking. I look down and see that the hem of her robe is soaked through, the cut is so deep, she's bleeding so much—"Come on, we have to go!"

My mind jolts back into gear as I shift my grasp on Candie, pulling her off the platform. The bowls of flowers and fruit clatter off the altar as I hoist Candie's injured body up and drag her forward.

The other disciples rush forward, their white robes billowing as they surround the stage.

"*Don't move!*" Candie bellows at them.

The entire crowd is caught in mid-motion, arms raised, faces frozen, paralyzed in place by Candie's command.

"Over here!" Faye's flagging us down from the very back of the theater, from under another arched doorway carved out of the wall. I struggle to maneuver Candie down the steps of the stage and up the aisles of the theater as she hisses in pain. Faye rushes us in as we finally make it to the doorway. We're a few feet into the tunnel before I realize Faye isn't with us. I twist to look over my shoulder.

Faye is still standing at the mouth of the tunnel, looking back at us.

"Come on!" I yell.

Behind her, the women have broken free from Candie's compulsion. They race up the aisles. Faye raises her hand, her mouth opening as if to say something to me. I reach out a hand to her, fingers straining.

Our hands never meet. The entrance of the tunnel seals up before me, a solid stone wall materializing, blocking us off from the theater.

"Faye! *Faye—!*" My fist slams down against the wall, pounding against the rocky surface.

Candie gasps, her body sagging in my arms. I crouch to help

her again. My hand throbs, pain radiating from my battered knuckles, but there's no time to stop. No way to turn back. I start moving forward again, as fast as I'm able to with the extra weight, stumbling out of the tunnel back into the maze of gray-tiled hallways.

"Which way do we go?" I glance at Candie, frantic. The deep red stain on Candie's robe has spread larger. I bunch up her bloody robe and have her press it against the wound on her thigh. It doesn't do much to stop the bleeding. "What do I do?"

"You should have left when I told you to," Candie says through gritted teeth. "Why didn't you just *listen* to me?"

"Because *you're* the whole reason I signed up for this night-mare in the first place!" I hiss back. "All I wanted was to see you again—"

I clamp my mouth shut when I see a familiar figure standing at the end of the hall.

Pink-and-white skirts puffing out over contorted legs. The edge of a short bob trailing against her chin, her face cast in shadow. It's the phantom I've been seeing everywhere. *Mina.* Her crooked, broken body turns and starts ambling down the hall. I tighten my hold on Candie, pulling her along.

We turn one corner, and then another, and I finally see where Mina is leading us, what she wanted to show me this entire time.

The wooden door, painted over with ancient runes and symbols.

I pull Candie forward until we're standing in front of it.

"Can you open it?" I ask.

Candie stares at the door in wonder, like she's confused why it's here. She draws her hand across the door's wood surface, leaving behind a smudged, bloody handprint. With a creak, the door opens.

We stumble back a step, startled.

The space behind the door is dark and cavelike, the walls jagged with uneven stone. Rectangular strips of paper talismans plaster the walls and hang from the ceiling. There are symbols and characters written on them, too, ones that resemble what's written on the outside of the door. Sitting at the very back of the cave is an ornate wooden table, with a single candle burning. There's something else placed on the center of the table. Candie and I shuffle forward to examine it.

It's a mask. Similar to the ceremonial masks, there is red outlining the eyeholes and painted across its small, wrinkled mouth.

Wrinkles. The mask has wrinkles.

A chill shoots through me as I lean in for a closer look. The mask is not made out of clay. Its surface is weathered, like dried leather. Like dried skin. But those huge eyes, that tiny chin and mouth. I recognize the familiar features.

"Is this the maiden's face?" I ask, horrified.

"They've kept a piece of her here all this time . . ." Candie's voice trembles.

Outside, the echo of footsteps is nearing, muttering voices rising from all directions. It sounds as if there's a crowd headed in our direction. Candie pushes away from my arms and turns for the door.

"What are you doing?!" I grab at her. "Don't go back out there!"

"I have to. They'll follow the trail of blood right to us." Candie resists my pull.

"You can barely stand; you can't take them all on!"

"Ms. Tao is the only one who has the same power that I do. I might stand a chance against the others." She winces with every word.

"No!" I cut her off resolutely. "There's something else we can try."

She turns to me, and I can see her gearing up for an argument.

"We can do the ritual to summon the maiden," I tell her. "You said a piece of the maiden's spirit is passed down through your ancestors' memories, right? Maybe she's been trapped this whole time. All the girls whose faces turned into hers kept saying they want to go home. Maybe if we set her free, we can end all of this."

Candie stares at me as the full weight of what I'm suggesting settles in her eyes. She shakes her head. "We don't have any of the items needed for the ritual. And we need at least three people."

"Mina is here," I say breathlessly. "Or at least, some form of her. Maybe being possessed by the maiden has kept Mina trapped, too. I've seen her everywhere. She's been following me this whole time, trying to lead me down here. Trying to show me this." I reach out and take Candie's hand, lacing our fingers together. "Trust me. Let's try it."

Candie's shoulders and chest rise with each harsh pant. After another moment of deliberation, she closes her fingers around mine. We sit down on the rocky ground, and together, we reach our other free hands into the vacant spaces next to us. Then we shut our eyes.

In the dark, Candie's labored breaths turn into wheezes. I grip her fingers tighter. We wait. One second. Two seconds. Three seconds. Four . . .

Something cold brushes up against my open palm, and my heart trips.

Slowly, stiff, icy fingers curl in against my outstretched hand. Jagged nails drag along the inside of my palm. I fight the urge to pull away. *Don't open your eyes*, Candie's warning from two years ago rings in my head. I grip on to that ghostly hand without hesitation.

Candie starts a summoning chant, singing in short bursts in between gasping for air. It sounds excruciating. But her voice erases every last lingering doubt I have. I grasp Candie's hand tightly in my left hand, and Mina's cold fingers with my right.

We're together again. All three of us.

That awful stench assaults me in a sweeping plume. The thick fingers of miasma force themselves into my nose and claw down my throat. This time, I don't fight it. I don't panic. I open my mouth and draw it all inside me with deep, welcoming gulps, allowing it to pool in and burrow into my lungs.

The presence arrives. It bears down on me from all sides, a giant hand closing into a fist with me at the center, unbearable pressure on my head, my shoulders, like it wants to crush me into oblivion.

Then the presence does something it didn't do last time. It speaks.

"Open your eyes," Mina's voice whispers.

Chapter 29

ETERNITY

I open my eyes and see nothing but green.

There are trees in every direction.

We're outdoors. In the woods.

The same dreamy, ephemeral forest Candie once brought us into.

Candie is standing next to me. I call out to her in relief, but like last time, my mouth opens and closes in silence. Candie points ahead of us, and I look in that direction. There's a girl standing with her back to us in the trees. The edges of her skirt ruffle, short hair shifting against her nape as though caught in a breeze, even though the air around me is stagnant and I feel no wind.

Mina! My lips shape her name.

Mina turns to glance over her shoulder. Her features aren't contorted—it's her face, her real face. Her limbs are not twisted and broken. Mina is whole again, and she's here with us, like she never left.

Candie and I shout at her, but nothing comes, our voices are stolen, our mouths strain with the desperate effort to produce sound. Mina turns away from us and walks into the trees.

We chase after her.

We trek through the heavy woods and come upon the familiar village. Mina walks in the direction of the huts, and we follow her through the gates.

The streets are crowded with people, and we're pushed along by the crowd toward the dais at the center of town. Atop it, the celestial maiden is surrounded by a circle of disciples. The women wear ritual masks, and I notice the mask design hasn't changed much over the hundreds of years that have passed since the scene playing out before us.

We watch as the circle of disciples sways and leaps. This time, I recognize the dance steps. I know them intimately now, the movements grafted into the marrow of my bones.

The maiden brandishes a dagger and proceeds to cut a lock of her hair.

"The maiden loved her family. She gave of herself freely, willingly," Mina's voice says beside us. "If they asked it of her, there was nothing she wouldn't do."

Suddenly, a man breaks out from the crowd and starts to climb the dais, reaching for the maiden, grabbing for her robe. Another one follows, and the crowd breaks into chaos, as more and more people swarm forward. The maiden's disciples form a protective circle around her and valiantly keep the crowd at bay.

"The villagers grew greedy." Mina turns to walk away from the commotion. I take one last glance over my shoulder, before following her.

"They were convinced that her divine body could cure all illnesses, grant blessings, guarantee fortunes, and that it held the key to eternal youth. They believed that her skin, her hair, her teeth, even her fingernails contained power. They wanted to take instead of waiting for the maiden to provide for them."

The path we're on winds through the huts and out the back gate of the village.

We continue to walk until we come upon a cliff.

"Eventually, the maiden made the decision to return to the heavens," Mina says.

The maiden is standing at the cliff's edge. Her husband is on his knees. He's crying, clinging to her robe. She leans down and pulls him up to his feet. She wipes the tears from his face and presses a kiss to his cheek. Then she turns. She spreads her arms out wide, the wind taking up the long sleeves of her white robe, sending them unfurling behind her.

She takes a step closer to the ledge.

Her husband lunges. He tackles her, pinning her to the ground.

The large crowd of villagers gathered behind him rushes forward. All of them are crying, wailing. The villagers mob her, they grab at her hair, tear at her robe, holding her down.

Candie and I are powerless to stop the violence, can only watch as the villagers capture the maiden and carry her off into the woods.

We chase after them, back through the trees, until we come across a hut hidden in the darkest part of the forest.

The hut has a wooden door, painted over with symbols.

A deep fear rattles me.

From between the trees comes a long procession. A dozen masked disciples, dressed in pristine white robes. As the women make their way up to the hut, the three of us fall into step with them, joining the line. The head disciple at the front pulls open the door, and we enter.

The smell hits me first. Putrid and harsh, the scent of rot and decay. Talisman papers are hung up on the wall and strung across the ceiling. There is nothing in the shack besides a wooden platform bed.

Lying on the bed is an emaciated woman. Her arms and legs are bound with chains, keeping her restrained to the platform. Her robe hangs loose around her shoulder; her face is covered with a mask.

It's the maiden.

"They wouldn't let her leave." Mina's voice echoes quietly in the hot, rancid space. "They were terrified that if she returned to the heavenly realm, she'd take all her blessings with her."

The disciples surround her bed. They throw themselves down on their hands and knees in apparent worship, but I can see the horrifying truth.

She is their deity, as well as their prisoner.

The platform is an altar of worship, and also a cage.

The head disciple kneels down before the maiden. She dips her hand into the terra cotta jar by the wooden platform and scoops out handfuls of brownish-red mud. Slowly, reverently, she applies the mud onto a patch of pale skin on the maiden's thigh.

All around the hut, the disciples are chanting and singing,

their voices rising and falling in unison. The head disciple pulls out a dagger. My stomach roils.

I know exactly what's about to happen next.

The disciple's dagger slices into the maiden's leg, cutting along the edge of the mud, just as Ms. Tao's knife had cut into Candie. The maiden's body thrashes. Behind her mask come low, agonized groans.

The disciple sets the bloody dagger aside as she peels back the layer of mud, taking a section of the maiden's skin with it. The women's voices rise higher. Some of them are prostrating themselves, others are dancing in circles around the altar in apparent ecstasy. The open wound on the maiden's leg is promptly dressed with a heavy slathering of the muddy concoction and bandages of white cloth.

The disciple finds a new patch of skin on the maiden's body and repeats the process.

It goes on like this, the singing and her howls mingling.

When the disciples finally file out of the hut, Mina, Candie, and I follow them outside and back to the village.

"Her disciples turned against her. They, too, were worried that the maiden's departure would mean they would no longer be blessed with her powers and her beauty," Mina says. "They took her robe—the one she needed in order to fly back to heaven—and sealed her away with powerful incantations. They kept her alive for a very long time, taking from her what they wanted."

There are unshed tears in Candie's eyes that she's trying to fight back. She must not have known anything about this dark chapter of her ancestor's history.

"The maiden's resentment grew, and it festered. Love turned

to hate and then to wrath," Mina tells us. "Her hopelessness coalesced into a curse that spread out across the island, changing the villagers' bodies."

As we approach the village again, we hear screaming. A woman runs out through the gates, clawing madly at her face. Wide eyes, sharp jaw, tiny chin.

Her face has become the maiden's.

Inside the village, a massacre is taking place. The townspeople are attacking one another with knives and farming tools. They gouge at one another's skin and slice at one another's faces.

"The villagers were convinced that the ones who resembled the maiden also held her power."

Candie looked like she might be ill.

Faye had described the facial transformation as being "touched by the maiden's spirit." She didn't mention anything about it being a harrowing curse. I wonder if Candie and Faye were even told the truth of what happened to the village.

"The disciples abandoned the villagers and the cursed island, taking the maiden with them, in pieces."

The row of masked, white-robed disciples emerges from the woods, each carrying a small parcel wrapped in white cloth. Some of the cloth is stained red around the edges.

They board the long boats docked on the shore.

"The disciples tried to break the curse. But as long as they coveted the maiden's powers, the curse persisted. And yet, they were still unwilling to give up." Mina watches the horizon as the long boats sail off. "So began the rituals. The disciples brought in outsiders in the hopes of passing on the curse and diverting the maiden's wrath away from themselves. Every generation, a descendant of the disciples would also be chosen to be sacrificed along with those cursed, in penance to the maiden. The sacrifice must endure the same pains that the maiden has suffered."

I remember Candie lying herself down on the altar, and my hands clench into fists.

"How do we stop this cycle?" I ask. The silencing spell that had restricted my voice is gone. I'm able to speak again.

"All she wants is to be free. And for that, she needs a vessel to carry her," Mina says to me. "Will you help her, Sunny? Will you deliver her freedom?"

Candie is shouting something next to me, alarmed. I can't hear a word she's saying.

"If you let her in, you can be with me like this, always," Mina says.

Candie's mouth forms the words *No! Take me!*

"I'll do it," I tell her without hesitating. "If she promises to end the curse, and not hurt anyone else, I'll set her free."

Mina holds out her hand to me.

I take it, giving the maiden my consent.

When I look up from our joined hands, Mina and I are standing on the edge of that rocky cliff. Candie is not here with us. This is the cliff where the maiden once stood before she was ambushed by the people who claimed to love her. I lean forward to glance down over the ledge.

There's nothing; the drop is endless into a black abyss.

"Will it hurt?" I ask.

"Not at all." Mina gives my hand a squeeze of assurance—the press of her palm so solid, so warm, like there's still blood in her veins.

"You're not really Mina, are you?" I ask with a sad smile.

"I am the part of her that has remained," she answers. "The part that is tethered to the maiden."

"I miss you," I tell her. Even if I'm speaking to nothing more than a wispy remnant of Mina's tattered soul, I need her to know this. "I keep waiting for it to get easier. For it to hurt less. But it hasn't stopped. Every day is torture. I miss you so much. And I'm sorry for everything."

"I know." She smiles that soft, soothing smile. "We'll be together again, soon."

I nod. My hand tightens around hers.

And we leap.

Chapter 30

ETERNITY

You hear—

Screaming. Yelling. Splattering. Wailing.

You feel incredible. A bright fire scorches through you, burning out everything that makes you weak. There's no more fear, no guilt, no shame, just—

Power.

You wonder if this is what Candie feels like when she forces others to submit to her will.

The other disciples are coming, but you're not afraid anymore.

You are free.

You think about snapping femurs and rupturing organs. You think about ribs splitting inside chests, breaths trapped within throats. A voice in your ear says, *Yes, just like that, they can't hurt you anymore. They deserve it. Keep going. Keep going.*

You think about stripping tendon from muscle. Loosening

teeth from gums. Applying pressure to eyeballs. Unraveling nerve endings.

The women in masks fall down, one after another.

The floor beneath your feet is sticky and red. A hungry void rips open inside you, demands *more.*

You think about your selfish mother, and the father who abandoned you without ever seeing your face. Your grandparents' cold dismissal. The stalker who wanted to put a bullet in you. You think about the messages telling you to kill yourself, that no one would miss you if you were gone. You think about Jin-hwan taking what he wanted from you, from Mina, leaving you both shattered. You think about all the girls like you, who sacrifice so much to be accepted, who bare their souls and twist themselves into impossible shapes for the world to enjoy, only to be torn apart and destroyed.

Your blood burns hotter. You want everything to burn.

You think of fire, and suddenly there is smoke, then flames, rising from the floor, engulfing the ceiling. Black smoke fills your vision, plunges into your lungs. You should be choking on it. You should feel the heat. But all you feel is rage.

"Sunny! Sunny, stop!"

Candie. She's calling you. Her voice is dim, far away.

You turn toward the sound.

There are fallen bodies all around you, strewn like human debris. Some are lying facedown, others collapsed against walls, torsos folded in half, legs broken backward at the knees.

Keep going, the voice says. *Keep going.*

"Don't let her take over! Push her back!"

Candie's command grips you, urges you, forces you into action, and you try, you want to do as she says, but you have no arms to push, no feet to steady yourself; you're slipping, slipping—

She hurt you, too, the voice says. *Don't let her hurt you again.*

Your hands grip Candie's neck, fingers constricting.

Yes, just like that, the voice affirms. *She's the worst of them all.* She hurt you the *most*.

"Stop . . . please . . ." Candie's fingers claw at yours, tugging, pulling.

Hurt her, the voice insists. *Hurt her like she hurt you.*

No, no . . .

You don't want this.

Your hands crush down harder on Candie's throat.

You don't want this!

You know why the maiden chose your body now. She wants to kill Candie, along with all the other disciples responsible for her endless torment.

No. Not her. You've had your revenge. Please not her!

You plead with the vengeful spirit wearing your body, with a voice you don't have.

You look down at yourself, your hands still tight around Candie's neck, and as you're squeezing the life from her, Candie whispers, "Come back to me . . . stay with me . . ."

Candie's cheeks are wet. She's crying. Tears spill from your rage-filled eyes. You beg the celestial maiden over and over.

Please. Please.

I know you just want to go home.

I'll help you. Whatever you want me to do. I'll do it.

Please spare her.

I'm sorry you were hurt.

I'm sorry you were betrayed.

But I love her.

You loved deeply once, too, didn't you?

Do you remember what it felt like?

To want to protect someone with your life?

The maiden's control over you loosens for a fraction of an instant, and you use the opening to reach for Candie, through the flames, through the smoke. You push and you fight, forcing your way back to her, twisting and expanding until you can feel your fingers again, your eyelids, your hair, your heartbeat.

You wrench your hands away from Candie's neck, hear her gasp for air.

And then her arms are around you. Holding you. Your throat bobs, then chokes, tasting the smoke, finally. It's so warm, in Candie's arms. You sink in against her, burrowing deep. Darkness washes over you in welcoming tides, pulling you toward oblivion.

You're so tired. Maybe you can rest now, just for a little bit.

Candie's tipping your face up, trying to look at you, trying to tell you something, her lips moving with urgency, but you can't hear anymore. And as your eyes fall shut, you think—

It's okay.

If her face is the last thing

You ever see.

You're

Okay with that.

Chapter 31

THEN

Two years ago

I'm hiding in a back room at the funeral home before the memorial, staring down at the notes in my hands. The brief eulogy I agreed to give. I read over the scribbled notes for the tenth time. It's shit. Every word is meaningless, every rehashed memory trite.

How can I possibly go out there and look into her parents' eyes—those empty, sunken pits of unimaginable sadness?

I don't have a right to share their grief.

I'm having trouble getting out of bed again. When I try to sleep, I have nightmares. Mina's exaggerated face peering back at me from the top of the railing. *Help me*, she begs. I race to her, but the harder I push, the farther she shrinks. And then she falls. Always just out of my reach.

I can't go one minute, one second, without running through

the series of events that led to Mina out there on the balcony. No matter what angle I look at it, rewind it, dissect it, analyze it, I arrive at the same conclusion.

It's my fault. Everything happened because of me.

If I hadn't done the things I did, for myself, for my own desperate need to be wanted and validated by someone, Mina would still be here.

Candie only tried to fix the mess I made.

"We'll release statements requesting privacy for you both," Ms. Tao tells us.

The media, as always, does not respect that and bombards our agency with requests for comments.

Shocked and grieving fans flood our socials, and my phone doesn't stop pinging with notifications until I turn it off entirely and shove it into a drawer. If Candie had tried to reach out to me, I never got her messages. I sink back into that dark place, hiding in my room, in my bed, from a world that just won't stop stripping away everything I hold dear.

Mama takes a leave from work for the first time in years and tries her best to perform motherhood. She makes me soup and brings it to my bedside. "You should eat something," she urges. "You haven't eaten today."

I can't eat. Everything I put into my mouth ends up in the toilet. Solids, liquids, nothing stays down.

"I don't know how to help you." Mama admits defeat after only a few days. But on the nights when I have night terrors, she'll sit by my sweat-drenched bedsheets and run her hand over my matted hair, humming Taiwanese folk songs quietly in the dark. She hasn't sung to me like this since I was five.

I couldn't refuse Mina's parents when they asked if I wanted to say a few words during the service. But now that I'm sitting here, I don't know how I'm supposed to do this, how I'm supposed to stand up there in front of all her loved ones, me, the culprit, the person who took Mina away from them.

I don't think I can do this.

A soft knock comes on the door, and I look up from the paper in my hands. Candie stands in the doorway in a somber black dress, black tights, black heels, dry-eyed and poised.

"It's time," she says.

My eyes drop back down to my notes. I shake my head. "I don't want to go out there."

"We have to. Her family needs our support."

"We're the last people who should be going up there and making a speech."

Candie's footfalls are quiet on the carpet as she walks up to me. "No matter what happened, it's important that we—"

"She trusted you. *We trusted you.*"

The bottomless anger and loathing I've inflicted on myself ricochets, changes direction, and launches full force at Candie. Her trying to direct me in this moment is having the opposite effect, stirring up vicious emotions that I don't know what to do with except use to lash out at her.

"How can you stand there and lecture me when this is your fault, too! Mina is lying outside in a casket! She's never coming back! Do you feel *anything*?!"

This pain is too much for me to carry alone. But Candie is fully cut off, detached from the whole event like she's merely an uninvolved bystander watching me come apart.

In the face of my rage, her expression remains unaltered.

"Go ahead. Blame me. Hate me," she says. "But for now, we need to put it all aside and go out there to support her family."

Candie reaches for my hand, but I pull away from her. Tears fall from my face onto the notepaper, smearing the words into squiggled wet blots.

"Why didn't you save her?" I sob.

Candie doesn't answer me. She stands there silently while I weep. I can't move. Can't will myself to get off this chair and stand. Everything has changed now. The Sunny and Candie from before are gone. Soon, they'll be joining Mina to be buried deep in the earth.

Who are the Sunny and Candie that Mina left behind?

What will become of us?

"Are you coming?" Candie asks.

What I want is for her to reach out and help guide me out of this. I can't do it by myself. But she doesn't. I already pushed her away. After another few moments of her silence and my quiet sniffling, she turns, her soft footsteps carrying her farther and farther away until she's gone.

Chapter 32

NOW

There's an ambient whirl of machinery somewhere to the left of me, and a steady *beep beep beep*.

I open my eyes to a white ceiling. Blinking, my gaze shifts into focus. I'm lying on my back. In a bed. My right hand is secured in a brace. IVs are taped to my arm, and there are oxygen tubes in my nose.

"Sunny? Sunny! Can you hear me?"

Hands land on my shoulders, the pressure light but insistent. I turn toward the familiar voice.

"Mama . . . ?" I croak out.

My mother's face looms in my field of vision. Her hair and makeup aren't nearly as immaculate as usual, and there are dark purple circles under her eyes. "Oh, thank god! You're awake!"

"Where am I?"

"You're in the hospital," my mother tells me. "You're safe. You're okay."

Mama gets up from her chair and starts hollering for the nurses. I try to sit up, but my limbs drag against my effort, weak and cumbersome. Is this another nightmare? Another illusion? Am I really here?

Nurses file into the room, moving around my bed in a flurry of blue as they check my vitals. The doctor arrives next, and she speaks in a calm, monotone voice, asking me if I remember what happened. When I don't answer, she goes on to explain that there was a terrible accident at the dance workshop. A gas leak that led to an explosion and fires. She tells me that I have a fractured wrist and an inhalation injury from breathing in smoke. That despite not suffering a head injury, I have been unconscious for almost two days.

Images flash, red on red, mangled bodies, torn skin, blood on the floor, flames on the walls. The maiden tied down in that hut in the woods. Her pain, her hatred expanding in my chest, pushing me out of my own body. My hands wrapped around Candie's neck.

A surge of strength shoots through me and I bolt up into a half-sitting position, hands grabbing at the nearest nurse, snatching at the front of her scrubs.

"Where's Candie? How is she? Can I see her?!"

It takes both nurses, the doctor, and Mama to placate me and force me down onto my back.

"Candie was already released from the hospital," Mama assures me.

"I have to see her; I have to talk to her."

"As soon as you get a little better; you're in no shape for visitors right now," Mama tries to tell me.

"You don't understand—I need to know if she's okay!"

"She's perfectly fine," Mama assures me. "According to the police, she pulled you and a bunch of other girls out of the burning building. She needed some stitches, but she's already been discharged. They should give her a medal. I'll make sure to contact her for you. Calm down. Please."

I try to relax and allow the doctor and nurses to finish their examination.

Once they leave the hospital room, I touch my hands to my face, pressing my fingers into the ridges and dips. I turn to glance at the window, but I can't clearly make out my reflection, can't tell whether I'm wearing my own face.

Mama starts ranting in Mandarin, like she tends to do when she's furious.

"I can't believe this happened. The sheer negligence! I'm going to go after the workshop, the property management company, the builder; they're all about to become intimately familiar with my lawyers."

"No, don't!" The intensity of my objection startles my mother. I try to cover quickly. "I don't want this to turn into another huge media circus. Please, Mama."

"I'll think about it." The distress in her voice is the closest she'll come to telling me *I love you.*

But for now, it's enough. I lie myself back down, dragging my sleep-laden body onto its side so I can face my mother, and I feel suddenly tired again.

"Mama?"

"Yes?"

"Can you sing for me a little?" I gather the scratchy hospital blanket around myself, the exhaustion setting in. "That Taiwanese song I like."

Her rage simmers. "Sure. Of course."

Mama reaches out to pull the blanket up over my shoulders. I don't fight the black tides when they sweep in and my eyelids fall shut, my mother's lullaby tucked against my ear.

When I open my eyes again from a hazy, dreamless sleep, it's dark outside my room window, and Candie is sitting in the hospital chair by my bed.

"Candie?"

She nods. The high collar of her blouse is buttoned all the way up, but I can see the edge of red bruising pressed into the skin of her neck. Bruises from my fingers. I look away the second I make the connection.

"Are you okay? My mom said you were fine, but . . ."

"I'm all right," Candie says, pressing a hand to her leg. "It looked much worse than it was."

Her answer comes too easily, a too-neat bow tied over a bloody wound. Neither of us walked away from this ordeal "all right." I bolt up, suddenly remembering.

"What about everyone else? Eugenia? D-did they find your cousin?"

Candie nods. "You were right. Freeing the maiden lifted her curse. The girls have all gone home to their families," Candie says. "But the lower chambers likely collapsed without Ms.

Tao holding up the illusion . . . I don't know if Yingyi managed to escape." She pauses, frowning deeply. "Do you remember what happened down there?"

"Bits and pieces," I mumble. "It's like a bad dream from a month ago. Did I . . ." My fingers clench around the bedsheets when I remember the screaming. The *crunching*.

"That wasn't you," Candie says firmly. "You didn't do any of that." Her hand reaches out to catch mine, squeezing down. "How do you feel now?"

"Well rested, actually." I roll one stiff shoulder. "This coma is the best sleep I've had in weeks."

She doesn't laugh, her eyes serious. "I mean, can you still feel her inside you?"

I shut my eyes and lift a hand to my chest, trying to feel for the heavy weight of the maiden's anger and resentment. "Not right now . . ."

I don't tell Candie that I had made a bargain with the maiden. Instead, I change the subject.

"You know, when I first showed up, instead of *What are you doing here?* you should have led with *This workshop is a trap and you're going to die.*"

"I *did* try to get you to leave," Candie retorts. "Multiple times."

The monitors let out soft pulsing beeps next to my bed.

"I lied to you," Candie says. "I don't have an aunt. And my mother died when I was eight months old."

"What happened to her?" I ask quietly.

"She was killed by my father. At least, that's what I was told," Candie says. "I was taught my whole life never to grow too close to any outsider. That those blessed by the maiden could drive others to obsession and madness."

I fall silent, letting her truth sink in deep.

"I was raised by Ms. Tao and the other disciples," Candie continues. "Worship of the maiden was all I knew. I learned to numb all my emotions and do what I was told, what was expected of me. You and Mina were the first real friends I had, and when I was around you . . . I felt like I could be myself."

Wordlessly, I reach out my hand to take Candie's. I feel a wrenching, profound sadness for her, knowing that her entire life had been shaped to suit someone else's agenda.

Her gaze drops down to her lap. "After what happened to Mina, I started questioning everything. How could the maiden take away someone so dear to me? I couldn't move on from the fact that . . . if Mina hadn't met me, she would still be alive. At Mina's funeral, you asked me why I didn't save her. I tried. I tried with everything I had to pull her off that balcony, and I couldn't. I let her slip out of my grasp . . ."

Her voice quivers and breaks. The edges of her eyes are wet.

"I'm sorry. For everything. Maybe the maiden cursed me, after all. I think there's something really wrong with me. All I can do is hurt people."

"Don't say that," I cut her off. "After everything we just went through, can we please just . . . forgive ourselves and start over?"

"I don't know how," Candie says, her tears falling.

My heart twists. Candie is retreating into herself before my eyes. I don't want to lose her again. Not after dragging ourselves out of that blood-soaked hell.

"Back there, I was nearly taken over by the maiden completely," I tell her. "But I heard you calling to me. You asked me to come back to you, to stay with you."

My words don't hold power the way Candie's do. But I summon all the resolve I have left, willing my feelings to finally have the strength to cross the divide and reach her.

"I don't know how you feel about me anymore. But I need you. I want to be with you. Will you let me?"

The confession leaves me, and I wait. Candie stares at me, her frame so frighteningly still, not a single eyelash fluttering. So I do the only thing I can think of.

I lean into Candie—past the guilt, the hurt, past all the things we were never able to articulate to each other—and push my lips to hers. She stiffens in surprise. I clutch at the front of her shirt, pulling her closer in against me. The tears on her cheeks wet my face.

Finally, she wraps her arms around my neck and kisses me back.

And in a single bound I leap across the years, back to that safe place, back into those arms, back to my *person*, the one I'd trade my life for.

It's always been her.

When we pull away from each other, light-headed, cheeks flushing, she surrenders.

"Okay," Candie says, breathless. "You win."

"Is that a yes?" I ask.

With a soft smile, Candie pushes me gently back down against the pillows and pulls the blankets up over my shoulders. "We'll figure it out," Candie promises. "After you leave the hospital."

That doesn't sound like a no. "Together?"

"Together." She nods.

Candie leans down and puts her forehead to mine, and we stay like that, just breathing with each other for a long time. The hospital room, the whole world, melts away.

"Can you tell me more about your life?" I whisper. "I want to know everything."

She sighs. "It's a really long story."

I gesture to the room around us. "I have a lot of time to kill."

Candie reaches out and brushes the messy bangs out of my eyes, tucking a tangled curl behind my ear. She sits up, then starts to tell me her story, from the beginning.

Chapter 33

NOW

"JNR Entertainment is holding auditions *in Houston next week; I think I'm going to do it."*

It's been a week since I got home from the hospital. I'm video chatting with Eugenia, who is completely undeterred by the "accident" and is already back on track, making her next moves. Her features look the way they're supposed to—angled, callous eyes, strong jawline, bold nose. The awful alchemy done to her face is fully reversed.

Her memory of what happened near the end of the program has also vanished, and she's fully convinced that the same person behind all the injuries was also the arsonist who caused the gas leak. All I can do is listen and agree with all her theories, occasionally offering misleading speculation that couldn't be further from the truth. A truth that will go with me to the grave.

"Aren't you supposed to head off to college next week?" I ask, tilting back in my desk chair.

"Nothing important happens at orientation; I can miss it. But if you don't hear from me in two weeks, call 911," Eugenia says.

"Are you really sure you're ready to go to an audition?" I know the chances of her running into another murderous cult are low, but anxiety still spikes through me. "Maybe you should give yourself some more time to recover."

"Just because you're throwing in the towel doesn't mean I am," Eugenia declares, then jabs a finger at me. *"You still owe me a Channing Tatum dance-off, by the way."*

I sigh. Of course she isn't going to heed my warning. "You talk a lot of shit for someone who hasn't debuted yet."

"That makes me the underdog, and the underdog always wins in the end."

We trade barbs easily, like we've known each other our whole lives. I would have never guessed that the one friend I would walk away with from all this would be Eugenia. Although, I'm still not entirely sure if Eugenia considers us friends or if she's just keeping tabs on me as she plots my downfall.

A knock comes on my bedroom door, and I look up to see Candie in the doorway.

I managed to convince Candie not to skip town until I was discharged. She's been staying at my house, and I was beginning to entertain the happy fantasy that she might permanently move in with me. But I see that stern look in her eyes, and I know what's coming.

"I gotta go. Talk to you later, Genie." I end the call, setting my phone down on my desk.

Candie moves across my room to sit down on my bed,

glancing at me with one raised eyebrow. "*Genie?* I didn't realize you two were so close now."

A smug grin tugs at the corners of my mouth. "You don't have to be jealous. We're just friends. Actually, you can be a little jealous. I would pay cash money to see you two in a fistfight."

She gives me a look of utter exasperation, and I savor it, steeling myself for the conversation that's about to happen.

"You're going to go look for your cousins, aren't you?" I ask.

Candie looks down, nodding silently.

She's been trying to reach her younger cousins with no avail, but Candie is certain that they're still out there, and she's determined to free Faye and the others from the disciples' control. It was only a matter of time before she needed to leave.

I cross the floor to sit down next to her on the bed. "When?"

"Tomorrow morning," Candie answers.

The devastation hits immediately. The tenuous ground we'd finally built back up beneath our feet splinters, brittle pieces of it already starting to crack away.

"If you want to go, I can't stop you." I touch my fingers to her chin, tilting her face up to me. "But you can't stop me from following you, either."

Her features immediately flood with alarm. "Sunny, *no.*"

"It works out perfectly"—I gesture with my hands as I illustrate the plan—"I was going to take a gap year before college, anyway. You know I don't believe in long-distance relationships anymore."

"It's too dangerous," she argues.

"So I'm supposed to sit back and watch you risk your life?" I fire back.

"That's not—!" Candie is at a loss for words, her mouth opening and closing without producing any sounds.

"How many times do I have to tell you. You don't have to tough everything out yourself. You're not alone, Candie."

She is silent, and I can tell from my many years of experience that her resolve is waning.

"You're not going to change your mind, are you?" she grumbles.

"Nope," I chirp. "Besides, someone's gotta be there to stop you when you're about to chop off a dick."

The short burst of laughter she lets out is involuntary but genuine. It's the first time I've heard it in years. I don't want to go without it ever again.

A smile rises on my lips, until I catch a flash of my reflection in the full-length mirror hung on the wall across from my bed.

Something is behind me. The shadow of a person, half hidden by the ridge of my shoulder. I whirl around in a panic. There's nothing behind me except for my pillows propped up against the headboard.

Candie stops laughing. Her striking brown eyes darken. "What's the matter?"

"Nothing." I rub a hand against my shoulder and glance back at the mirror, at my own forced smile and pinched expression. "It's nothing."

That night, we sleep curled up against each other in my bed.

I dream about dancing. I'm spinning and leaping on a sparkling white beach.

There's a woman standing in the ocean. She points a long slender finger out to the horizon. Then she turns, beckoning me forward, and I dance down to the water, into the rolling waves.

My eyes snap open. I'm standing outside my house, on the front lawn.

Above me, the moon swells high in the midnight black sky. My bare toes curl into the wet dirt, and I shiver against the night wind. Behind me, the front door of the house flies open, and I turn to see Candie rushing toward me, arms outstretched. She pulls me in against her, shielding me from the cold.

"I woke up and you were gone," she gasps. "What are you doing out here?"

I turn to look at the sky.

"The maiden is awake. I can feel her stirring inside." I lean my head down against Candie's shoulder and shut my eyes. "She wants to find the other pieces of herself, to become whole again. She wants to track down the other disciples. I think she'll lead you back to your family," I whisper. "She'll lead you home."

We leave together on a Tuesday.

Surprisingly, Mama doesn't object when I tell her that I'm taking an extended hiatus from show business to go on a long road trip with Candie. She even stays home from work the morning we're set to leave to see us off.

"What exactly are you two planning to do on this soul-searching journey, again?" Mama asks, nursing her mug of coffee on the front porch as I drop my last bag into the trunk.

"There are people in trouble out there. We're going to go help them," I explain without explaining.

Mama wrinkles her nose. "You didn't get roped into some strange cult, did you?"

"Our leader prefers to call it a *happiness movement*," I say sarcastically, pushing the car trunk shut and circling back around to the driver's side.

Mama takes a long sip from her mug. Even after a near-death experience, these moments of vulnerability between us haven't gotten any less awkward.

"Mama, I want you to know that I really appreciate all the support you've given me in my career," I tell her. "But I don't know if I can ever let go of the idea that if enough people praised me, recognized me, took my picture, asked for my autograph, that I'd finally feel like I'm worth something. And I don't want to keep giving up pieces of myself to others just to feel loved. Maybe someday in the future when I've figured things out more I'll give it another shot, but not right now."

She considers my words, then says, "As long as you're at peace with your decision."

"I think it's the best decision I've ever made," I reply.

"Hmm. Do you have a full tank of gas?"

"Yup."

"Checked your tire pressure?"

"Uh-huh."

"Remember to pull over to rest if you're getting tired instead of drinking energy drinks. Those things will make your heart explode."

"What's the percentage of lung cancer that's directly linked to smoking? Seventy percent? Eighty?"

"Get off my property." Mama points out to the road. "And I'm starting nicotine patches tomorrow."

I give her a *Sure, okay* smile and wave as I pull open the car door to get in the driver's seat. "I'll text you when we get to our first stop."

In the passenger seat, Candie's looking at the navigation app on her phone. She's wearing red-framed sunglasses.

"Want to stop by DC on our way?" I ask, pulling on my seatbelt. "I've never been."

"I thought the road trip thing was just a cover story for your mom?" Candie looks over.

"It is. But if we're going to go out in a blaze of glory rescuing your cousins, we might as well enjoy some cool museums beforehand, right?"

"Okay." Candie starts tapping on the navigation route to change it.

"Wow, really? That easy?" I slide my own sunglasses on as I start to back out of the driveway. "I always thought you'd be a high-maintenance girlfriend, but you're really proving me wrong so far."

A small laugh tumbles out of her, shaking her shoulders. "Please. We both know *you* are the high-maintenance one."

I reach out a hand to shove playfully at her before looking into the rearview mirror to check for oncoming cars. Light bounces across its rectangular glass surface, and for a split second, there's a flash of a woman sitting in the back seat.

I slam on the brakes, my hands clenching the steering wheel. When I glance in the rearview mirror again, the back seat is empty.

"What is it?" Candie asks.

"Nothing." I shake my head.

But we both know it isn't nothing.

Candie stares at me, her eyes obscured behind the dark lenses of her sunglasses. She reaches over the center console and wraps her hand around mine.

"No matter what happens from here," she says, "you won't be alone, either."

I roll the windows down because in this heat, the AC takes at least five minutes to kick in. When I turn the steering wheel, my wrist feels a little heavier than it should. There's a phantom weight pulling under my skin, a strange itching in my gums, and maybe the shadow of a ghost in the back seat. But it's all right, because the radio is playing an upbeat pop anthem reminiscent of an old Sweet Cadence single, and Candie is humming along to it, turning to me to say something. *I like this song*, she shouts, the wind sweeping through her voice and her hair.

We drive north, the brutal mid-August Georgia sun beating down on the road ahead, the hot haze making bits of asphalt glimmer like crushed diamonds.

Acknowledgments

This book was written in 2020, when I was scared and lost and grieving much like most of the world. Working on it got me through the darkest times, and I want to thank you first, dear reader, for picking it up and going on this journey with me.

Thank you so much to my incredible editor Kate Meltzer, for championing my weird bloody tale, and understanding the vision of horror and romance I was going for, and saying, "I think we can take this *further*." Thank you to Emilia Sowersby, assistant editor extraordinaire, for everything you do, and for being one of *GGF*'s first supporters. All my gratitude to my agent John Cusick, who has guided me through this wild ride with so much enthusiasm and patience.

Thank you so much to the brilliant team at Macmillan: Morgan Rath, Teresa Ferraiolo, Leigh Ann Higgins, Mia Moran, Emily Stone, Katy Miller, Ilana Worrell, Elizabeth Peskin, and Jennifer Healey. To the design team, Samira Iravani and Beth Clark, thank you for the absolutely jaw-dropping cover. Thank you to the Roaring Brook team, Allison Verost and Connie Hsu, for your enthusiastic early support. And thank you to the subrights team, Kristin Dulaney, Kaitlin Loss, and Jordan Winch.

To Sarah Chung, best friend, devil sister, my first creative partner, I never would have written a single word without you. I owe it all to every cringe fic we wrote in the eighth grade (who what when where why), every comic we drew in French class, every hour we spent laughing on our thinking curb.

To Ming Chow, the original member of Team Gorgeous, my twin, thank you for your endless steadfast friendship and support, I will forever cherish our years together as the two Asian girls living in a small Southern town.

To Nora Elghazzawi, my war buddy, you saw this story through from the very first draft to the very final one, *GGF* literally would not exist without you. Thank you for sharing all those highs and lows, for laughing and crying with me, know that you are amazing and I will always be your biggest fan.

Thank you to the best critique group ever, the ladies who kept me focused and motivated (and laughing) through the pandemic, and gave me the confidence to finish this story: Flor Salcedo, S. Isabelle, Candace Buford, Maya Prasad, Michele Bacon, and Tanya Aydelott.

Thank you to Emily X. R. Pan and Nova Ren Suma for creating *Foreshadow* and giving me my first publishing credit.

To the amazing authors who came before me, Malinda Lo, Cindy Pon, Joan He, and many others, thank you for paving the way so stories like mine could enter the world.

To my family, Baba, Mama, and David, thank you for the support and love that allowed me to reach the horizons I was aiming for.

To my daughter, who told me she was proud of me and that even if my books are not "famous" I am "famous in her heart," thank you for changing my world for the better in every single way.

And finally, to lao gong. You are my rock, my anchor, my voice of reason when I get too neurotic. Thank you for being my person for the past twenty (!!) years, for walking nearly every stage of life with me, and for being the first to believe in me, and to keep believing in me during all the years I was "trying to write my book" by asking me how that novel was coming along. Well, it's DONE NOW :P Eye knee.

LINDA CHENG

was born in Taiwan and spent her childhood moving between cultures and continents. She received her BFA from the Savannah College of Art and Design and worked as an art director across South Carolina and Georgia, where she developed a deep love for sweet tea, grits, and Southern gothic stories. She currently resides in Vancouver, Canada, with her family. *Gorgeous Gruesome Faces* is her debut novel.

LYCHENGWRITES.COM

@LYCHENGWRITES